The
CHINESE PARROT

BY
EARL DERR BIGGERS

Charlie Chan
Mysteries

New York
P. F. COLLIER & SON COMPANY
PUBLISHERS

CONTENTS

THE CHINESE PARROT

CHAPTER I

THE PHILLIMORE PEARLS

ALEXANDER EDEN stepped from the misty street into the great, marble-pillared room where the firm of Meek and Eden offered its wares. Immediately, behind show-cases gorgeous with precious stones or bright with silver, platinum and gold, forty resplendent clerks stood at attention. Their morning coats were impeccable, lacking the slightest suspicion of a wrinkle, and in the left lapel of each was a pink carnation, as fresh and perfect as though it had grown there.

Eden nodded affably to right and left and went on his way, his heels clicking cheerily on the spotless tile floor. He was a small man, gray-haired and immaculate, with a quick keen eye and the imperious manner that so well became his position. For the clan of Meek, having duly inherited the earth, had relinquished that inheritance and passed to the great beyond, leaving Alexander Eden the sole owner of the best-known jewelry store west of the Rockies.

Arriving at the rear of the shop, he ascended a brief stairway to the luxurious suite of offices on the mezzanine floor where he spent his days. In the anteroom of the suite he encountered his secretary.

1

"Ah, good morning, Miss Chase," he said.

The girl answered with a smile. Eden's eye for beauty, developed by long experience in the jewel trade, had not failed him when he picked Miss Chase. She was an ash blonde with violet eyes; her manners were exquisite; so was her gown. Bob Eden, reluctant heir to the business, had been heard to remark that entering his father's office was like arriving for tea in a very exclusive drawing-room.

Alexander Eden glanced at his watch. "In about ten minutes," he announced, "I expect a caller—an old friend of mine—Madame Jordon, of Honolulu. When she arrives, show her in at once."

"Yes, Mr. Eden," replied the girl.

He passed on into his own room, where he hung up his hat, coat and stick. On his broad, gleaming desk lay the morning mail; he glanced at it idly, but his mind was elsewhere. In a moment he strolled to one of the windows and stood there gazing at the façade of the building across the way.

The day was not far advanced, and the fog that had blanketed San Francisco the night before still lingered in the streets. Staring into that dull gray mist Eden saw a picture, a picture that was incongruously all color and light and life. His thoughts had traveled back down the long corridor of the years, and in that imagined scene outside the window he himself moved, a slim dark boy of seventeen.

Forty years ago—a night in Honolulu, the gay happy Honolulu of the monarchy. Behind a bank of ferns in one corner of the great Phillimore living-room Berger's band was playing, and over the polished floor young

Alec Eden and Sally Phillimore danced together. The boy stumbled now and then, for the dance was a new-fangled one called the two-step, lately introduced into Hawaii by a young ensign from the *Nipsic*. But perhaps it was not entirely his unfamiliarity with the two-step that muddled him, for he knew that in his arms he held the darling of the islands.

Some few are favored by fortune out of all reason, and Sally Phillimore was one of these. Above and beyond her beauty, which would have been sufficient in itself, she seemed, in that simple Honolulu society, the heiress of all the ages. The Phillimore fortunes were at their peak, Phillimore ships sailed the seven seas, on thousands of Phillimore acres the sugar-cane ripened toward a sweet, golden harvest. Looking down, Alec Eden saw hanging about the girl's white throat, a symbol of her place and wealth, the famous pearl necklace Marc Phillimore had brought home from London, and for which he had paid a price that made all Honolulu gasp.

Eden, of Meek and Eden, continued to stare into the fog. It was pleasant to relive that night in Hawaii, a night filled with magic and the scent of exotic blossoms, to hear again the giddy laughter, the distant murmur of the surf, the soft croon of island music. Dimly he recalled Sally's blue eyes shining up at him. More vivid-ly—for he was nearly sixty now, and a business man—he saw again the big lustrous pearls that lay on her breast, reflecting the light with a warm glow—

Oh, well—he shrugged his shoulders. All that was forty years ago, and much had happened since. Sally's marriage to Fred Jordan, for example, and then, a few years later, the birth of her only child, of Victor. Eden smiled grimly. How ill-advised she had been when she named that foolish, wayward boy.

He went over to his desk and sat down. No doubt it was some escapade of Victor, he reflected, that was responsible for the scene shortly to be enacted here in this office on Post Street. Yes, of course, that was it. Victor, lurking in the wings, was about to ring down the final curtain on the drama of the Phillimore pearls.

He was deep in his mail when, a few moments later, his secretary opened the door and announced: "Madame Jordan is calling."

Eden rose. Sally Jordan was coming toward him over the Chinese rug. Gay and sprightly as ever—how valiantly she had battled with the years! "Alec—my dear old friend—"

He took both her fragile hands in his. "Sally! I'm mighty glad to see you. Here." He drew a big leather chair close to his desk. "The post of honor for you. Always."

Smiling, she sat down. Eden went to his accustomed place behind his desk. He took up a paper-knife and balanced it; for a man of his poise he appeared rather ill at ease. "Ah—er—how long have you been in town?"

"Two weeks—I think—yes, two weeks last Monday."

"You're not living up to your promise, Sally. You didn't let me know."

"But I've had such a gay round," she protested. "Victor is always so good to me."

"Ah, yes—Victor—he's well, I hope." Eden looked away, out the window. "Fog's lifting, isn't it? A fine day, after all—"

"Dear old Alec." She shook her head. "No good

beating round the bush. Never did believe in it. Get down to business—that's my motto. It's as I told you the other day over the telephone. I've made up my mind to sell the Phillimore pearls."

He nodded. "And why not? What good are they, anyhow?"

"No, no," she objected. "It's perfectly true—they're no good to me. I'm a great believer in what's fitting—and those gorgeous pearls were meant for youth. However, that's not the reason I'm selling. I'd hang on to them if I could. But I can't. I—I'm broke, Alec."

He looked out the window again.

"Sounds absurd, doesn't it?" she went on. "All the Phillimore ships—the Phillimore acres—vanished into thin air. The big house on the beach—mortgaged to the hilt. You see—Victor—he's made some unfortunate investments—"

"I see," said Eden softly.

"Oh, I know what you're thinking, Alec. Victor's a bad, bad boy. Foolish and careless and—and worse, perhaps. But he's all I've got, since Fred went. And I'm sticking by him."

"Like the good sport you are," he smiled. "No, I wasn't thinking unkindly of Victor, Sally. I—I have a son myself."

"Forgive me," she said. "I should have asked before. How's Bob?"

"Why, he's all right, I guess. He may come in before you leave—if he happens to have had an early breakfast."

"Is he with you in the business?"

Eden shrugged. "Not precisely. Bob's been out of

college three years now. One of those years was spent in the South Seas, another in Europe, and the third— from what I can gather—in the card-room of his club. However, his career does seem to be worrying him a bit. The last I heard he was thinking of the newspaper game. He has friends on the papers." The jeweler waved his hand about the office. "This sort of thing, Sally—this thing I've given my life to—it's a great bore to Bob."

"Poor Alec," said Sally Jordan softly. "The new generation is so hard to understand. But—it's my own troubles I came to talk about. Broke, as I told you. Those pearls are all I have in the world."

"Well—they're a good deal," Eden told her.

"Enough to help Victor out of the hole he's in. Enough for the few years left me, perhaps. Father paid ninety thousand for them. It was a fortune at that time— but to-day—"

"To-day," Eden repeated. "You don't seem to realize, Sally. Like everything else, pearls have greatly appreciated since the 'eighties. To-day that string is worth three hundred thousand if it's worth a cent."

She gasped. "Why, it can't be. Are you sure? You've never seen the necklace—"

"Ah—I was wondering if you'd remember," he chided. "I see you don't. Just before you came in I was thinking back—back to a night forty years ago, when I was visiting my uncle in the islands. Seventeen—that's all I was—but I came to your dance, and you taught me the two-step. The pearls were about your throat. One of the memorable nights of my life."

"And of mine," she nodded. "I remember now. Father had just brought the necklace from London, and it was the first time I'd worn it. Forty years ago—ah, Alec, let's hurry back to the present. Memories—sometimes they hurt." She was silent for a moment. "Three hundred thousand, you say."

"I don't guarantee I can get that much," he told her. "I said the necklace was worth it. But it isn't always easy to find a buyer who will meet your terms. The man I have in mind—"

"Oh—you've found some one—"

"Well—yes—I have. But he refuses to go above two hundred and twenty thousand. Of course, if you're in a hurry to sell—"

"I am," she answered. "Who is this Midas?"

"Madden," he said. "P. J. Madden."

"Not the big Wall Street man? The Plunger?"

"Yes. You know him?"

"Only through the newspapers. He's famous, of course, but I've never seen him."

Eden frowned. "That's curious," he said. "He appeared to know you. I had heard he was in town, and when you telephoned me the other day, I went at once to his hotel. He admitted he was on the lookout for a string as a present for his daughter, but he was pretty cold at first. However, when I mentioned the Phillimore pearls, he laughed. 'Sally Phillimore's pearls,' he said. 'I'll take them.' 'Three hundred thousand,' I said. 'Two hundred and twenty and not a penny more,' he answered. And looked at me with those eyes of his—as well try to bargain with this fellow here." He indicated a small bronze Buddha on his desk.

Sally Jordan seemed puzzled. "But Alec—he couldn't know me. I don't understand. However, he's offering a fortune, and I want it, badly. Please hurry and close with him before he leaves town."

Again the door opened at the secretary's touch. "Mr. Madden, of New York," said the girl.

"Yes," said Eden. "We'll see him at once." He turned to his old friend. "I asked him to come here this morning and meet you. Now take my advice and don't be too eager. We may be able to boost him a bit, though I doubt it. He's a hard man, Sally, a hard man. The newspaper stories about him are only too true."

He broke off suddenly, for the hard man he spoke of stood upon his rug. P. J. himself, the great Madden, the hero of a thousand Wall Street battles, six feet and over and looming like a tower of granite in the gray clothes he always affected. His cold blue eyes swept the room like an Arctic blast.

"Ah, Mr. Madden, come in," said Eden, rising. Madden advanced farther into the room, and after him came a tall languid girl in expensive furs and a lean, precise-looking man in a dark blue suit.

"Madame Jordan, this is Mr. Madden, of whom we have just been speaking," Eden said.

"Madame Jordan," repeated Madden, bowing slightly. He had dealt so much in steel it had got somehow into his voice. "I've brought along my daughter Evelyn, and my secretary, Martin Thorn."

"Charmed, I'm sure," Eden answered. He stood for a moment gazing at this interesting group that had invaded his quiet office—the famous financier, cool, competent, conscious of his power, the slender haughty girl upon whom, it was reported, Madden lavished all the affection of his later years, the thin intense secretary, subserviently in the background but for some reason not so negligible as he might have been. "Won't you all sit down, please?" the jeweler continued. He arranged chairs. Madden drew his close to the desk; the air seemed charged with his presence; he dwarfed them all.

"No need of any preamble," said the millionaire. "We've come to see those pearls."

Eden started. "My dear sir—I'm afraid I gave you the wrong impression. The pearls are not in San Francisco at present."

Madden stared at him. "But when you told me to come here and meet the owner—"

"I'm so sorry—I meant just that."

Sally Jordan helped him out. "You see, Mr. Madden, I had no intention of selling the necklace when I came here from Honolulu. I was moved to that decision by events after I reached here. But I have sent for it—"

The girl spoke. She had thrown back the fur about her neck, and she was beautiful in her way, but cold and hard like her father—and just now, evidently, unutterably bored. "I thought of course the pearls were here," she said, "or I should not have come."

"Well, it isn't going to hurt you," her father snapped. "Mrs. Jordan, you say you've sent for the necklace?"

"Yes. It will leave Honolulu to-night, if all goes well. It should be here in six days."

"No good," said Madden. "My daughter's starting to-night for Denver. I go south in the morning, and in a week I expect to join her in Colorado and we'll travel east together. No good, you see."

"I will agree to deliver the necklace anywhere you say," suggested Eden.

"Yes—I guess you will." Madden considered. He turned to Madame Jordan. "This is the identical string of pearls you were wearing at the old Palace Hotel in 1889?" he asked.

She looked at him in surprise. "The same string," she answered.

"And even more beautiful than it was then, I'll wager," Eden smiled. "You know, Mr. Madden, there is an old superstition in the jewelry trade that pearls assume the personality of their wearer and become somber or bright, according to the mood of the one they adorn. If that is true, this string has grown more lovely through the years."

"Bunk," said Madden rudely. "Oh, excuse me—I don't mean that the lady isn't charming. But I have no sympathy with the silly superstitions of your trade—or of any other trade. Well, I'm a busy man. I'll take the string—at the price I named."

Eden shook his head. "It's worth at least three hundred thousand, as I told you."

"Not to me. Two hundred and twenty—twenty now to bind it and the balance within thirty days after the delivery of the string. Take it or leave it."

He rose and stared down at the jeweler. Eden was an adept at bargaining, but somehow all his cunning left him as he faced this Gibraltar of a man. He looked helplessly toward his old friend.

"It's all right, Alec," Madame Jordan said. "I accept."

"Very good," Eden sighed. "But you are getting a great bargain, Mr. Madden."

"I always get a great bargain," replied Madden. "Or

I don't buy." He took out his check-book. "Twenty thousand now, as I agreed."

For the first time the secretary spoke; his voice was thin and cold and disturbingly polite. "You say the pearls will arrive in six days?"

"Six days or thereabouts," Madame Jordan answered.

"Ah, yes." An ingratiating note crept in. "They are coming by—"

"By a private messenger," said Eden sharply. He was taking a belated survey of Martin Thorn. A pale high forehead, pale green eyes that now and then popped disconcertingly, long, pale, grasping hands. Not the jolliest sort of playmate to have around, he reflected. "A private messenger," he repeated firmly.

"Of course," said Thorn. Madden had written the check and laid it on the jeweler's desk. "I was thinking, Chief—just a suggestion," Thorn went on. "If Miss Evelyn is to return and spend the balance of the winter in Pasadena, she will want to wear the necklace there. We'll still be in that neighborhood six days from now, and it seems to me—"

"Who's buying this necklace?" cut in Madden. "I'm not going to have the thing carried back and forth across the country. It's too risky in these days when every other man is a crook."

"But father," said the girl, "it's quite true that I'd like to wear it this winter—"

She stopped. P. J. Madden's crimson face had gone purple, and he was tossing his great head. It was a quaint habit he had when opposed, the newspapers said. "The necklace will be delivered to me in New York," he remarked to Eden, ignoring his daughter and Thorn.

"I'll be in the south for some time—got a place in Pasadena and a ranch on the desert, four miles from Eldorado. Haven't been down there for quite a while, and unless you look in on these caretakers occasionally, they get slack. As soon as I'm back in New York I'll wire you, and you can deliver the necklace at my office. You'll have my check for the balance within thirty days."

"That's perfectly agreeable to me," Eden said. "If you'll wait just a moment I'll have a bill of sale drawn, outlining the terms. Business is business—as you of all men understand."

"Of course," nodded Madden. The jeweler went out.

Evelyn Madden rose. "I'll meet you down-stairs, father. I want to look over their stock of jade." She turned to Madame Jordan. "You know, one finds better jade in San Francisco than anywhere else."

"Yes, indeed," smiled the older woman. She rose and took the girl's hands. "Such a lovely throat, my dear—I was saying just before you came—the Phillimore pearls need youth. Well, they're to have it at last. I hope you will wear them through many happy years."

"Why—why, thank you," said the girl, and went.

Madden glanced at his secretary. "Wait for me in the car," he ordered. Alone with Madame Jordan, he looked at her grimly. "You never saw me before, did you?" he inquired.

"I'm so sorry. Have I?"

"No—I suppose not. But I saw you. Oh, we're well along in years now, and it does no harm to speak of these things. I want you to know it will be a great satisfaction to me to own that necklace. A deep wound and an old one is healed this morning."

She stared at him. "I don't understand."

"No, of course you don't. But in the 'eighties you used to come from the islands with your family and stop at the Palace Hotel. And I—I was a bell-hop at that same hotel. I often saw you there—I saw you once when you were wearing that famous necklace. I thought you were the most beautiful girl in the world—oh, why not—we're both—er—"

"We're both old now," she said softly.

"Yes—that's what I mean. I worshiped you, but I—I was a bell-hop—you looked through me—you never saw me. A bit of furniture, that's all I was to you. Oh, I tell you, it hurt my pride—a deep wound, as I said. I swore I'd get on—I knew it, even then. I'd marry you. We can both smile at that now. It didn't work out—even some of *my* schemes never worked out. But to-day I own your pearls—they'll hang about my daughter's neck. It's the next best thing. I've bought you out. A deep wound in my pride, but healed at last."

She looked at him, and shook her head. Once she might have resented this, but not now. "You're a strange man," she said.

"I am what I am," he answered. "I had to tell you. Otherwise the triumph would not have been complete."

Eden came in. "Here you are, Mr. Madden. If you'll sign this—thank you."

"You'll get a wire," said Madden. "In New York, remember, and nowhere else. Good day." He turned to Madame Jordan and held out his hand.

She took it, smiling. "Good-by. I'm not looking through you now. I see you at last."

"And what do you see?"

"A terribly vain man. But a likable one."

"Thank you. I'll remember that. Good-by."

He left them. Eden sank wearily into a chair. "Well, that's that. He rather wears one out. I wanted to stick for a higher figure, but it looked hopeless. Somehow, I knew he always wins."

"Yes," said Madame Jordan, "he always wins."

"By the way, Sally, I didn't want you to tell that secretary who was bringing the pearls. But you'd better tell me."

"Why, of course. Charlie's bringing them."

"Charlie?"

"Detective-Sergeant Chan, of the Honolulu police. Long ago, in the big house on the beach, he was our number-one boy."

"Chan. A Chinese?"

"Yes. Charlie left us to join the police force, and he's made a fine record there. He's always wanted to come to the mainland, so I've had it all arranged—his leave of absence, his status as a citizen, everything. And he's coming with the pearls. Where could I have found a better messenger? Why—I'd trust Charlie with my life—no, that isn't very precious any more. I'd trust him with the life of the one I loved dearest in the world."

"He's leaving to-night, you said."

"Yes—on the *President Pierce*. It's due late next Thursday afternoon."

The door opened, and a good-looking young man stood on the threshold. His face was lean and tanned, his manner poised and confident, and his smile had just left Miss Chase day-dreaming in the outer office. "Oh, I'm sorry, dad—if you're busy. Why—look who's here!"

"Bob," cried Madame Jordan. "You rascal—I was hoping to see you. How are you?"

"Just waking into glorious life," he told her. "How are you, and all the other young folks out your way?"

"Fine, thanks. By the way, you dawdled too long over breakfast. Just missed meeting a very pretty girl."

"No, I didn't. Not if you mean Evelyn Madden. Saw her down-stairs as I came in—she was talking to one of those exiled grand dukes we employ to wait on the customers. I didn't linger—she's an old story now. Been seeing her everywhere I went for the past week."

"I thought her very charming," Madame Jordan said.

"But an iceberg," objected the boy. "B-r-r—how the wintry winds do blow in her vicinity. However, I guess she comes by it honestly. I passed the great P. J. himself on the stairs."

"Nonsense. Have you ever tried that smile of yours on her?"

"In a way. Nothing special—just the old trade smile. But look here—I'm on to you. You want to interest me in the obsolete institution of marriage."

"It's what you need. It's what all young men need."

"What for?"

"As an incentive. Something to spur you on to get the most out of life."

Bob Eden laughed. "Listen, my dear. When the fog begins to drift in through the Gate, and the lights begin to twinkle on O'Farrell Street—well, I don't want to be hampered by no incentive, lady. Besides, the girls aren't what they were when you were breaking hearts."

"Rot," she answered. "They're very much nicer. The young men are growing silly. Alec, I'll go along."

"I'll get in touch with you next Thursday," the elder Eden said. "By the way—I'm sorry it wasn't more, for your sake."

"It was an amazing lot," she replied. "I'm very happy." Her eyes filled. "Dear dad—he's taking care of me still," she added, and went quickly out.

Eden turned to his son. "I judge you haven't taken a newspaper job yet?"

"Not yet." The boy lighted a cigarette. "Of course, the editors are all after me. But I've been fighting them off."

"Well, fight them off a little longer. I want you to be free for the next two or three weeks. I've a little job for you myself."

"Why of course, dad." He tossed a match into a priceless Kang-Hsi vase. "What sort of job? What do I do?"

"First of all, you meet the *President Pierce* late next Thursday afternoon."

"Sounds promising. I presume a young woman, heavily veiled, comes ashore——"

"No. A Chinese comes ashore."

"A what?"

"A Chinese detective from Honolulu, carrying in his pocket a pearl necklace worth over a quarter of a million dollars."

Bob Eden nodded. "Yes. And after that——"

"After that," said Alexander Eden thoughtfully. "who can say? That may be only the beginning."

CHAPTER II

A T SIX o'clock on the following Thursday evening,
Alexander Eden drove to the Stewart Hotel. All
day a February rain had spattered over the town, bringing an early dusk. For a moment Eden stood in the
doorway of the hotel, staring at the parade of bobbing
umbrellas and at the lights along Geary Street, glowing
a dim yellow in the dripping mist. In San Francisco
age does not matter—much, and he felt like a boy again
as he rode up in the elevator to Sally Jordan's suite.

She was waiting for him in the doorway of her sitting-
room, lovely as a girl in a soft clinging dinner gown of
gray. Caste tells, particularly when one has reached the
sixties, Eden thought as he took her hand.

"Ah, Alec," she smiled. "Come in. You remember
Victor."

Victor stepped forward eagerly, and Eden looked at
him with interest. He had not seen Sally Jordan's son
for some years and he noted that, at thirty-five, Victor
began to show the strain of his giddy career as man about
town. His brown eyes were tired, as though they had
looked at the bright lights too long, his face a bit puffy,
his waistline far too generous. But his attire was perfection; evidently his tailor had yet to hear of the failing
Phillimore fortunes.

17

"Come in, come in," said Victor gaily. His heart was light, for he saw important money in the offing. "As I understand it, to-night's the night."

"And I'm glad it is," Sally Jordan added. "I shall be happy to get that necklace off my mind. Too great a burden at my age."

Eden sat down. "Bob's gone to the dock to meet the *President Pierce*," he remarked. "I told him to come here at once with your Chinese friend."

"Ah, yes," said Sally Jordan.

"Have a cocktail," suggested Victor.

"No, thanks," Eden replied. Abruptly he rose and strode about the room.

Mrs. Jordan regarded him with concern. "Has anything happened?" she inquired.

The jeweler returned to his chair. "Well, yes— something has happened," he admitted. "Something— well, something rather odd."

"About the necklace, you mean?" asked Victor with interest.

"Yes," said Eden. He turned to Sally Jordan. "You remember what Madden told us, Sally? Almost his last words. 'New York, and nowhere else.'"

"Why, yes—I remember," she replied.

"Well, he's changed his mind," frowned the jeweler. "Somehow, it doesn't seem like Madden. He called me up this morning from his ranch down on the desert, and he wants the necklace delivered there."

"On the desert?" she repeated, amazed.

"Precisely. Naturally, I was surprised. But his instructions were emphatic, and you know the sort of man he is. One doesn't argue with him. I listened to what he had to say, and agreed. But after he had rung off, I got to thinking. What he had said that morning at my office, you know. I asked myself—was it really Madden talking? The voice had an authentic ring—but even so— well, I determined to take no chances."

"Quite right, too," nodded Sally Jordan.

"So I called him back. I had a devil of a time finding his number, but I finally got it from a business associate of his here in town. Eldorado 76. I asked for P. J. Madden and I got him. Oh, it was Madden right enough."

"And what did he say?"

"He commended me for my caution, but his orders were even more emphatic than before. He said he had heard certain things that made him think it risky to take the necklace to New York at this time. He didn't explain what he meant by that. But he added that he'd come to the conclusion that the desert was an ideal place for a transaction of this sort. The last place in the world any one would come looking for a chance to steal a quarter of a million dollar necklace. Of course he didn't say all that over the wire, but that was what I gathered."

"He's absolutely right, too," said Victor.

"Well, yes—in a way, he is. I've spent a lot of time on the desert myself. In spite of the story writers, it's the most law-abiding place in America to-day. Nobody ever locks a door, or so much as thinks of thieves. Ask the average rancher about police protection, and he'll look surprised and murmur something about a sheriff several hundred miles away. But for all that——"

Eden got up again and walked anxiously about the room. "For all that—or rather, for those very reasons,

I don't like the idea at all. Suppose somebody did want
to play a crooked game—what a setting for it! Away
out there on that ocean of sand, with only the Joshua
trees for neighbors. Suppose I send Bob down there
with your necklace, and he walks into a trap. Madden
may not be at that lonely ranch. He may have gone east.
He may even, by the time Bob gets there, have gone
west—as they said in the war. Lying out on the desert,
with a bullet in him—"

Victor laughed derisively. "Look here, your imagination is running away with you," he cried.

Eden smiled. "Maybe it is," he admitted. "Begins
to look as though I were growing old, eh, Sally?" He
took out his watch. "But where's Bob? Ought to be
here by now. If you don't mind, I'll use your telephone."

He called the dock, and came away from the phone
with a still more worried look. "The *President Pierce*
got in a full forty-five minutes ago," he announced.
"Half an hour should bring them here."

"Traffic's rather thick at this hour," Victor reminded
him.

"Yes—that's right, too," Eden agreed. "Well, Sally,
I've told you the situation. What do you think?"

"What should she think?" Victor cut in. "Madden's
bought the necklace and wants it delivered on the desert.
It isn't up to us to question his orders. If we do, he
may get annoyed and call the whole deal off. No, our
job is to deliver the pearls, get his receipt, and wait for
his check." His puffy white hands twitched eagerly.

Eden turned to his old friend. "Is that your opinion,
Sally?"

"Why, yes, Alec," she said. "I fancy Victor is

right." She looked at her son proudly. Eden also looked at him, but with a vastly different expression.

"Very good," he answered. "Then there is no time to be lost. Madden is in a great hurry, as he wants to start for New York very soon. I shall send Bob with the necklace at eleven o'clock to-night—but I absolutely refuse to send him alone."

"I'll go along," Victor offered.

Eden shook his head. "No," he objected, "I prefer a policeman, even though he does belong to a force as far away as Honolulu. This Charlie Chan—do you think, Sally, that you could persuade him to go with Bob?"

She nodded. "I'm sure of it. Charlie would do any-thing for me."

"All right—that's settled. But where the devil are they? I tell you, I'm worried—"

The telephone interrupted him, and Madame Jordan went to answer it. "Oh—hello, Charlie," she said. "Come right up. We're on the fourth floor—number 492. Yes. Are you alone?" She hung up the receiver and turned back into the room. "He says he is alone," she announced.

"Alone," repeated Eden. "Why—I don't understand that—" He sank weakly into a chair.

A moment later he looked up with interest at the chubby little man his hostess and her son were greeting warmly at the door. The detective from Honolulu stepped farther into the room, an undistinguished figure in his Western clothes. He had round fat cheeks, an ivory skin, but the thing about him that caught Eden's attention was the expression in his eyes, a look of keen brightness that made the pupils gleam like black buttons in the yellow light.

"Alec," said Sally Jordan, "this is my old friend, Charlie Chan. Charlie—Mr. Eden."

Chan bowed low. "Honors crowd close on this mainland," he said. "First I am Miss Sally's old friend, and now I meet Mr. Eden."

Eden rose. "How do you do," he said.

"Have a good crossing, Charlie?" Victor asked.

Chan shrugged. "All time big Pacific Ocean suffer sharp pain down below, and toss about to prove it. Maybe from sympathy, I am in same fix."

Eden came forward. "Pardon me if I'm a little abrupt—but my son—he was to meet your ship—"

"So sorry," Chan said, regarding him gravely. "The fault must indubitably be mine. Kindly overlook my stupidity, but there was no meeting at dock."

"I can't understand it," Eden complained again.

"For some few minutes I linger round gang-board," Chan continued. "No one ventures to approach out of rainy night. Therefore I engage taxi and hurry to this spot."

"You've got the necklace?" Victor demanded.

"Beyond any question," Chan replied. "Already I have procured room in this hotel, partly disrobing to remove same from money-belt about waist." He tossed an innocent-looking string of beads down upon the table. "Regard the Phillimore pearls at journey's end," he grinned. "And now a great burden drops from my shoulders with a most delectable thud."

Eden, the jeweler, stepped forward and lifted the string in his hands. "Beautiful," he murmured, "beautiful. Sally, we should never have let Madden have them at the price. They're perfectly matched—I don't know that I ever saw—" He stared for a moment into the rosy glow of the pearls, then laid them again on the table. "But Bob—where is Bob?"

"Oh, he'll be along," remarked Victor, taking up the necklace. "Just a case of missing each other."

"I am the faulty one," insisted Chan. "Shamed by my blunder—"

"Maybe," said Eden. "But—now that you have the pearls, Sally, I'll tell you something else. I didn't want to worry you before. This afternoon at four o'clock some one called me—Madden again, he said. But something in his voice—anyhow, I was wary. Pearls were coming on the *President Pierce,* were they? Yes. And the name of the messenger? Why should I tell him that, I inquired. Well, he had just got hold of some inside facts that made him feel the string was in danger, and he didn't want anything to happen. He was in a position to help in the matter. He insisted, so I finally said: 'Very good, Mr. Madden. Hang up your receiver and I'll call you back in ten minutes with the information you want.' There was a pause, then I heard him hang up. But I didn't phone the desert. Instead I had that call traced, and I found it came from a pay-station in a cigar store at the corner of Sutter and Kearny Streets."

Eden paused. He saw Charlie Chan regarding him with deep interest.

"Can you wonder I'm worried about Bob?" the jeweler continued. "There's some funny business going on, and I tell you I don't like it—"

A knock sounded on the door, and Eden himself

opened it. His son stepped into the room, debonair and smiling. At sight of him, as so often happens in such a situation, the anxious father's worry gave way to a deep rage.

"You're a hell of a business man," he cried.

"Now, father—no compliments," laughed Bob Eden. "And me wandering all over San Francisco in your service."

"I suppose so. That's about what you would be doing, when it was your job to meet Mr. Chan at the dock."

"Just a moment, dad." Bob Eden removed a glistening rain coat. "Hello, Victor. Madame Jordan. And this, I imagine, is Mr. Chan."

"So sorry to miss meeting at dock," murmured Chan. "All my fault, I am sure—"

"Nonsense," cried the jeweler. "His fault, as usual. When, in heaven's name, are you going to show a sense of responsibility?"

"Now, dad. And a sense of responsibility just what I've only this minute stopped showing nothing else but."

"Good lord—what language is that? You didn't meet Mr. Chan, did you?"

"Well, in a way, I didn't—"

"In a way? In a way!"

"Precisely. It's a long story, and I'll tell it if you'll stop interrupting with these unwarranted attacks on my character. I'll sit down, if I may. I've been about a bit, and I'm tired."

He lighted a cigarette. "When I came out of the club about five to go to the dock, there was nothing in sight but a battered old taxi that had seen better days. I jumped in. When I got down on the Embarcadero I noticed that the driver was a pretty disreputable lad with a scar on one cheek and a cauliflower ear. He said he'd wait for me, and he said it with a lot of enthusiasm. I went into the pier-shed. There was the *President Pierce* out in the harbor, fumbling round trying to dock. In a few minutes I noticed a man standing near me—a thin chilly-looking lad with an overcoat, the collar up about his ears, and a pair of black spectacles. I guess I'm psychic— he didn't look good to me. I couldn't tell, but somehow he seemed to be looking at me from back of those smoked windows. I moved to the other side of the shed. So did he. I went to the street. He followed. Well, I drifted back to the gang-plank, and old Chilly Bill came along."

Bob Eden paused, smiling genially about him. "Right then and there I came to a quick decision. I'm remarkable that way. I didn't have the pearls, but Mr. Chan did. Why tip off the world to Mr. Chan? So I just stood there staring hopefully at the crowd landing from the old *P. P.* Presently I saw the man I took to be Mr. Chan come down the plank, but I never stirred. I watched him while he looked about, then I saw him go out to the street. Still the mysterious gent behind the windows stuck closer than a bill collector. After everybody was ashore, I went back to my taxi and paid off the driver. 'Was you expecting somebody on the ship?' he asked. 'Yes,' I told him. 'I came down to meet the Dowager Empress of China, but they tell me she's dead.' He gave me a dirty look. As I hurried away the man with the black glasses came up. 'Taxi, Mister,' said Cauliflower Ear. And old Glasses got in. I had to meander through the rain all the way to the S. P. station before I could find another cab. Just as I drove away from the station along came Cauliflower Ear in his splendid equipage. He followed along behind, down Third, up Market to Powell, and finally to the St. Francis. I went in the front door of the hotel and out the side, on to Post. And there was Cauliflower Ear and his fare, drifting by our store. As I went in the front door of the club, my dear old friends drew up across the street. I escaped by way of the kitchen, and slipped over here. I fancy they're still in front of the club—they loved me like a brother." He paused. "And that, dad, is the long but thrilling story of why I did not meet Mr. Chan."

Eden smiled. "By jove, you've got more brains than I thought. You were perfectly right. But look here, Sally—I like this less than ever. That necklace of yours isn't a well-known string. It's been in Honolulu for years. Easy as the devil to dispose of it, once it's stolen. If you'll take my advice, you'll certainly not send it off to the desert—"

"Why not?" broke in Victor. "The desert's the very place to send it. Certainly this town doesn't look any too good."

"Alec," said Sally Jordan, "we need the money. If Mr. Madden is down at Eldorado, and asks for the necklace there, then let's send it to him immediately and get his receipt. After that—well, it's his lookout. His worry. Certainly I want it off my hands as soon as may be."

Eden sighed. "All right. It's for you to decide. Bob will take it at eleven, as we planned. Provided—well, provided you make the arrangement you promised—provided he doesn't go alone." He looked toward Charlie Chan who was standing at the window watching, fascinated, the noisy life of Geary Street far below.

"Charlie," said Sally Jordan.

"Yes, Miss Sally." He turned, smiling, to face her.

"What was that you said about the burden dropping from your shoulders? The delectable thud?"

"Now vacation begins," he said. "All my life I have unlimited yearning to face the wonders of this mainland. Moment are now at hand. Care-free and happy, not like crossing on ship. There all time pearls rest heavy on stomach, most undigestible, like sour rice. Not so now."

Madame Jordan shook her head. "I'm sorry, Charlie," she said. "I'm going to ask you to eat one more bowl of sour rice. For me—for auld lang syne."

"I do not quite grasp meaning," he told her.

She outlined the plan to send him with Bob Eden to the desert. His expression did not change.

"I will go," he promised gravely.

"Thank you, Charlie," said Sally Jordan softly.

"In my youth," he continued, "I am house-boy in the Phillimore mansion. Still in my heart like old-time garden bloom memories of kindness never to be repaid." He saw Sally Jordan's eyes bright and shining with tears. "Life would be dreary waste," he finished, "if there was no thing called loyalty."

Very flowery, thought Alexander Eden. He sought to introduce a more practical note. "All your expenses will be paid, of course. And that vacation is just postponed for a few days. You'd better carry the pearls—you have the belt, and besides, no one knows your connection with the affair. Thank heaven for that."

"I will carry them," Chan agreed. He took up the string from the table. "Miss Sally, toss all worry out of mind. When this young man and I encounter proper person, pearls will be delivered. Until then, I guard them well."

"I'm sure you will," smiled Madame Jordan.

"Well, that's settled," said Eden. "Mr. Chan, you and my son will take the eleven o'clock ferry to Richmond, which connects with the train to Barstow. There you'll have to change to another train for Eldorado, but you should reach Madden's ranch to-morrow evening. If he is there and everything seems in order—"

"Why should everything be in order?" broke in Victor. "If he's there—that's enough."

"Well, of course, we don't want to take any undue risk," Eden went on. "But you two will know what to do when you reach there. If Madden's at the ranch, give him the string and get his receipt. That lets us out. Mr. Chan, we will pick you up here at ten-thirty. Until then, you are free to follow your own inclination."

"Present inclination," smiled Chan, "means tub filled with water, steaming hot. At ten-thirty in entrance hall of hotel I will be waiting, undigestible pearls on stomach, as before. Good-by. Good-by." He bobbed to each in turn and went out.

"I've been in the business thirty-five years," said Eden, "but I never employed a messenger quite like him before."

"Dear Charlie," said Sally Jordan. "He'll protect those pearls with his life."

Bob Eden laughed. "I hope it doesn't go as far as that," he remarked. "I've got a life, too, and I'd like to hang on to it."

"Won't you both stay to dinner?" suggested Sally Jordan.

"Some other time, thanks," Alexander Eden answered. "I don't think it wise we should keep together to-night. Bob and I will go home—he has a bag to pack, I imagine. I don't intend to let him out of my sight until train time."

"One last word," said Victor. "Don't be too squeamish when you get down on that ranch. If Madden's in danger, that's no affair of ours. Put those pearls in his hand and get his receipt. That's all."

Eden shook his head. "I don't like the look of this, Sally. I don't like this thing at all."

"Don't worry," she smiled. "I have every confidence in Charlie—and in Bob."

"Such popularity must be deserved," said Bob Eden. "I promise I'll do my best. Only I hope that lad in the overcoat doesn't decide to come down to the desert and warm up. Somehow, I'm not so sure I'd be a match for him—once he warmed up."

CHAPTER III

A N HOUR later Charlie Chan rode down in the elevator to the bright lobby of his hotel. A feeling of heavy responsibility again weighed upon him, for he had restored to the money-belt about his bulging waist the pearls that alone remained of all the Phillimore fortune. After a quick glance about the lobby, he went out into Geary Street.

The rain no longer fell and for a moment he stood on the curb, a little, wistful, wide-eyed stranger, gazing at a world as new and strange to him as though he had wakened to find himself on Mars. The sidewalk was crowded with theater-goers; taxis honked in the narrow street; at intervals sounded the flippant warning of cable-car bells, which is a tune heard only in San Francisco, a city with a voice and a gesture all its own.

Unexplored country to Charlie Chan, this mainland, and he was thrilled by the electric gaiety of the scene before him. Old-timers would have told him that what he saw was only a dim imitation of the night life of other days, but he had no memories of the past, and hence nothing to mourn. Seated on a stool at a lunch-counter he ate his evening meal—a stool and a lunch-counter, but it was adventure enough for one who had never known Billy Bogan's Louvre Café, on the site of which now stands the

Bank of Italy—adventure enough for one who had no happy recollections of Delmonico's on O'Farrell Street or of the Odeon or the Pup or the Black Cat, bright spots blotted out forever now. He partook heartily of the white man's cooking, and drank three cups of steaming tea.

A young man, from his appearance perhaps a clerk, was eating a modest dinner at Chan's side. After a few words concerned with the sugar bowl, Chan ventured to address him further.

"Please pardon the abrupt advance of a newcomer," he said. "For three hours I am free to wander the damp but interesting streets of your city. Kindly mention what I ought to see."

"Why—I don't know," said the young man, surprised. "Not much doing any more. San Francisco's not what it used to be."

"The Barbary Coast, maybe," suggested Chan.

The young man snorted. "Gone forever. The Thalia, the Elko, the Midway—say, they're just memories now. Spider Kelley is over in Arizona, dealing in land. Yes, sir—all those old dance-halls are just garages to-day—or maybe ten cent flop-houses. But look here—this is New Year's Eve in Chinatown. However—" He laughed. "I guess I don't need to tell you that."

Chan nodded. "Ah yes—the twelfth of February. New Year's Eve."

Presently he was back on the sidewalk, his keen eyes sparkling with excitement. He thought of the somnolent thoroughfares of Honolulu by night—Honolulu, where every one goes home at six, and stays there. How different here in this mainland city. The driver of a sightseeing bus approached him and also spoke of Chinatown.

"Show you the old opium dens and the fan-tan joints," he promised, but after a closer look moved off and said no more of his spurious wares.

At a little after eight, the detective from the islands left the friendly glow of Union Square and, drifting down into the darker stretches of Post Street, came presently to Grant Avenue. A loiterer on the corner directed him to the left, and he strolled on. In a few moments he came to a row of shops displaying cheap Oriental goods for the tourist eye. His pace quickened; he passed the church on the crest of the hill and moved on down into the real Chinatown.

Here a spirit of carnival filled the air. The façade of every Tong House, outlined by hundreds of glowing incandescent lamps, shone in yellow splendor through the misty night. Throngs milled on the narrow sidewalks— white sightseers, dapper young Chinese lads in collegecut clothes escorting slant-eyed flappers attired in their best, older Chinese shuffling along on felt-clad feet, each secure in the knowledge that his debts were paid, his house scoured and scrubbed, the new year auspiciously begun.

At Washington Street Chan turned up the hill. Across the way loomed an impressive building—four gaudy stories of light and cheer. Gilt letters in the transom over ,the door proclaimed it the home of the Chan Family Society. For a moment the detective stood, family pride uppermost in his thoughts.

A moment later he was walking down the dim, almost deserted pavement of Waverly Place. A bright-eyed boy of his own race offered him a copy of the Chinese Daily Times. He bought it and moved on, his gaze intent on dim house numbers above darkened doorways.

Presently he found the number he sought, and climbed a shadowy stair. At a landing where crimson and gold-lettered strips of paper served as a warning to evil spirits he paused, and knocked loudly at a door. It was opened, and against the light from within stood the figure of a Chinese, tall, with a gray meager beard and a loose-fitting, embroidered blouse of black satin.

For a moment neither spoke. Then Chan smiled. "Good evening, illustrious Chan Kee Lim," he said in pure Cantonese. "Is it that you do not know your unworthy cousin from the islands?"

A light shone in the narrow eyes of Kee Lim. "For a moment, no," he replied. "Since you come in the garb of a foreign devil, and knock on my door with the knuckles, as rude foreign devils do. A thousand welcomes. Deign to enter my contemptible house."

Still smiling, the little detective went inside. The room was anything but contemptible, as he saw at once. It was rich with tapestries of Hang-chiu silk, the furniture was of teakwood, elaborately carved. Fresh flowers bloomed before the ancestral shrine, and everywhere were Chinese lilies, the pale, pungent sui-sin-fah, symbol of the dawning year. On the mantel, beside a tiny Buddha of Ningpo wood, an American alarm clock ticked noisily.

"Please sit in this wretched chair," Kee Lim said. "You arrive unexpectedly as August rain. But I am happy to see you." He clapped his hands and a woman entered. "My wife, Chan So," the host explained. "Bring rice cakes, and my Dew of Roses wine," he ordered.

He sat down opposite Charlie Chan, and regarded him across a teakwood table on which were sprays of fresh almond blossoms. "There was no news of your coming" he remarked.

Chan shrugged. "No. It was better so. I come on a mission. On business," he added, in his best Rotary Club manner.

Kee Lim's eyes narrowed. "Yes—I have heard of your business," he said.

The detective was slightly uncomfortable. "You do not approve?" he ventured.

"It is too much to say that I do not approve," Kee Lim returned. "But I do not quite understand. The foreign devil police—what has a Chinese in common with them?"

Charlie smiled. "There are times, honorable cousin," he admitted, "when I do not quite understand myself."

The reed curtains at the rear parted, and a girl came into the room. Her eyes were dark and bright; her face pretty as a doll's. To-night, in deference to the holiday, she wore the silken trousers and embroidered jacket of her people, but her hair was bobbed and her walk, her gestures, her whole manner all too obviously copied from her American sisters. She carried a tray piled high with New Year delicacies.

"My daughter, Rose," Kee Lim announced. "Behold, our famous cousin from Hawaii." He turned to Charlie Chan. "She, too, would be an American, insolent as the daughters of the foolish white men."

The girl laughed. "Why not? I was born here. I went to American grammar schools. And now I work American fashion."

"Work?" repeated Charlie, with interest.

"The Classics of Girlhood are forgotten," explained Kee Lim. "All day she sits in the Chinatown telephone exchange, shamelessly talking to a wall of teakwood that flashes red and yellow eyes."

"Is that so terrible?" asked the girl, with a laughing glance at her cousin.

"A most interesting labor," surmised Charlie.

"I'll tell the world it is," answered the girl in English, and went out. A moment later she returned with a battered old wine jug. Into Swatow bowls she poured two hot libations—then, taking a seat on the far side of the room, she gazed curiously at this notable relative from across the seas. Once she had read of his exploits in the San Francisco papers.

For an hour or more Chan sat, talking with his cousin of the distant days when they were children in China. Finally he glanced toward the mantel. "Does that clock speak the truth?" he asked.

Kee Lim shrugged. "It is a foreign devil clock," he said. "And therefore a great liar."

Chan consulted his watch. "With the keenest regret," he announced, "I find I must walk my way. To-night my business carries me far from here—to the desert that lies in the south. I have had the presumption, honest and industrious cousin, to direct my wife to send to your house any letters of importance addressed to me. Should a message arrive in my absence, you will be good enough to hold it here awaiting my return. In a few days, at most, I will walk this way again. Meanwhile I go beyond the reach of messengers."

The girl rose and came forward. "Even on the desert," she said, "there are telephones."

Charlie looked at her with sudden interest. "On the desert," he repeated.

"Most assuredly. Only two days ago I had a long distance call for a ranch near Eldorado. A ranch named— but I do not remember."

"Perhaps—the ranch of Madden," said Chan hope-fully.

She nodded. "Yes—that was the name. It was a most unusual call."

"And it came from Chinatown?"

"Of course. From the bowl shop of Wong Ching, in Jackson Street. He desired to speak to his relative, Louie Wong, caretaker on Madden's Ranch. The number, Eldorado 76."

Chan dissembled his eagerness, but his heart was beating faster. He was of the foreign devil police now. "Perhaps you heard what was said?"

"Louie Wong must come to San Francisco at once. Much money and a fine position awaited him here—"

"Haie!" cut in Kee Lim. "It is not fitting that you reveal thus the secrets of your white devil profession. Even to one of the family of Chan."

"You are right, ever wise cousin," Charlie agreed. He turned to the girl. "You and I, little blossom, will meet again. Even though the desert has telephones, I am beyond reach there. Now, to my great regret, I must go."

Kee Lim followed him to the door. He stood there on the reed mat, stroking his thin beard and blinking. "Farewell, notable cousin. On that long journey of yours upon which you now set out—walk slowly."

"Farewell," Charlie answered. "All my good wishes for happiness in the new year." Suddenly he found himself speaking English. "See you later," he called, and hurried down the stairs.

Once in the street, however, he obeyed his cousin's parting injunction, and walked slowly indeed. A startling bit of news, this, from Rose, the telephone operator.

Louie Wong was wanted in San Francisco—wanted by his relative Wong Ching, the bowl merchant. Why?

An old Chinese on a corner directed him to Jackson Street, and he climbed its steep sidewalk until he reached the shop of Wong Ching. The brightly lighted window was filled with Swatow cups and bowls, a rather beautiful display, but evidently during this holiday season the place was not open for business, for the curtains on the door were drawn. Chan rattled the latch for a full minute, but no one came.

He crossed the street, and took up a post in a dark doorway opposite. Sooner or later his summons would be answered. On a near-by balcony a Chinese orchestra was playing, the whanging flute, the shrill plink of the moon-kwan, the rasping cymbals and the drums filled the night with a blissful dissonance. Presently the musicians ceased, the din died away, and Chan heard only the click of American heels and the stealthy swish of felt slippers passing his hiding-place.

In about ten minutes the door of Wong Ching's shop opened and a man came out. He stood looking cautiously up and down the dim street. A thin man in an overcoat which was buttoned close about him—a chilly-seeming man. His hat was low over his eyes, and as a further means of deceit he wore dark spectacles. Charlie Chan permitted a faint flash of interest to cross his chubby face.

The chilly man walked briskly down the hill, and stepping quickly from the doorway, Chan followed at a distance. They emerged into Grant Avenue; the dark-spectacled one turned to the right. Still Chan followed; this was child's play for him. One block, two, three. They came to a cheap hotel, the Killarney, on one of

Grant Avenue's corners, and the man in the overcoat went inside.

Glancing at his watch, Chan decided to let his quarry escape, and turned in the direction of Union Square. His mind was troubled. "This much even a fool could grasp," he thought. "We move toward a trap. But with eyes open—with eyes keenly open."

Back in his tiny hotel room, he restored to his inexpensive suit-case the few articles he had previously removed. Returning to the desk, he found that his trunk had reached the hotel, but had not yet been taken upstairs. He arranged for its storage until his return, paid his bill, and sitting down in a great leather chair in the lobby, with his suit-case at his feet, he waited patiently.

At precisely ten-thirty Bob Eden stepped inside the door of the hotel and beckoned. Following the young man to the street, Chan saw a big limousine drawn up to the curb.

"Jump in, Mr. Chan," said the boy, taking his bag. As the detective entered the darkened interior, Alexander Eden greeted him from the gloom. "Tell Michael to drive slowly—I want to talk," called the older man to his son. Bob Eden spoke to the chauffeur, then leaped into the car and it moved off down Geary Street.

"Mr. Chan," said the jeweler in a low voice, "I am very much disturbed."

"More events have taken place?" suggested Chan.

"Decidedly," Eden replied. "You were not in the room this afternoon when I spoke of a telephone call I had received from a pay-station at Sutter and Kearny Streets." He repeated the details. "This evening I called into consultation Al Draycott, head of the Gale Detective

Agency, with which I have affiliations. I asked him to investigate and, if possible, find that man in the overcoat Bob saw at the dock. An hour ago he reported that he had located our man with no great difficulty. He has discovered him—"

"At the Killarney Hotel, perhaps, on Grant Avenue," suggested Chan, dissembling a deep triumph.

"Good lord," gasped Eden. "You found him, too. Why—that's amazing—"

"Amazing luck," said Chan. "Please pardon rude interruption. Will not occur again."

"Well, Draycott located this fellow, and reports that he is Shaky Phil Maydorf, one of the Maydorf brothers, as slick a pair of crooks as ever left New York for their health. The fellow suffers from malaria, I believe, but otherwise he is in good form and, it seems, very much interested in our little affairs. But Mr. Chan,—your own story,—how in the world did you find him too?"

Chan shrugged. "Successful detective," he said, "is plenty often man on whom luck turns smiling face. This evening I bask in most heart-warming grin." He told of his visit to Chan Lee Kim, of the telephone call to the desert from Wong's bowl shop, and of his seeing the man in the overcoat leaving the shop. "After that, simple matter to hound him to hotel," he finished.

"Well, I'm more disturbed than ever," Eden said. "They have called the caretaker away from Madden's ranch. Why? I tell you I don't like this business—"

"Nonsense, father," Bob Eden protested. "It's rather interesting."

"Not to me. I don't welcome the attention of these Maydorfs—and where, by the way, is the other one?

They are not the modern type of crook—the moron brand
that relies entirely on a gun. They are men of brains—
old-fashioned outlaws who are regarded with respect by
the police whom they have fought for many years. I
called Sally Jordan and tried to abandon the whole pro-
ceeding—but that son of hers. He's itching to get the
money, and he's urging her to go ahead. So what can I
do? If it was any one else I'd certainly drop out of the
deal—but Sally Jordan—well, she's an old friend. And
as you said this afternoon, Mr. Chan, there is such a
thing as loyalty in the world. But I tell you I'm sending
you two down there with the deepest reluctance."

"Don't you worry, dad. It's going to be great fun,
I'm sure. All my life I've wanted to be mixed up in a
good exciting murder. As a spectator, of course."

"What are you talking about?" the father demanded.

"Why, Mr. Chan here is a detective, isn't he? A detective on a vacation. If you've ever read a mystery story
you know that a detective never works so hard as when
he's on a vacation. He's like the postman who goes for a
long walk on his day off. Here we all, all set. We've
got our bright and shining mark, our millionaire—P. J.
Madden, one of the most famous financiers in America.
I tell you, poor P. J. is doomed. Ten to one Mr. Chan
and I will walk into that ranch house and find him dead
on the first rug we come to."

"This is no joking matter," Eden rebuked severely.
"Mr. Chan—you seem to be a man of considerable ability.
Have you anything to suggest?"

Charlie smiled in the dark car. "Flattery sounds sweet
to any ear," he remarked. "I have, it is true, inclination
for making humble suggestion."

"Then, for heaven's sake, make it," Eden said.

"Pray give the future a thought. Young Mr. Eden and I walk hand in hand, like brothers, on to desert ranch. What will spectator say? Aha, they bring pearls If not, why come together for strength?"

"Absolutely true," Eden agreed.

"Then why travel side by side?" Charlie continued. "It is my humble hint that Mr. Bob Eden arrive alone at ranch. Answering all inquiries he says no, he does not carry pearls. So many dark clouds shade the scene, he is sent by honorable father to learn if all is well. When he is sure of that, he will telegraph necklace be sent at once, please."

"A good idea," Eden said. "Meanwhile—"

"At somewhat same hour," Chan went on, "there stumble on to ranch weary old Chinese, seeking employment. One whose clothes are of a notable shabbiness, a wanderer over sand, a what you call—a desert rat. Who would dream that on the stomach of such a one repose those valuable Phillimore pearls?"

"Say—that's immense," cried Bob Eden enthusiastically.

"Might be," admitted Chan. "Both you and old Chinese look carefully about. If all is well, together you approach this Madden and hand over necklace. Even then, others need not know."

"Fine," said the boy. "We'll separate when we board the train. If you're in doubt at any time, just keep your eye on me, and tag along. We're due in Barstow tomorrow at one-fifteen, and there's a train to Eldorado at three-twenty, which arrives about six. I'm taking it, and you'd better do the same. One of my newspaper friends here has given me a letter to a fellow named Will Holley, who's editor of a little paper at Eldorado. I'm going to invite him to have dinner with me, then I'll drive out to Madden's. You, of course, will get out some other way. As somebody may be watching us, we won't speak on our journey. Friends once, but strangers now. That's the idea, isn't it?"

"Precisely the notion," agreed Chan.

The car had stopped before the ferry building. "I have your tickets here," Alexander Eden said, handing over a couple of envelopes. "You have lower berths, in the same car, but at different ends. You'll find a little money there for expenses, Mr. Chan. I may say that I think your plan is excellent—but for heaven's sake, be careful, both of you. Bob, my boy—you're all I've got. I may have spoken harshly to you, but I—I—take care of yourself."

"Don't you worry, dad," Bob Eden said. "Though you'll never believe it, I'm grown up. And I've got a good man with me."

"Mr. Chan," Eden said. "Good luck. And thank you a thousand times."

"Don't talk about it," smiled Charlie. "Happiest walk of postman's life is on his holiday. I will serve you well. Good-by."

He followed Bob Eden through the gates and on to the ferryboat. A moment later they had slipped out upon the black waters of the harbor. The rain was gone, the sky spattered with stars, but a chill wind blew through the Gate. Charlie stood alone by the rail; the dream of his life had come true; he knew the great mainland at last. The flaming ball atop the Ferry Building receded; the yellow lamps of the city marched up the hills and down again. He thought of the tiny island that was his home, of the house on Punchbowl Hill where his wife and children patiently awaited his return. Suddenly he was appalled at the distance he had come.

Bob Eden joined him there in the dark, and waved his hand toward the glow in the sky above Grant Avenue. "A big night in Chinatown," he said.

"Very large night," agreed Chan. "And why not? To-morrow is the first day of the new year. Of the year 4869."

"Great Scott," smiled Eden. "How time flies. A Happy New Year to you."

"Similar one to you," said Chan.

The boat plowed on. From the prison island of Alcatraz a cruel, relentless searchlight swept at intervals the inky waters. The wind was bitter now.

"I'm going inside," shivered Bob Eden. "This is good-by, I guess."

"Better so," admitted Charlie. "When you are finally at Madden's ranch, look about for that desert rat."

Alone, he continued to stare at the lamps of the city, cold and distant now, like the stars.

"A desert rat," he repeated softly, "with no fondly feeling for a trap."

CHAPTER IV

DUSK was falling in the desert town of Eldorado
when, on Friday evening, Bob Eden alighted from
the train at a station that looked like a little red schoolhouse gone wrong. His journey down from San Francisco to Barstow had been quite without incident. At
that town, however, a rather disquieting thing had happened. He had lost all trace of Charlie Chan.

It was in the Barstow lunch-room that he had last seen
the detective from the islands, busy with a cup of steaming tea. The hour of three-twenty and the Eldorado
train being some distance off, he had gone for a stroll
through the town. Returning about three, he had looked
in vain for the little Chinese policeman. Alone he had
boarded the train and now, as he stared up and down the
dreary railroad tracks, he perceived that he had been the
only passenger to alight at this unpromising spot.

Thinking of the fortune in "undigestible" pearls on
the detective's person, he was vaguely alarmed. Had
Chan met with some unfortunate accident? Or perhaps—
who could say? What did they really know about this
Charlie Chan? Every man is said to have his price, and
this was an overwhelming temptation to put in the way
of an underpaid detective from Honolulu. But no—Bob
Eden recalled the look in Chan's eyes when he had prom-

44

ised Sally Jordan to guard those pearls well. The Jordans
no doubt had good reason for their faith in an old friend.
But suppose Shaky Phil Maydorf was no longer in San
Francisco—

Resolutely Bob Eden put these thoughts aside and,
rounding the station, entered a narrow strip of ground
which was, rather pathetically, intended for a park. February had done its worst, and up above the chill evening
wind from the desert blew through the stark branches of
Carolina poplars and cottonwoods. Crossing a gravel
path almost hidden by a mass of yellow leaves, he stood
on the curb of the only pavement in Eldorado.

Against the background of bare brown hills, he saw
practically the entire town at a glance. Across the way
a row of scraggly buildings proclaimed yet another Main
Street—a bank, a picture theater, the Spot Cash Store,
the News Bureau, the post-office, and towering above the
rest, a two-story building that announced itself as the
Desert Edge Hotel. Eden crossed the street, and thread-
ing his way between dusty automobiles parked head-on
at the curb, approached the door of the latter. On the
double seat of a shoe-shining stand two ranchers lolled
at ease, and stared at him with mild interest as he went
inside.

An electric lamp of modest candle-power burned
above the desk of the Desert Edge, and a kindly old man
read a Los Angeles paper in its dim company.

"Good evening," said Bob Eden.

"Evenin'," answered the old man

"I wonder if I might leave this suit-case in your
check-room for a while?" the boy inquired.

"Check-room, hell," replied the old man. "Just throw

her down anywhere. Ain't lookin' fer a room, I suppose. Make you a special rate."

"No," said Eden. "I'm sorry."

" 'Sall right," answered the proprietor. "Not many are."

"I'd like to find the office of the *Eldorado Times*," Eden informed him.

"Round corner on First," murmured the old man, deep in his pink newspaper again.

Bob Eden went to the corner, and turned off. His feet at once left Eldorado's solitary sidewalk for soft crunching sand. He passed a few buildings even meaner than those on Main Street, a plumber's shop, a grocer's, and came to a little yellow shack which bore on its window the fading legend: "The Eldorado Times. Job Printing Neatly Done." There was no light inside, and crossing a narrow, dilapidated porch, he saw a placard on the door. Straining his eyes in the dusk, he read:

"Back in an hour—
God knows why.
Will Holley."

Smiling, Eden returned to the Desert Edge. "How about dinner?" he inquired.

"Wonderin' about it myself," admitted the old man. "We don't serve meals here. Lose a little less that way."

"But there must be a restaurant—"

"Sure there is. This is an up-to-date town." He nodded over his shoulder. "Down beyond the bank—the Oasis Café."

Thanking him, Bob Eden departed. Behind unwashed windows he found the Oasis dispensing its dubious cheer.

A long high counter and a soiled mirror running the length of it suggested that in other days this had been an oasis indeed.

The boy climbed on to one of the perilously high stools. At his right, too close for comfort, sat a man in overalls and jumper, with a week's growth of beard on his lean hard face. At his left, equally close but somehow not so much in the way, was a trim girl in khaki riding breeches and blouse.

A youth made up to resemble a motion-picture sheik demanded his order, and from a soiled menu he chose the Oasis Special—"steak and onions, French fried, bread and butter and coffee. Eighty cents." The sheik departed languidly.

Awaiting the special, Bob Eden glanced into the smoky mirror at the face of the girl beside him. Not so bad, even in that dim reflection. Corn yellow hair curling from under the brim of a felt hat; a complexion that no beauty parlor had originated. He held his left elbow close so that she might have more room for the business that engrossed her.

His dinner arrived, a plenteous platter of food—but no plate. He glanced at his neighbors. Evidently plates were an affectation frowned upon in the Oasis. Taking up a tarnished knife and fork, he pushed aside the underbrush of onions and came face to face with his steak.

First impressions are important, and Bob Eden knew at once that this was no meek, complacent opponent that confronted him. The steak looked back at him with an air of defiance that was amply justified by what followed. After a few moments of unsuccessful battling, he summoned the sheik. "How about a steel knife?" he inquired.

"Only got three and they're all in use," the waiter replied.

Bob Eden resumed the battle, his elbows held close, his muscles swelling. With set teeth and grim face he bore down and cut deep. There was a terriffic screech as his knife skidded along the platter, and to his horror he saw the steak rise from its bed of gravy and onions and fly from him. It traveled the grimy counter for a second, then dropped on to the knees of the girl and thence to the floor.

Eden turned to meet her blue eyes filled with laughter. "Oh, I'm so sorry," he said. "I thought it was a steak, and it seems to be a lap dog."

"And I hadn't any lap," she cried. She looked down at her riding breeches. "Can you ever forgive me? I might have caught it for you. It only goes to show—women should be womanly."

"I wouldn't have you any different," Bob Eden responded gallantly. He turned to the sheik. "Bring me something a little less ferocious," he ordered.

"How about the pot roast?" asked the youth.

"Well, how about it?" Eden repeated. "Fetch it along and I'll fight another round. I claim a foul on that one. And say—bring this young woman a napkin."

"A what? A napkin. We ain't got any. I'll bring her a towel."

"Oh, no—please don't," cried the girl. "I'm all right, really."

The sheik departed.

"Somehow," she added to Eden, "I think it wiser not to introduce an Oasis towel into this affair."

"You're probably right," he nodded. "I'll pay for the damage, of course."

She was still smiling. "Nonsense. I ought to pay for the steak. It wasn't your fault. One needs long practise to eat in the crowded arena of the Oasis."

He looked at her, his interest growing every minute. "You've had long practise?" he inquired.

"Oh, yes. My work often brings me this way."

"Your—er—your work?"

"Yes. Since your steak seems to have introduced us, I may tell you I'm with the moving pictures."

Of course, thought Eden. The desert was filled with movie people these days. "Ah—have I ever seen you in the films?" he ventured.

She shrugged. "You have not—and you never will. I'm not an actress. My job's much more interesting. I'm a location finder."

Bob Eden's pot roast arrived, mercifully cut into small pieces by some blunt instrument behind the scenes. "A location finder. I ought to know what that is."

"You certainly ought to. It's just what it sounds like. I travel about hunting backgrounds. By the Vandeventer Trail to Piñon Flat, down to the Salton Sea or up to the Morongos—all the time trying to find something new, something the dear old public will mistake for Algeria, Araby, the South Seas."

"Sounds mighty interesting."

"It is, indeed. Particularly when one loves this country as I do.'

"You were born here, perhaps?"

"Oh, no. I came out with dad to Doctor Whitcomb's—it's five miles from here, just beyond the Madden ranch—some years ago. When—when dad left me I had to get a job, and—but look here, I'm telling you the story of my life."

"Why not?" asked Eden. "Women and children always confide in me. I've got such a fatherly face. By
the way, this coffee is terrible."

"Yes, isn't it?" she agreed. "What will you have for
dessert? There are two kinds of pie—apple, and the
other's out. Make your selection."

"I've made it," he replied. "I'm taking the one that's
out." He demanded his check. "Now, if you'll let me
pay for your dinner—"

"Nothing of the sort," she protested.

"But after the way my steak attacked you."

"Forget it. I've an expense account, you know. If
you say any more, I'll pay your check."

Ignoring the jar of toothpicks hospitably offered by
a friendly cashier, Bob Eden followed her to the street
Night had fallen; the sidewalk was deserted. On the
false front of a long low building with sides of corrugated
tin, a sad little string of electric lights proclaimed that
gaiety was afoot.

"Whither away?" Bob Eden said. "The movies?"

"Heavens, no. I remember that one. It took ten
years off my young life. Tell me, what are you doing
here? People confide in me, too. Stranger, you don't
belong."

"No, I'm afraid I don't," Eden admitted. "It's a
complicated story but I'll inflict it on you anyhow, some
day. Just at present I'm looking for the editor of the
Eldorado Times. I've got a letter to him in my pocket."

"Will Holley?"

"Yes. You know him?"

"Everybody knows him. Come with me. He ought
to be in his office now."

They turned down First Street. Bob Eden was pleasantly conscious of the slim lithe figure walking at his side.
He had never before met a girl so modestly confident, so
aware of life and unafraid of it. These desert towns
were delightful.

A light was burning in the newspaper office, and
under it a frail figure sat hunched over a typewriter. As
they entered Will Holley rose, removing a green shade
from his eyes. He was a thin tall man of thirty-five or
so, with prematurely gray hair and wistful eyes.

"Hello, Paula," he said.

"Hello, Will. See what *I* found at the Oasis Café."

Holley smiled. "You would find him," he said.
"You're the only one I know who can discover anything
worth while in Eldorado. My boy, I don't know who you
are, but run away before this desert gets you."

"I've a letter to you, Mr. Holley," Eden said. He
took it from his pocket. "It's from an old friend of
yours—Harry Fladgate."

"Harry Fladgate," repeated Holley softly. He read
the letter through. "A voice from the past," he said.
"The past when we were boys together on the old *Sun*,
in New York. Say—that was a newspaper!" He was
silent for a moment, staring out at the desert night.
"Harry says you're here on business of some sort," he
added.

"Why, yes," Eden replied. "I'll tell you about it
later. Just at present I want to hire a car to take me out
to the Madden ranch."

"You want to see P. J. himself?"

"Yes, just as soon as possible. He's out there, isn't
he?"

Holley nodded. "Yes—he's supposed to be. How-ever, I haven't seen him. It's rumored he came by motor the other day from Barstow. This young woman can tell you more about him than I can. By the way, have you two met each other, or are you just taking a stroll to-gether in the moonlight?"

"Well, the fact is—" smiled Eden. "Miss—er—she just let a steak of mine get away from her in the Oasis. I had to credit her with an error in the infield, but she made a splendid try. However, as to names—and all that—"

"So I perceive," said Holley. "Miss Paula Wendell, may I present Mr. Bob Eden. Let us not forget our book of etiquette, even here in the devil's garden."

"Thanks, old man," remarked Eden. "No one has ever done me a greater kindness. Now that we've been introduced, Miss Wendell, and I can speak to you at last, tell me—do you know Mr. Madden?"

"Not exactly," she replied. "It isn't given such hum-ble folk to know the great Madden. But several years ago my company took some pictures at his ranch—he has rather a handsome house there, with a darling patio. The other day we got hold of a script that fairly screamed for the Madden patio. I wrote him, asking permission to use his place, and he answered—from San Francisco—that he was coming down and would be glad to grant our request. His letter was really most kind."

The girl sat down on the edge of Holley's typewriter table. "I got to Eldorado two nights ago, and drove out to Madden's at once. And—well, it was rather queer—what happened. Do you want to hear all this?"

"I certainly do," Bob Eden assured her.

"The gate was open, and I drove into the yard. The lights of my car flashed suddenly on the barn door, and I saw a bent old man with a black beard and a pack on his back—evidently an old-time prospector such as one meets occasionally, even to-day, in this desert country. It was his expression that startled me. He stood like a frightened rabbit in the spotlight, then darted away. I knocked at the ranch house door. There was a long delay, then finally a man came, a pale, excited-looking man—Madden's secretary, Thorn, he said he was. I give you my word—Will's heard this before—he was trembling all over. I told him my business with Madden, and he was very rude. He informed me that I positively could not see the great P. J. 'Come back in a week,' he said, over and over. I argued and pleaded—and he shut the door in my face."

"You couldn't see Madden," repeated Bob Eden slowly. "Anything else?"

"Not much. I drove back to town. A short distance down the road my lights picked up the little old prospector again. But when I got to where I thought he was, he'd disappeared utterly. I didn't investigate—I just stepped on the gas. My love for the desert isn't so keen after dark."

Bob Eden took out a cigarette. "I'm awfully obliged," he said. "Mr. Holley, I must get out to Madden's at once. If you'll direct me to a garage—"

"I'll do nothing of the sort," Holley replied. "An old flivver that answers to the name of Horace Greeley happens to be among my possessions at the moment, and I'm going to drive you out."

"I couldn't think of taking you away from your work."

'Oh, don't joke like that. You're breaking my heart. My work! Here I am, trying to string one good day's work along over all eternity, and you drift in and start to kid me—"

"I'm sorry," said Eden. "Come to think of it, I did see your placard on the door."

Holley shrugged. "I suppose that was just cheap cynicism. I try to steer clear of it. But sometimes— sometimes—"

They went together out of the office, and Holley locked the door. The deserted, sad little street stretched off to nowhere in each direction. The editor waved his hand at the somnolent picture.

"You'll find us all about out here," he said, "the exiles of the world. Of course, the desert is grand, and we love it—but once let a doctor say 'you can go' and you couldn't see us for the dust. I don't mind the day-time so much—the hot friendly day—but the nights—the cold lonely nights."

"Oh, it isn't so bad, Will," said the girl gently.

"Oh no, it isn't so bad," he admitted. "Not since the radio—and the pictures. Night after night I sit over there in that movie theater, and sometimes, in a news-reel or perhaps in a feature, I see Fifth Avenue again, Fifth Avenue at Forty-second, with the motors, and the lions in front of the library, and the women in furs. But I never see Park Row." The three of them walked along in silence through the sand. "If you love me, Paula," added Will Holley softly, "there's a location you'll find. A story about Park Row, with the crowds under the El, and the wagons backed up to the rear door of the post-office, and Perry's Drug Store and the gold dome of the

World. Give me a film of that, and I'll sit in the Strand watching it over and over until these old eyes go blind."

"I'd like to," said the girl. "But those crowds under the Elevated wouldn't care for it. What they want is the desert—the broad open spaces away from the roar of the town."

Holley nodded. "I know. It's a feeling that's spread over America these past few years like some dread epidemic. I must write an editorial about it. The French have a proverb that describes it—'Wherever one is not, that is where the heart is.' "

The girl held out her hand. "Mr. Eden, I'm leaving you here—leaving you for a happy night at the Desert Edge Hotel."

"But I'll see you again," Bob Eden said quickly. "I must."

"You surely will. I'm coming out to Madden's ranch to-morrow. I have that letter of his, and this time I'll see him—you bet I'll see him—if he's there."

"If he's there," repeated Bob Eden thoughtfully. "Good night. But before you go—how do you like your steaks?"

"Rare," she laughed.

"Yes—I guess one was enough. However, I'm very grateful to that one."

"It was a lovely steak," she said. "Good night."

Will Holley led the way to an aged car parked before the hotel. "Jump in," he said. "It's only a short run."

"Just a moment—I must get my bag," Eden replied. He entered the hotel and returned in a moment with his suit-case. which he tossed into the tonneau. "Horace Greeley's ready," Holley said. "Come west, young man."

Eden climbed in and the little car clattered down Main Street. "This is mighty kind of you," the boy said.

"It's a lot of fun," Holley answered. "You know, I've been thinking. Old P. J. never gives an interview, but you can't tell—I might be able to persuade him. These famous men sometimes let down a little when they get out here. It would be a big feather in my cap. They'd hear of me on Park Row again."

"I'll do all I can to help," Bob Eden promised.

"That's good of you," Holley answered. The faint yellow lights of Eldorado grew even fainter behind them. They ascended a rough road between two small hills—barren, unlovely piles of badly assorted rocks. "Well, I'm going to try it," the editor added. "But I hope I have more luck than the last time."

"Oh—then you've seen Madden before?" Eden asked with interest.

"Just once," Holley replied. "Twelve years ago, when I was a reporter in New York. I'd managed to get into a gambling house on Forty-fourth Street, a few doors east of Delmonico's. It didn't have a very good reputation, that joint, but there was the great P. J. Madden himself, all dolled up in evening clothes, betting his head off. They said that after he'd gambled all day in Wall Street, he couldn't let it alone—hung round the roulette wheels in that house every night."

"And you tried to interview him?"

"I did. I was a fool kid, with lots of nerve. He had a big railroad merger in the air at the time, and I decided to ask him about it. So I went up to him during a lull in the betting. I told him I was on a newspaper—and that was as far as I got. 'Get the hell out of here,' he

roared. 'You know I never give interviews.' " Holley
laughed. "That was my first and only meeting with P.
J. Madden. It wasn't a very propitious beginning, but
what I started that night on Forty-fourth Street I'm
going to try to finish out here to-night."

They reached the top of the grade, the rocky hills
dropped behind them, and they were in a mammoth doorway leading to a strange new world. Up amid the
platinum stars a thin slice of moon rode high, and far
below in that meager light lay the great gray desert,
lonely and mysterious.

CHAPTER V

CAREFULLY Will Holley guided his car down the steep, rock-strewn grade. "Go easy, Horace," he murmured. Presently they were on the floor of the desert, the road but a pair of faint wheel tracks amid the creosote brush and mesquite. Once their head-lights caught a jack-rabbit, sitting firmly on the right of way; the next instant he was gone forever.

Bob Eden saw a brief stretch of palm trees back of a barbed-wire fence, and down the lane between the trees the glow of a lonely window.

"Alfalfa ranch," Will Holley explained.

"Why, in heaven's name, do people live out here?" Eden asked.

"Some of them because they can't live anywhere else," the editor answered. "And at that—well, you know it isn't a bad place to ranch it. Apples, lemons, pears—"

"But how about water?"

"It's only a desert because not many people have taken the trouble to bore for water. Just go down a ways, and you strike it. Some go down a couple of hundred feet—Madden only had to go thirty odd. But that was Madden luck. He's near the bed of an underground river."

58

They came to another fence; above it were painted
signs and flags fluttering yellow in the moonlight.

"Don't tell me that's a subdivision," Eden said.

Holley laughed. "Date City," he announced. "Here
in California the subdivider, like the poor, is always with
us. Date City where, if you believe all you're told,
every dime is a baby dollar. No one lives there yet—
but who knows? We're a growing community—see my
editorial in last week's issue."

The car plowed on. It staggered a bit now, but
Holley's hands were firm on the wheel. Here and there
a Joshua tree stretched out hungry black arms as though
to seize these travelers by night, and over that gray waste
a dismal wind moaned constantly, chill and keen and
biting. Bob Eden turned up the collar of his top coat.

"I can't help thinking of that old song," he said.
"You know—about the lad who guaranteed to love somebody 'until the sands of the desert grow cold.' "

"It wasn't much of a promise," agreed Holley.
"Either he was a great kidder, or he'd never been on the
desert at night. But look here—is this your first experience with this country? What kind of a Californian are
you?"

"Golden Gate brand," smiled Eden. "Yes, it's true,
I've never been down here before. Something tells me
I've missed a lot."

"You sure have. I hope you won't rush off in a
hurry. By the way, how long do you expect to be here?"

"I don't know," replied Eden. He was silent for a
moment; his friend at home had told him that Holley
could be trusted, but he really did not need that assurance.
One look into the editor's friendly gray eyes was

sufficient. "Holley, I may as well tell you why I've come," he continued. "But I rely on your discretion. This isn't an interview."

"Suit yourself," Holley answered. "I can keep a secret if I have to. But tell me or not, just as you prefer."

"I prefer to tell you," Eden said. He recounted Madden's purchase of the Phillimore pearls, his request for their delivery in New York, and then his sudden unexpected switch to the desert. "That, in itself, was rather disturbing," he added.

"Odd, yes," agreed Holley.

"But that wasn't all," Bob Eden went on. Omitting only Charlie Chan's connection with the affair, he told the whole story—the telephone call from the cigar store in San Francisco, the loving solicitude at the dock and after of the man with the dark glasses, the subsequent discovery that this was Shaky Phil Maydorf, a guest at the Killarney Hotel, and last of all, the fact that Louie Wong had been summoned from the Madden ranch by his relative in Chinatown. As he related all this out there on that lonesome desert, it began to take on a new and ominous aspect, the future loomed dark and thrilling. Had that great opening between the hills been, in reality, the gateway to adventure? Certainly it looked the part. "What do you think?" he finished.

"Me?" said Holley. "I think I'm not going to get that interview."

"You don't believe Madden is at the ranch?"

"I certainly don't. Look at Paula's experience the other night. Why couldn't she see him? Why didn't he hear her at the door and come to find out what the row was about? Because he wasn't there. My lad, I'm glad you didn't venture out here alone. Particularly if you've brought the pearls—as I presume you have."

"Well, in a way, I've got them. About this Louie Wong? You know him, I suppose?"

"Yes. And I saw him at the station the other morning. Look at to-morrow's *Eldorado Times* and you'll find the big story, under the personals. 'Our respected fellow townsman, Mr. Louie Wong, went to San Francisco on business last Wednesday.'"

"Wednesday, eh? What sort of lad is Louie?"

"Why—he's just a Chinaman. Been in these parts a long time. For the past five years he's stayed at Madden's ranch the year round, as caretaker. I don't know a great deal about him. He's never talked much to any one round here—except the parrot."

"The parrot? What parrot?"

"His only companion on the ranch. A little gray Australian bird that some sea captain gave Madden several years ago. Madden brought the bird—its name is Tony—here to be company for the old caretaker. A rough party, Tony—used to hang out in a barroom on an Australian boat. Some of his language when he first came was far from pretty. But they're clever, those Australian parrots. You know, from associating with Louie, this one has learned to speak Chinese."

"Amazing," said Bob Eden.

"Oh, not so amazing as it sounds. A bird of that sort will repeat anything it hears. So Tony rattles along in two languages. A regular linguist. The ranchers round here call him the Chinese parrot." They had reached a little group of cottonwoods and pepper trees sheltering a handsome adobe ranch house—an oasis on the bare plain. "Here we are at Madden's," Holley said. "By the way—have you got a gun?"

"Why, no," Bob Eden replied. "I didn't bring any. I thought that Charlie—"

"What's that?"

"No matter. I'm unarmed."

"So am I. Walk softly, son. By the way, you might open that gate, if you will."

Bob Eden got out and, unlatching the gate, swung it open. When Holley had steered Horace Greeley inside the yard, Eden shut the gate behind him. The editor brought his car to a stop twenty feet away, and alighted.

The ranch house was a one-story structure, eloquent of the old Spanish days in California before Iowa came. Across the front ran a long low veranda, the roof of which sheltered four windows that were glowing warmly in the chill night. Holley and the boy crossed the tile floor of the porch, and came to a big front door, strong and forbidding.

Eden knocked loudly. There was a long wait. Finally the door opened a scant foot, and a pale face looked out. "What is it? What do you want?" inquired a querulous voice. From inside the room came the gay lilt of a fox-trot.

"I want to see Mr. Madden," Bob Eden said. "Mr. P. J. Madden."

"Who are you?"

"Never mind. I'll tell Madden who I am. Is he here?"

The door went shut a few inches. "He's here, but he isn't seeing any one."

"He'll see me, Thorn," said Eden sharply. "You're Thorn, I take it. Please tell Madden that a messenger from Post Street, San Francisco, is waiting."

The door swung instantly open, and Martin Thorn was as near to beaming as his meager face permitted.

"Oh, pardon me. Come in at once. We've been expecting you. Come in—ah—er—gentlemen." His face clouded as he saw Holley. "Excuse me just a moment."

The secretary disappeared through a door at the rear, and left the two callers standing in the great living-room of the ranch house. To step from the desert into a room like this was a revelation. Its walls were of paneled oak; rare etchings hung upon them; there were softly shaded lamps standing by tables on which lay the latest magazines—even a recent edition of a New York Sunday newspaper. At one end, in a huge fireplace, a pile of logs was blazing, and in a distant corner a radio ground out dance music from some far orchestra.

'Say, this is home, sweet home," Bob Eden remarked. He nodded to the wall at the opposite end of the room from the fireplace. "And speaking of being unarmed—"

"That's Madden's collection of guns," Holley explained. "Wong showed it to me once. They're loaded. If you have to back away, go in that direction." He looked dubiously about. "You know, that sleek lad didn't say he was going for Madden."

"I know he didn't," Eden replied. He studied the room thoughtfully. One great question worried him— where was Charlie Chan?

They stood there, waiting. A tall clock at the rear of the room struck the hour of nine, slowly, deliberately. The fire sputtered; the metallic tinkle of jazz flowed on.

Suddenly the door through which Thorn had gone opened suddenly behind them, and they swung quickly about. In the doorway, standing like a tower of granite in the gray clothes he always affected, was the man Bob Eden had last seen on the stairs descending from his father's office, Madden, the great financier—P. J. himself.

Bob Eden's first reaction was one of intense relief, as of a burden dropping from his shoulders with a "most delectable thud." But almost immediately after came a feeling of disappointment. He was young, and he craved excitement. Here was the big desert mystery crashing about his ears, Madden alive and well, and all their fears and premonitions proving groundless. Just a tame handing over of the pearls—when Charlie came—and then back to the old rut again. He saw Will Holley smiling.

"Good evening, gentleman," Madden was saying. "I'm very glad to see you. Martin," he added to his secretary, who had followed him in, "turn off that confounded racket. An orchestra, gentlemen—an orchestra in the ballroom of a hotel in Denver. Who says the day of miracles is past?" Thorn silenced the jazz; it died with a gurgle of protest. "Now," inquired Madden, "which of you comes from Post Street?"

The boy stepped forward. "I am Bob Eden, Mr. Madden. Alexander Eden is my father. This is my friend, a neighbor of yours, Mr. Will Holley of the *Eldorado Times*. He very kindly drove me out here."

"Ah, yes." Madden's manner was genial. He shook hands. "Draw up to the fire, both of you. Thorn—cigars, please." With his own celebrated hands he placed chairs before the fireplace.

"I'll sit down just a moment," Holley said. "I'm not stopping. I realize that Mr. Eden has some business with you, and I'll not intrude. But before I go, Mr. Madden—"

"Yes," said Madden sharply, biting the end from a cigar.

"I—I don't suppose you remember me," Holley continued.

Madden's big hand poised with the lighted match. "I never forget a face. I've seen yours before. Was it in Eldorado?"

Holley shook his head. "No—it was twelve years ago—on Forty-fourth Street, New York. At"—Madden was watching him closely—"at a gambling house just east of Delmonico's. One winter's night—"

"Wait a minute," cut in the millionaire. "Some people say I'm getting old—but listen to this. You came to me as a newspaper reporter, asking an interview. And I told you to get the hell out of there."

"Splendid," laughed Holley.

"Oh, the old memory isn't so bad, eh? I remember perfectly. I used to spend many evenings in that place—until I discovered the game was fixed. Yes, I dropped a lot of spare change there. Why didn't you tell me it was a crooked joint?"

Holley shrugged. "Well, your manner didn't encourage confidences. But what I'm getting at, Mr. Madden—I'm still in the newspaper game, and an interview from you—"

"I never give 'em," snapped the millionaire.

"I'm sorry," said Holley. "An old friend of mine runs a news bureau in New York, and it would be a big triumph for me if I could wire him something from you. On the financial outlook, for example. The first interview from P. J. Madden."

"Impossible," answered Madden.

"I'm sorry to hear you say that, Mr. Madden," Bob Eden remarked. "Holley here has been very kind to me, and I was hoping with all my heart you would overlook your rule this once."

Madden leaned back, and blew a ring of smoke toward the paneled ceiling. "Well," he said, and his voice was somehow gentler, "you've taken a lot of trouble for me, Mr. Eden, and I'd like to oblige you." He turned to Holley. "Look here—nothing much, you know. Just a few words about business prospects for the coming year."

"That would be extremely kind of you, Mr. Madden."

"Oh, it's all right. I'm away out here, and I feel a bit differently about the newspapers than I do at home. I'll dictate something to Thorn—suppose you run out here to-morrow about noon."

"I certainly will," said Holley, rising. "You don't know what this means to me, sir. I must hurry back to town." He shook hands with the millionaire, then with Bob Eden. His eyes as he looked at the latter said: "Well, everything's all right, after all. I'm glad." He paused at the door. "Good-by—until to-morrow," he added. Thorn let him out.

The door had barely closed behind the editor when Madden leaned forward eagerly. His manner had changed; suddenly, like an electric shock, the boy felt the force of this famous personality. "Now, Mr. Eden," he began briskly, "you've got the pearls, of course?"

Eden felt extremely silly. All their fears seemed so futile here in this bright, home-like room. "Well, as a matter of fact—" he stammered.

A glass door at the rear of the room opened, and some one entered. Eden did not look round; he waited. Presently the newcomer stepped between him and the fire. He saw a plump little Chinese servant, with worn trousers and velvet slippers, and a loose jacket of Canton crêpe. In his arms he carried a couple of logs. "Maybe you wantee catch 'um moah fiah, hey, boss?" he said in a dull voice. His face was quite expressionless. He threw the logs into the fireplace and as he turned, gave Bob Eden a quick look. His eyes were momentarily sharp and bright—like black buttons in the yellow light. The eyes of Charlie Chan.

The little servant went noiselessly out. "The pearls," insisted Madden quickly. "What about the pearls?" Martin Thorn came closer.

"I haven't got them," said Bob Eden slowly.

"What! You didn't bring them?"

"I did not."

The huge red face of Madden purpled suddenly, and he tossed his great head—the old gesture of annoyance of which the newspapers often spoke. "In heaven's name, what's the matter with you fellows, anyhow?" he cried. "Those pearls are mine—I've bought them, haven't I? I've asked for them here—I want them."

"Call your servant." The words were on the tip of Bob Eden's tongue. But something in that look Charlie Chan had given him moved him to hesitate. No, he must first have a word with the little detective.

"Your final instructions to my father were that the

pearls must be delivered in New York," he reminded
Madden.

"Well, what if they were? I can change my mind,
can't I?"

"Nevertheless, my father felt that the whole affair
called for caution. One or two things happened—"

"What things?"

Eden paused. Why go over all that? It would sound
silly, perhaps—in any case, was it wise to make a confi-
dant of this cold, hard man who was glaring at him with
such evident disgust? "It is enough to say, Mr. Madden,
that my father refused to send that necklace down here
into what might be a well-laid trap."

"Your father's a fool," cried Madden.

Bob Eden rose, his face flushed. "Very well—if you
want to call the deal off—"

"No, no. I'm sorry. I spoke too quickly. I apologize. Sit down." The boy resumed his chair. "But I'm
very much annoyed. So your father sent you here to
reconnoiter?"

"He did. He felt something might have happened to
you."

"Nothing ever happens to me unless I want it to,"
returned Madden, and the remark had the ring of truth.
"Well, you're here now. You see everything's all right.
What do you propose to do?"

"I shall call my father on the telephone in the morning, and tell him to send the string at once. If I may,
I'd like to stay here until it comes."

Again Madden tossed his head. "Delay—delay—I
don't like it. I must hurry back east. I'd planned to
leave here for Pasadena early in the morning, put the

pearls in a vault there, and then take a train to New York."

"Ah," said Eden. "Then you never intended to give that interview to Holley?"

Madden's eyes narrowed. "What if I didn't? He's of no importance, is he?" Bruskly he stood up. "Well, if you haven't got the pearls, you haven't got them. You can stay here, of course. But you're going to call your father in the morning—early—I warn you I won't stand for any more delay."

"I agree to that," replied Eden. "And now, if you don't mind—I've had a hard day—"

Madden went to the door, and called. Charlie Chan came in.

"Ah Kim," said Madden, "this gentleman has the bedroom at the end of the left wing. Over here." He pointed. "Take his suit-case."

"Allight, boss," replied the newly christened Ah Kim. He picked up Eden's bag.

"Good night," said Madden. "If you want anything, this boy will look after you. He's new here, but I guess he knows the ropes. You can reach your room from the patio. I trust you'll sleep well."

"I know I shall," said Eden. "Thank you so much. Good night."

He crossed the patio behind the shuffling figure of the Chinese. Above, white and cool, hung the desert stars. The wind blew keener than ever. As he entered the room assigned him he was glad to see that a fire had been laid. He stooped to light it.

"Humbly begging pardon," said Chan. "That are my work."

Eden glanced toward the closed door. "What became of you? I lost you at Barstow."

"Thinking deep about the matter," said Chan softly, "I decide not to await train. On auto truck belonging to one of my countrymen, among many other vegetables, I ride out of Barstow. Much better I arrive on ranch in warm daylight. Not so shady look to it. I am Ah Kim, the cook. How fortunate I mastered that art in far-away youth."

"You're darned good," laughed Eden.

Chan shrugged. "All my life," he complained, "I study to speak fine English words. Now I must strangle all such in my throat, lest suspicion rouse up. Not a happy situation for me."

"Well, it won't last long," replied Eden. "Everything's all right, evidently."

Again Chan shrugged, and did not answer.

"It is all right, isn't it?" Eden asked with sudden interest.

"Humbly offering my own poor opinion," said Chan, "it are not so right as I would be pleased to have it."

Eden stared at him. "Why—what have you found out?"

"I have found nothing whatever."

"Well, then—"

"Pardon me," Chan broke in. "Maybe you know—Chinese are very psychic people. Can not say in ringing words what is wrong here. But deep down in heart—"

"Oh, forget that," cut in Eden. "We can't go by instinct now. We came to deliver a string of pearls to Madden, if he proved to be here, and get his receipt. He's here, and our course is simple. For my part, I'm not taking any chances. I'm going to give him those pearls now."

Chan looked distressed. "No, no, please! Speaking humbly for myself—"

"Now, see here, Charlie—if I may call you that?"

"Greatly honored, to be sure."

"Let's not be foolish, just because we're far from home on a desert. Chinese may be psychic people, as you say. But I see myself trying to explain that to Victor Jordan—and to dad. All we were to find out was whether Madden was here or not. He is. Please go to Madden at once and tell him I want to see him in his bedroom in twenty minutes. When I go in you wait outside his door, and when I call you—come. We'll hand over our burden then and there."

"An appalling mistake," objected Chan.

"Why? Can you give me one definite reason?"

"Not in words, which are difficult. But—"

"Then I'm very sorry, but I'll have to use my own judgment. I'll take the full responsibility. Now, really, I think you'd better go—"

Reluctantly, Charlie went. Bob Eden lighted a cigarette and sat down before the fire. Silence had closed down like a curtain of fog over the house, over the desert, over the world. An uncanny silence that nothing, seemingly, would ever break.

Eden thought deeply. What had Charlie Chan been talking about, anyhow? Rot and nonsense. They loved to dramatize things, these Chinese. Loved to dramatize themselves. Here was Chan playing a novel rôle, and his complaint against it was not sincere. He wanted to go on playing it, to spy around and imagine vain things.

Well, that wasn't the American way. It wasn't Bob Eden's way.

The boy looked at his watch. Ten minutes since Charlie had left him; in ten minutes more he would go to Madden's room and get those pearls off his hands forever. He rose and walked about. From his window opposite the patio he looked out across the dim gray desert to the black bulk of distant hills. Ye gods, what a country. Not for him, he thought. Rather street lamps shining on the pavements, the clamor of cable-cars, crowds, crowds of people. Confusion and—noise. Something terrible about this silence. This lonely silence—

A horrible cry shattered the night. Bob Eden stood, frozen. Again the cry, and then a queer, choked voice: "Help! Help! Murder!" The cry. "Help! Put down that gun! Help! Help!"

Bob Eden ran out into the patio. As he did so, he saw Thorn and Charlie Chan coming from the other side. Madden—where was Madden? But again his suspicion proved incorrect—Madden emerged from the living-room and joined them.

Again came the cry. And now Bob Eden saw, on a perch ten feet away, the source of the weird outburst. A little gray Australian parrot was hanging there uncertainly, screeching its head off.

"That damn bird," cried Madden angrily. "I'm sorry, Mr. Eden—I forgot to tell you about him. It's only Tony, and he's had a wild past, as you may imagine."

The parrot stopped screaming and blinked solemnly at the little group before him. "One at a time, gentlemen, please," he squawked.

Madden laughed. "That goes back to his barroom

days," he said. "Picked it up from some bartender, I suppose."

"One at a time, gentlemen, please."

"It's all right, Tony," Madden continued. "We're not lined up for drinks. And you keep quiet. I hope you weren't unduly alarmed, Mr. Eden. There seems to have been a killing or two in those barrooms where Tony used to hang out. Martin,"—he turned to his secretary—"take him to the barn and lock him up."

Thorn came forward. Bob Eden thought that the secretary's face was even paler than usual in the moonlight. He held out his hands to the parrot. Did Eden imagine it, or were the hands really trembling? "Here, Tony," said Thorn. "Nice Tony. You come with me." Gingerly he unfastened the chain from Tony's leg.

"You wanted to see me, didn't you?" Madden said. He led the way to his bedroom, and closed the door behind them. "What is it? Have you got those pearls, after all?"

The door opened, and the Chinese shuffled into the room.

"What the devil do you want?" cried Madden.

"You allight, boss?"

"Of course, I'm all right. Get out of here."

"Tomallah," said Charlie Chan in his rôle of Ah Kim, and a glance that was full of meaning passed between him and Bob Eden. "Tomallah nice day, you bet. See you tomallah, gentlemen."

He departed, leaving the door open. Eden saw him moving across the patio on silent feet. He was not waiting outside Madden's door.

"What was it you wanted?" Madden persisted.

Bob Eden thought quickly. "I wanted to see you alone for just a moment. This Thorn—you can trust him, can't you?"

Madden snorted. "You give me a pain," he said. "Any one would think you were bringing me the Bank of England. Of course, Thorn's all right. He's been with me for fifteen years."

"I just wanted to be sure," Eden answered. "I'll get hold of dad early in the morning. Good night."

He returned to the patio. The secretary was hurrying in from his unwelcome errand. "Good night, Mr. Thorn," Eden said.

"Oh—er—good night, Mr. Eden," answered the man. He passed furtively from sight.

Back in his room, Eden began to undress. He was both puzzled and disturbed. Was this adventure to be as tame as it looked? Still in his ears rang the unearthly scream of the parrot. After all, had it been in a barroom that Tony picked up that hideous cry for help?

CHAPTER VI

TONY'S HAPPY NEW YEAR

FORGETTING the promise he had made to rise and telephone his father early in the morning, Bob Eden lingered on in the pleasant company of his couch. The magnificent desert sunrise, famous wherever books are sold, came and went without the seal of his approval, and a haze of heat spread over the barren world. It was nine o'clock when he awoke from a most satisfactory sleep and sat up in bed.

Staring about the room, he gradually located himself on the map of California. One by one the events of the night before came back to him. First of all the scene at the Oasis—that agile steak eluding him with diabolic cunning—the girl whose charming presence made the dreary café an oasis indeed. The ride over the desert with Will Holley, the bright and cheery living-room of the ranch house, the fox-trot from a Denver orchestra. Madden, leaning close and breathing hard, demanding the Phillimore pearls. Chan in his velvet slippers, whispering of psychic fears and dark premonitions. And then the shrill cry of the parrot out of the desert night.

Now, however, the tense troubled feeling with which he had gone to bed was melting away in the yellow sunshine of the morning. The boy began to suspect that he

75

had made rather a fool of himself in listening to the little detective from the islands. Chan was an Oriental, also a policeman. Such a combination was bound to look at almost any situation with a jaundiced eye. After all he, Bob Eden, was here as the representative of Meek and Eden, and he must act as he saw fit. Was Chan in charge of this expedition, or was he?

The door opened, and on the threshold stood Ah Kim, in the person of Charlie Chan.

"You come 'long, boss," said his confederate loudly. "You ac' lazy bimeby you no catch 'um bleckfast."

Having said which, Charlie gently closed the door and came in, grimacing as one who felt a keen distaste.

"Silly talk like that hard business for me," he complained. "Chinese without accustomed dignity is like man without clothes, naked and ashamed. You enjoy long, restful sleep, I think."

Eden yawned. "Compared to me last night, Rip Van Winkle had insomnia."

"That's good. Humbly suggest you tear yourself out of that bed now. The great Madden indulges in nervous fit on living-room rug."

Eden laughed. "Suffering, is he? Well, we'll have to stop that." He tossed aside the covers.

Chan was busy at the curtains. "Favor me by taking a look from windows," he remarked. "On every side desert stretches off like floor of eternity. Plenty acres of unlimitable sand."

Bob Eden glanced out. "Yes, it's the desert, and there's plenty of it, that's a fact. But look here—we ought to talk fast while we have the chance. Last night you made a sudden change in our plans."

"Presuming greatly—yes."

"Why?"

Chan stared at him. "Why not? You yourself hear parrot scream out of the dark. 'Murder. Help. Help. Put down gun.'"

Eden nodded. "I know. But that probably meant nothing."

Charlie Chan shrugged. "You understand parrot does not invent talk. Merely repeats what others have remarked."

"Of course," Eden agreed. "And Tony was no doubt repeating something he heard in Australia, or on a boat. I happen to know that all Madden said of the bird's past was the truth. And I may as well tell you, Charlie, that looking at things in the bright light of the morning, I feel we acted rather foolishly last night. I'm going to give those pearls to Madden before breakfast."

Chan was silent for a moment. "If I might presume again, I would speak a few hearty words in praise of patience. Youth, pardon me, is too hot around the head. Take my advice, please, and wait."

"Wait. Wait for what?"

"Wait until I have snatched more conversation out of Tony. Tony very smart bird—he speaks Chinese. I am not so smart—but so do I."

"And what do you think Tony would tell you?"

"Tony might reveal just what is wrong on this ranch," suggested Chan.

"I don't believe anything's wrong," objected Eden.

Chan shook his head. "Not very happy position for me," he said, "that I must argue with bright boy like you are."

"But listen, Charlie," Eden protested. "I promised to call my father this morning. And Madden isn't an easy man to handle."

"Hoo malimali," responded Chan.

"No doubt you're right," Eden said. "But I don't understand Chinese."

"You have made natural error," Chan answered. "Pardon me while I correct you. That are not Chinese. It are Hawaiian talk. Well known in islands—hoo malimali—make Madden feel good by a little harmless deception. As my cousin Willie Chan, captain of All-Chinese baseball team, translate with his vulgarity, kid him along."

"Easier said than done," replied Eden.

"But you are clever boy. You could perfect it. Just a few hours, while I have talk with the smart Tony."

Eden considered. Paula Wendell was coming out this morning. Too bad to rush off without seeing her again. "Tell you what I'll do," he said. "I'll wait until two o'clock. But when the clock strikes two, if nothing has happened in the interval, we hand over those pearls. Is that understood?"

"Maybe," nodded Chan.

"You mean maybe it's understood?"

"Not precisely. I mean maybe we hand over pearls." Eden looked into the stubborn eyes of the Chinese, and felt rather helpless. "However," Chan added, "accept my glowing thanks. You are pretty good. Now proceed toward the miserable breakfast I have prepared."

"Tell Madden I'll be there very soon."

Chan grimaced. "With your kind permission, I will alter that message slightly, losing the word very. In memory of old times, there remains little I would not do

for Miss Sally. My life, perhaps—but by the bones of
my honorable ancestors, I will not say 'velly.' " He went
out.

On his perch in the patio, opposite Eden's window,
Tony was busy with his own breakfast. The boy saw
Chan approach the bird, and pause. "Hoo la ma," cried
the detective.

Tony looked up, and cocked his head on one side.
"Hoo la ma," he replied, in a shrill, harsh voice.

Chan went nearer, and began to talk rapidly in
Chinese. Now and then he paused, and the bird replied
amazingly with some phrase out of Chan's speech. It
was, Bob Eden reflected, as good as a show.

Suddenly from a door on the other side of the patio,
the man Thorn emerged. His pale face was clouded with
anger.

"Here," he cried loudly. "What the devil are you
doing?"

"Solly, boss," said the Chinese. "Tony nice litta fellah.
Maybe I take 'um to cook house."

"You keep away from him," Thorn ordered. "Get
me—keep away from that bird."

Chan shuffled off. For a long moment Thorn stood
staring after him, anger and apprehension mingled in his
look. As Bob Eden turned away, he was deep in thought.
Was there something in Chan's attitude, after all?

He hurried into the bath, which lay between his room
and the vacant bedroom beyond. When he finally joined
Madden, he thought he perceived the afterglow of that
nervous fit still on the millionaire's face.

"I'm sorry to be late," he apologized. "But this
desert air—"

"I know," said Madden. "It's all right—we haven't lost any time. I've already put in that call for your father."

"Good idea," replied the boy, without any enthusiasm. "Called his office, I suppose?"

"Naturally."

Suddenly Eden remembered. This was Saturday morning, and unless it was raining in San Francisco, Alexander Eden was by now well on his way to the golf links at Burlingame. There he would remain until late to-night at least—perhaps over Sunday. Oh, for a bright day in the north!

Thorn came in, sedate and solemn in his blue serge suit, and looked with hungry eyes toward the table standing before the fire. They sat down to the breakfast prepared by the new servant, Ah Kim. A good breakfast it was, for Charlie Chan had not forgotten his early training in the Phillimore household. As it progressed, Madden mellowed a bit.

"I hope you weren't alarmed last night by Tony's screeching," he said presently.

"Well—for a minute," admitted Eden. "Of course, as soon as I found out the source of the racket, I felt better."

Madden nodded. "Tony's a colorless little beast, but he's had a scarlet past," he remarked.

"Like some of the rest of us," Eden suggested.

Madden looked at him keenly. "The bird was given me by a sea captain in the Australian trade. I brought him here to be company for my caretaker, Louie Wong."

"I thought your boy's name was Ah Kim," said Eden, innocently.

"Oh—this one. This isn't Wong. Louie was called suddenly to San Francisco the other day. This Ah Kim just happened to drift in most opportunely yesterday. He's merely a stop-gap until Louie comes back."

"You're lucky," Eden remarked. "Such good cooks as Ah Kim are rare."

"Oh, he'll do," Madden admitted. "When I come west to stay, I bring a staff with me. This is a rather unexpected visit."

"Your real headquarters out here are in Pasadena, I believe?" Eden inquired.

"Yes—I've got a house there, on Orange Grove Avenue. I just keep this place for an occasional week-end— when my asthma threatens. And it's good to get away from the mob, now and then." The millionaire pushed back from the table, and looked at his watch. "Ought to hear from San Francisco any minute now," he added hopefully.

Eden glanced toward the telephone in a far corner. "Did you put the call in for my father, or just for the office?" he asked.

"Just for the office," Madden replied. "I figured that if he was out, we could leave a message."

Thorn came forward. "Chief, how about that interview for Holley?" he inquired.

"Oh, the devil!" Madden said. "Why did I let myself in for that?"

"I could bring the typewriter in here," began the secretary.

"No—we'll go to your room. Mr. Eden, if the telephone rings, please answer it."

The two went out. Ah Kim arrived on noiseless feet

to clear away the breakfast. Eden lighted a cigarette, and dropped into a chair before the fire, which the blazing sun outside made rather superfluous.

Twenty minutes later, the telephone rang. Eden leaped to it, but before he reached the table where it stood, Madden was at his side. He had hoped to be alone for this ordeal, and sighed wearily. At the other end of the wire he was relieved to hear the cool, melodious voice of his father's well-chosen secretary.

"Hello," he said. "This is Bob Eden, at Madden's ranch down on the desert. And how are you this bright and shining morning?"

"What makes you think it's a bright and shining morning up here?" asked the girl.

Eden's heart sank. "Don't tell me it isn't. I'd be broken-hearted."

"Why?"

"Why! Because, while you're beautiful at any time, I like to think of you with the sunlight on your hair—"

Madden laid a heavy hand on his shoulder. "What the blazes do you think you're doing—making a date with a chorus girl? Get down to business."

"Excuse it, please," said Eden. "Miss Chase, is my father there?"

"No. This is Saturday, you know. Golf."

"Oh yes—of course. Then it *is* a nice day. Well, tell him to call me here if he comes in. Eldorado 76."

"Where is he?" demanded Madden eagerly.

"Out playing golf," the boy answered.

"Where? What links?"

Bob sighed. "I suppose he's at Burlingame," he said over the wire.

Then—oh, excellent young woman, thought the boy—
the secretary answered: "Not to-day. He went with
some friends to another links. He didn't say which."

"Thank you so much," Eden said. "Just leave the
message on his desk, please." He hung up.

"Too bad," he remarked cheerfully. "Gone off to play
golf somewhere, and nobody knows where."

Madden swore. "The old simpleton. Why doesn't
he attend to his business—"

"Look here, Mr. Madden," Eden began.

"Golf, golf, golf," stormed Madden. "It's ruined
more good men than whisky. I tell you, if I'd fooled
round on golf links, I wouldn't be where I am to-day. If
your father had any sense—"

"I've heard about enough," said Eden, rising.

Madden's manner changed suddenly. "I'm sorry,"
he said. "But this is annoying, you must admit. I
wanted that necklace to start to-day."

"The day's young," Eden reminded him. "It may get
off yet."

"I hope so," Madden frowned. "I'm not accustomed
to this sort of dilly-dallying, I can tell you that."

His great head was tossing angrily as he went out.
Bob Eden looked after him, thoughtfully. Madden, master of many millions, was putting what seemed an undue
emphasis on a little pearl necklace. The boy wondered.
His father was getting on in years—he was far from the
New York markets. Had he made some glaring mistake
in setting a value on that necklace? Was it, perhaps,
worth a great deal more than he had asked, and was Madden fuming to get hold of it before the jeweler learned
his error and perhaps called off the deal? Of course,

Alexander Eden had given his word, but even so, Madden might fear a slip-up.

The boy strolled idly out into the patio. The chill night wind had vanished and he saw the desert of song and story, baking under a relentless sun. In the sandy little yard of the ranch house, life was humming along. Plump chickens and haughty turkeys strutted back of wire enclosures. He paused for a moment to stare with interest at a bed of strawberries, red and tempting. Up above, on the bare branches of the cottonwoods, he saw unmistakable buds, mute promise of a grateful shade not far away.

Odd how things lived and grew, here in this desolate country. He took a turn about the grounds. In one corner was a great reservoir half filled with water—a pleasant sight that must be on an August afternoon. Coming back to the patio, he stopped to speak to Tony, who was sitting rather dejectedly on his perch.

"Hoo la ma," he said.

Tony perked up. "Sung kai yat bo," he remarked.

"Yes, and a great pity, too," replied Eden facetiously.

"Gee fung low hop," added Tony, somewhat feebly.

"Perhaps, but I heard different," said Eden, and moved on. He wondered what Chan was doing. Evidently the detective thought it best to obey Thorn's command that he keep away from the bird. This was not surprising, for the windows of the secretary's room looked out on Tony's perch.

Back in the living-room, Eden took up a book. At a few minutes before twelve he heard the asthmatic cough of Horace Greeley in the yard and rising, he admitted Will Holley. The editor was smiling and alert.

"Hello," Eden said. "Madden's in there with Thorn, getting out the interview. Sit down." He came close. "And please remember that I haven't brought those pearls. My business with Madden is still unfinished."

Holley looked at him with sudden interest. "I get you. But I thought last night that everything was lovely. Do you mean—"

"Tell you later," interrupted Eden. "I may be in town this afternoon." He spoke in a louder tone. "I'm glad you came along. I was finding the desert a bit flat when you flivvered in."

Holley smiled. "Cheer up. I've got something for you. A veritable storehouse of wit and wisdom." He handed over a paper. "This week's issue of the *Eldorado Times*, damp from the presses. Read about Louie Wong's big trip to San Francisco. All the news to fit the print."

Eden took the proffered paper—eight small pages of mingled news and advertisements. He sank into a chair. "Well," he said, "it seems that the Ladies' Aid Supper last Tuesday night was notably successful. Not only that, but the ladies responsible for the affair labored assiduously and deserve much credit."

"Yes, but the real excitement's inside," remarked Holley. "On page three. There you'll learn that coyotes are getting pretty bad in the valley. A number of people are putting out traps."

"Under those circumstances," Eden said, "how fortunate that Henry Gratton is caring for Mr. Dickey's chickens during the latter's absence in Los Angeles."

Holley rose, and stared for a moment down at his tiny newspaper. "And once I worked with Mitchell on the *New York Sun*," he misquoted sadly. "Don't let

Harry Fladgate see that, will you? When Harry knew me I was a newspaper man." He moved off across the room. "By the way, has Madden shown you his collection of firearms?"

Bob Eden rose, and followed. "Why no—he hasn't."

"It's rather interesting. But dusty—say, I guess Louie was afraid.to touch them. Nearly every one of these guns has a history. See—there's a typewritten card above each one. 'Presented to P. J. Madden by Til Taylor'—Taylor was one of the best sheriffs Oregon ever had. And here—look at this one—it's a beauty. Given to Madden by Bill Tilghman. That gun, my boy, saw action on Front Street in the old Dodge City days."

"What's the one with all the notches?" Eden asked.

"Used to belong to Billy the Kid," said Holley. "Ask them about Billy over in New Mexico. And here's one Bat Masterson used to tote. But the star of the collection"—Holley's eyes ran over the wall—"the beauty of the lot—" He turned to Eden. "It isn't there," he said.

"There's a gun missing?" inquired Eden slowly.

"Seems to be. One of the first Colts made—a forty-five—it was presented to Madden by Bill Hart, who's staged a lot of pictures round here." He pointed to an open space on the wall. "There's where it used to be," he added, and was moving away.

Eden caught his coat sleeve. "Wait a minute," he said in a low, tense voice. "Let me get this. A gun missing. And the card's gone, too. You can see where the tacks held it in place."

"Well, what's all the excitement—" began Holley surprised.

Eden ran his finger over the wall. "There's no dust

where that card should be. What does that mean? That
Bill Hart's gun has been removed within the last few
days."

"My boy," said Holley. "What are you talking
about—"

"Hush," warned Eden. The door opened and Madden, followed by Thorn, entered the room. For a moment the millionaire stood, regarding them intently.

"Good morning, Mr. Holley," he said. "I've got your
interview here. You're wiring it to New York, you say?"

"Yes. I've queried my friend there about it this
morning. I know he'll want it."

"Well, it's nothing startling. I hope you'll mention
in the course of it where you got it. That will help to
soothe the feelings of the boys I've turned down so often
in New York. And you won't change what I've said?"

"Not a comma," smiled Holley. "I must hurry back
to town now. Thank you again, Mr. Madden."

"That's all right," said Madden. "Glad to help you
out."

Eden followed Holley to the yard. Out of earshot of
the house, the editor stopped.

"You seemed a little het up about that gun. What's
doing?"

"Oh, nothing, I suppose," said Eden. "On the other
hand—"

"What?"

"Well, Holley, it strikes me that something queer may
have happened lately on this ranch."

Holley stared. "It doesn't sound possible. However,
don't keep me in suspense."

"I've got to. It's a long story, and Madden mustn't

see us getting too chummy. I'll come in this afternoon, as I promised."

Holley climbed into his car. "All right," he said. "I can wait, I guess. See you later, then."

Eden was sorry to watch Horace Greeley stagger down the dusty road. Somehow the newspaper man brought a warm, human atmosphere to the ranch, an atmosphere that was needed there. But a moment later he was sorry no longer, for a little speck of brown in the distance became a smart roadster, and at its wheel he saw the girl of the Oasis, Paula Wendell.

He held open the gate, and with a cheery wave of her hand the girl drove past him into the yard.

"Hello," he said, as she alighted. "I was beginning to fear you weren't coming."

"I overslept," she explained. "Always do, in this desert country. Have you noticed the air? People who are in a position to know tell me it's like wine."

"Had a merry breakfast, I suppose?"

"I certainly did. At the Oasis."

"You poor child. That coffee."

"I didn't mind. Will Holley says that Madden's here."

"Madden? That's right—you do want to see Madden, don't you? Well, come along inside."

Thorn was alone in the living-room. He regarded the girl with a fishy eye. Not many men could have managed that, but Thorn was different.

"Thorn," said Eden. "Here's a young woman who wants to see Mr. Madden."

"I have a letter from him," the girl explained, "offering me the use of the ranch to take some pictures. You may remember—I was here Wednesday night."

"I remember," said Thorn sourly. "And I regret very much that Mr. Madden can not see you. He also asks me to say that unfortunately he must withdraw the permission he gave you in his letter."

"I'll accept that word from no one but Mr. Madden himself," returned the girl, and a steely light flamed suddenly in her eyes.

"I repeat—he will not see you," persisted Thorn.

The girl sat down. "Tell Mr. Madden his ranch is charming," she said. "Tell him I am seated in a chair in his living-room and that I shall certainly continue to sit here until he comes and speaks to me himself."

Thorn hesitated a moment, glaring angrily. Then he went out.

"I say—you're all right," Eden laughed.

"I aim to be," the girl answered, "and I've been on my own too long to take any nonsense from a mere secretary."

Madden blustered in. "What is all this—"

"Mr. Madden," the girl said, rising and smiling with amazing sweetness, "I was sure you'd see me. I have here a letter you wrote me from San Francisco. You recall it, of course."

Madden took the letter and glanced at it. "Yes, yes—of course. I'm very sorry, Miss Wendell, but since I wrote that certain matters have come up—I have a business deal on—" He glanced at Eden. "In short, it would be most inconvenient for me to have the ranch overrun with picture people at this time. I can't tell you how I regret it."

The girl's smile vanished. "Very well," she said, "but it means a black mark against me with the company. The people I work for don't accept excuses—only results. I have told them everything was arranged."

"Well, you were a little premature, weren't you?"

"I don't see why. I had the word of P. J. Madden. I believed—foolishly, perhaps—the old rumor that the word of Madden was never broken."

The millionaire looked decidedly uncomfortable. "Well—I—er—of course I never break my word. When did you want to bring your people here?"

"It's all arranged for Monday," said the girl.

"Out of the question," replied Madden. "But if you could postpone it a few days—say, until Thursday." Once more he looked at Eden. "Our business should be settled by Thursday," he added.

"Unquestionably," agreed Eden, glad to help.

"Very well," said Madden. He looked at the girl, and his eyes were kindly. He was no Thorn. "Make it Thursday, and the place is yours. I may not be here then myself, but I'll leave word to that effect."

"Mr. Madden, you're a dear," she told him. "I knew I could rely on you."

With a disgusted look at his employer's back, Thorn went out.

"You bet you can," said Madden, smiling pleasantly. He was melting fast. "And the record of P. J. Madden is intact. His word is as good as his bond—isn't that so?"

"If any one doubts it, let him ask me," replied the girl.

"It's nearly lunch time," Madden said. "You'll stay?"

"Well—I—really, Mr. Madden—"

"Of course she'll stay," Bob Eden broke in. "She's eating at a place in Eldorado called the Oasis, and if she doesn't stay, then she's just gone and lost her mind."

The girl laughed. "You're all so good to me," she said.

"Why not?" inquired Madden. "Then it's settled. We need some one like you around to brighten things up. Ah Kim," he added, as the Chinese entered, "another place for lunch. In about ten minutes, Miss Wendell."

He went out. The girl looked at Bob Eden. "Well, that's that. I knew it would be all right, if only he would see me."

"Naturally," said Eden. "Everything in this world would be all right, if every man in it could only see you."

"Sounds like a compliment," she smiled.

"Meant to be," replied the boy. "But what makes it sound so cumbersome? I must brush up on my social chatter."

"Oh—then it was only chatter?"

"Please—don't look too closely at what I say. I may tell you I've got a lot on my mind just now. I'm trying to be a business man, and it's some strain."

"Then you're not a real business man?"

"Not a real anything. Just sort of drifting. You know, you made me think, last night."

"I'm proud of that."

"Now—don't spoof me. I got to thinking—here you are, earning your living—luxurious pot roasts at the Oasis and all that—while I'm just father's little boy. I shouldn't be surprised if you inspired me to turn over a new leaf."

"Then I shan't have lived in vain." She nodded toward the far side of the room. "What in the world is the meaning of that arsenal?"

"Oh—that's gentle old Madden's collection of fire-

arms. A hobby of his. Come on over and I'll teach you
to call each one by name."

Presently Madden and Thorn returned, and Ah Kim
served a perfect lunch. At the table Thorn said nothing,
but his employer, under the spell of the girl's bright eyes,
talked volubly and well. As they finished coffee, Bob
Eden suddenly awoke to the fact that the big clock near
the patio windows marked the hour as five minutes of
two. At two o'clock! There was that arrangement with
Chan regarding two o'clock. What were they to do? The
impassive face of the Oriental as he served lunch had told
the boy nothing.

Madden was in the midst of a long story about his
early struggle toward wealth, when the Chinese came
suddenly into the room. He stood there, and though he
did not speak, his manner halted the millionaire as effec-
tively as a pistol shot.

"Well, well, what is it?" Madden demanded.

"Death," said Ah Kim solemnly in his high-pitched
voice. "Death unevitable end. No wolly. No solly."

"What in Sam Hill are you talking about?" Madden
inquired. Thorn's pale green eyes were popping.

"Poah litta Tony," went on Ah Kim.

"What about Tony?"

"Poah litta Tony enjoy happly noo yeah in Hades-
land," finished Ah Kim.

Madden was instantly on his feet, and led the way to
the patio. On the stone floor beneath his perch lay the
lifeless body of the Chinese parrot.

The millionaire stooped and picked up the bird.
"Why—poor old Tony," he said. "He's gone west. He's
dead."

Eden's eyes were on Thorn. For the first time since he met that gentleman he thought he detected the ghost of a smile on the secretary's pale face.

"Well, Tony was old," continued Madden. "A very old boy. And as Ah Kim says, death is inevitable—" He stopped, and looked keenly at the expressionless face of the Chinese. "I've been expecting this," he added. "Tony hasn't seemed very well of late. Here, Ah Kim"—he handed over all that was mortal of Tony—"you take and bury him somewhere."

"I take 'um," said Ah Kim, and did so.

In the big living-room the clock struck twice, loud and clear. Ah Kim, in the person of Charlie Chan, was moving slowly away, the bird in his arms. He was muttering glibly in Chinese. Suddenly he looked back over his shoulder.

"Hoo malimali," he said clearly.

Bob Eden remembered his Hawaiian.

CHAPTER VII

THE POSTMAN SETS OUT

THE THREE men and the girl returned to the living-
room, but Madden's flow of small talk was stilled,
and the sparkle was gone from his luncheon party.

"Poor Tony," the millionaire said when they had sat
down. "It's like the passing of an old friend. Five years
ago he came to me." He was silent for a long time, staring into space.

Presently the girl rose. "I really must be getting back
to town," she announced. "It was thoughtful of you to
invite me to lunch, Mr. Madden, and I appreciate it. I
can count on Thursday, then?"

"Yes—if nothing new comes up. In that case, where
could I reach you?"

"I'll be at the Desert Edge—but nothing must come
up. I'm relying on the word of P. J. Madden."

"Nothing will, I'm sure. Sorry you have to go."

Bob Eden came forward. "I think I'll take a little
fling at city life myself," he said. "If you don't mind,
I'd like to ride into Eldorado with you."

"Delighted," she smiled. "But I'm not sure I can
bring you back."

"Oh no—I don't want you to. I'll walk back."

"You needn't do that," said Madden. "It seems that

94

Ah Kim can drive a flivver—a rather remarkable boy, Ah Kim." He was thoughtfully silent for a moment. "I'm sending him to town later in the afternoon for supplies. Our larder's rather low. He'll pick you up." The Chinese entered to clear away. "Ah Kim, you're to bring Mr. Eden back with you this evening."

"Allight. I bling 'um," said Ah Kim, without interest.

"I'll meet you in front of the hotel any time you say," suggested Eden.

Ah Kim regarded him sourly. "Maybe flive 'clock," he said.

"Fine. At five then."

"You late, you no catch 'um lide," warned the Chinese.

"I'll be there," the boy promised. He went to his room and got a cap. When he returned, Madden was waiting.

"In case your father calls this afternoon, I'll tell him you want that matter rushed through," he said.

Eden's heart sank. He hadn't thought of that. Suppose his father returned to the office unexpectedly—but no, that was unlikely. And it wouldn't do to show alarm and change his plans now.

"Surely," he remarked carelessly. "If he isn't satisfied without a word from me, tell him to call again about six."

When he stepped into the yard, the girl was skilfully turning her car about. He officiated at the gate, and joined her in the sandy road.

The car moved off and Eden got his first unimpeded look at this queer world Holley had called the devil's garden. "Plenty acres of unlimitable sand," Chan had said, and that about summed it up. Far in the distance was a touch of beauty—a cobalt sky above snow-capped mountains. But elsewhere he saw only desert, a great gray interminable blanket spattered with creosote brush. All the trees, all the bushes, were barbed and cruel and menacing—a biznaga, pointing like a finger of scorn toward the sky, an unkempt palo verde, the eternal Joshua trees, like charred stumps that had stood in the path of a fire. Over this vast waste played odd tricks of light and shade, and up above hung the sun, a living flame, merciless, ineffably pure, and somehow terrible.

"Well, what do you think of it?" asked the girl.

Eden shrugged. "Hell's burnt out and left the embers," he remarked.

She smiled. "The desert is an acquired taste," she explained. "No one likes it at first. I remember the night, long ago, when I got off the train at Eldorado with poor dad. A little girl from a Philadelphia suburb—a place that was old and settled and civilized. And there I stood in the midst of this savage-looking world. My heart broke."

"Poor kid," said Eden. "But you like it now?"

"Yes—after a while—well, there's a sort of weird beauty in this sun-drenched country. You waken to it in the course of time. And in the spring, after the rains— I'd like to take you over round Palm Springs then. The verbena is like a carpet of old rose, and the ugliest trees put forth the most delicate and lovely blossoms. And at any time of the year there's always the desert nights, with the pale stars overhead, and the air full of peace and calm and rest."

"Oh, no doubt it's a great place to rest," Eden agreed. "But as it happens, I wasn't very tired."

"Who knows?" she said. "Perhaps before we say

good-by I can initiate you into the Very Ancient Order of Lovers of the Desert. The requirements for membership are very strict. A sensitive soul, a quick eye for beauty—oh, a very select group, you may be sure. No riff-raff on our rolls."

A blatant sign hung before them. "Stop! Have you bought your lot in Date City?" From the steps of a tiny real estate office a rather shabby young man leaped to life. He came into the road and held up his hand. Obligingly the girl stopped her car.

"Howdy, folks," said the young man. "Here's the big opportunity of your life—don't pass it by. Let me show you a lot in Date City, the future metropolis of the desert."

Bob Eden stared at the dreary landscape. "Not interested," he said.

"Yeah. Think of the poor devils who once said that about the corner of Spring and Sixth, Los Angeles. Not interested—and they could have bought it for a song. Look ahead. Can you picture this street ten years hence?"

"I think I can," Eden replied. "It looks just the way it does to-day."

"Blind!" rebuked the young man. "Blind! This won't be the desert forever. Look!" He pointed to a small lead pipe surrounded by a circle of rocks and trying to act like a fountain. From its top gurgled an anemic stream. "What's that! Water, my boy, water, the pure, life-giving elixir, gushing madly from the sandy soil. What does that mean? I see a great city rising on this spot, skyscrapers and movie palaces, land five thousand a front foot—land you can buy to-day for a paltry two dollars."

"I'll take a dollar's worth," remarked Eden.

"I appeal to the young lady," continued the real-estate man. "If that ring on the third finger of her left hand means anything, it means a wedding." Startled, Bob Eden looked, and saw a big emerald set in platinum. "You, miss—you have vision. Suppose you two bought a lot to-day and held it for your—er—for future generations. Wealth, wealth untold—I'm right, ain't I, miss?"

The girl looked away. "Perhaps you are," she admitted. "But you've made a mistake. This gentleman is not my fiancé."

"Oh," said the youth, deflating.

"I'm only a stranger, passing through," Eden told him.

The salesman pulled himself together for a new attack. "That's it—you're a stranger. You don't understand. You can't realize that Los Angeles looked like this once."

"It still does—to some people," suggested Bob Eden gently.

The young man gave him a hard look. "Oh—I get you," he said. "You're from San Francisco." He turned to the girl. "So this ain't your fiancé, eh, lady? Well—hearty congratulations."

Eden laughed. "Sorry," he said.

"I'm sorry, too," returned the salesman. "Sorry for you, when I think of what you're passing up. However, you may see the light yet, and if you ever do, don't forget me. I'm here Saturdays and Sundays, and we have an office in Eldorado. Opportunity's knocking, but of course if you're from Frisco, you're doing the same. Glad to have met you, anyhow."

They left him by his weak little fountain, a sad but hopeful figure.

"Poor fellow," the girl remarked, as she stepped on the gas. "The pioneer has a hard time of it."

Eden did not speak for a moment. "I'm an observing little chap, aren't I?" he said at last.

"What do you mean?"

"That ring. I never noticed it. Engaged, I suppose?"

"It looks that way, doesn't it?"

"Don't tell me you're going to marry some movie actor who carries a vanity case."

"You should know me better that that."

"I do, of course. But describe this lucky lad. What's he like?"

"He likes me."

"Naturally." Eden lapsed into silence.

"Not angry, are you?" asked the girl.

"Not angry," he grinned, "but terribly, terribly hurt. I perceive you don't want to talk about the matter."

"Well—some incidents in my life I really should keep to myself. On such short acquaintance."

"As you wish," agreed Eden. The car sped on. "Lady," he said presently, "I've known this desert country, man and boy, going on twenty-four hours. And believe me when I tell you, miss, it's a cruel land—a cruel land."

They climbed the road that lay between the two piles of brown rock pretending to be mountains, and before them lay Eldorado, huddled about the little red station. The town looked tiny and helpless and forlorn. As they alighted before the Desert Edge Hotel, Eden said:

"When shall I see you again?"

"Thursday, perhaps."

"Nonsense. I shall probably be gone by then, I must see you soon."

"I'll be out your way in the morning. If you like, I'll pick you up."

"That's kind of you—but morning's a long way off," he said. "I'll think of you to-night, eating at the Oasis. Give my love to that steak, if you see it. Until to-morrow, then—and can't I buy you an alarm clock?"

"I shan't oversleep—much," she laughed. "Good-by."

"Good-by," answered Eden. "Thanks for the buggy ride."

He crossed the street to the railroad station, which was also the telegraph office. In the little cubby-hole occupied by the agent, Will Holley stood, a sheaf of copy paper in his hand.

"Hello," he said. "Just getting that interview on the wire. Were you looking for me?"

"Yes, I was," Eden replied. "But first I want to send a wire of my own."

The agent, a husky youth with sandy hair, looked up. "Say, Mister, no can do. Mr. Holley here's tied up things forever."

Holley laughed. "That's all right. You can cut in with Mr. Eden's message, and then go back."

Frowning, Eden considered the wording of his rather difficult telegram. How to let his father know the situation without revealing it to the world? Finally he wrote:

"Buyer here, but certain conditions make it advisable we treat him to a little hoo malimali. Mrs. Jordan will translate. When I talk with you over telephone promise to send valuable package at once then forget it. Any confidential message for me care Will Holley, *Eldorado Times*. They have nice desert down here but too full of mystery for frank and open young business man like your loving son. Bob."

He turned the yellow slip over to the worried telegrapher, with instructions to send it to his father's office, and in duplicate to his house. "How much?" he asked.

After some fumbling with a book, the agent named a sum, which Eden paid. He added a tip, upsetting the boy still further.

"Say, this is some day here," announced the telegrapher. "Always wanted a little excitement in my life, but now it's come I guess I ain't ready for it. Yes, sir—I'll send it twice—I know—I get you—"

Holley gave the boy a few directions about the Madden interview, and returned with Bob Eden to Main Street.

"Let's drop over to the office," the editor said. "Nobody there now, and I'm keen to know what's doing out at Madden's."

In the bare little home of the *Eldorado Times*, Eden took a chair that was already partly filled with exchanges, close to the editor's desk. Holley removed his hat and replaced it with an eye-shade. He dropped down beside his typewriter.

"My friend in New York grabbed at that story," he said. "It was good of Madden to let me have it. I understand they're going to allow me to sign it, too—the name of Will Holley back in the big papers again. But look here—I was surprised by what you hinted out at the ranch this morning. It seemed to me last night that everything was O. K. You didn't say whether you had that necklace with you or not, but I gathered you had—"

"I haven't," cut in Eden.

"Oh—it's still in San Francisco?"

"No. My confederate has it."

"Your what?"

"Holley, I know that if Harry Fladgate says you're all right, you are. So I'm going the whole way in the matter of trusting you."

"That's flattering—but suit yourself."

"Something tells me we'll need your help," Eden remarked. With a glance round the deserted office, he explained the real identity of the servant, Ah Kim.

Holley grinned. "Well, that's amusing, isn't it? But go on. I get the impression that although you arrived at the ranch last night to find Madden there and everything, on the surface, serene, such was not the case. What happened?"

"First of all, Charlie thought something was wrong. He sensed it. You know the Chinese are a very psychic race."

Holley laughed. "Is that so? Surely you didn't fall for that guff. Oh, pardon me—I presume you had some better reason for delay?"

"I'll admit it sounded like guff to me—at the start. I laughed at Chan and prepared to hand over the pearls at once. Suddenly out of the night came the weirdest cry for help I ever expect to hear."

"What! Really? From whom?"

"From your friend, the Chinese parrot. From Tony."

"Oh—of course," said Holley. "I'd forgotten him. Well, that probably meant nothing."

"But a parrot doesn't invent," Eden reminded him. "It merely repeats. I may have acted like a fool, but

I hesitated to produce those pearls." He went on to tell how, in the morning, he had agreed to wait until two o'clock while Chan had further talk with Tony, and ended with the death of the bird just after lunch. "And there the matter rests," he finished.

"Are you asking my advice?" said Holley. "I hope you are, because I've simply got to give it to you."

"Shoot," Eden replied.

Holley smiled at him in a fatherly way. "Don't think for a moment I wouldn't like to believe there's some big melodrama afoot at Madden's ranch. Heaven knows little enough happens round here, and a thing like that would be manna from above. But as I look at it, my boy, you've let a jumpy Chinese lead you astray into a bad case of nerves."

"Charlie's absolutely sincere," protested Eden.

"No doubt of that," agreed Holley. "But he's an Oriental, and a detective, and he's simply got to detect. There's nothing wrong at Madden's ranch. True, Tony lets out weird cries in the night—but he always has."

"You've heard him, then?"

"Well, I never heard him say anything about help and murder, but when he first came I was living out at Doctor Whitcomb's, and I used to hang round the Madden ranch a good deal. Tony had some strange words in his small head. He'd spent his days amid violence and crime. It's nothing to wonder at that he screamed as he did last night. The setting on the desert, the dark, Charlie's psychic talk—all that combined to make a mountain out of a molehill, in your eyes."

"And Tony's sudden death this noon?"

"Just as Madden said. Tony was as old as the hills—

even a parrot doesn't live forever. A coincidence, yes—
but I'm afraid your father won't be pleased with you, my
boy. First thing you know P. J. Madden, who is hot and
impetuous, will kick you out and call the transaction off.
And I can see you back home explaining that you didn't
close the deal because a parrot on the place dropped dead.
My boy, my boy—I trust your father is a gentle soul.
Otherwise he's liable to annihilate you."

Eden considered. "How about that missing gun?"

Holley shrugged. "You can find something queer
almost anywhere, if you look for it. The gun was gone—
yes. What of it? Madden may have sold it, given it
away, taken it to his room."

Bob Eden leaned back in his chair. "I guess you're
right, at that. Yes, the more I think about it, here in
the bright light of afternoon, the more foolish I feel."
Through a side window he saw a flivver swing up before
the grocery store next door, and Charlie Chan alight. He
went out on to the porch.

"Ah Kim," he called.

The plump little Chinese detective approached and,
without a word, entered the office.

"Charlie," said Bob Eden, "this is a friend of mine,
Mr. Will Holley. Holley, meet Detective-Sergeant Chan,
of the Honolulu Police."

At mention of his name, Chan's eyes narrowed.
"How do you do," he said coldly.

"It's all right," Eden assured him. "Mr. Holley can
be trusted—absolutely. I've told him everything."

"I am far away in strange land," returned Chan.
"Maybe I would choose to trust no one—but that, no
doubt, are my heathen churlishness. Mr. Holley will
pardon, I am sure."

"Don't worry, said Holley. "I give you my word. I'll tell no one."

Chan made no reply, in his mind, perhaps, the memory of other white men who had given their word.

"It doesn't matter, anyhow," Eden remarked. "Charlie, I've come to the decision that we're chasing ghosts. I've talked things over with Mr. Holley, and from what he says, I see that there's really nothing wrong out at the ranch. When we go back this evening we'll hand over those pearls and head for home." Chan's face fell. "Cheer up," added the boy. "You, yourself, must admit that we've been acting like a couple of old women."

An expression of deeply offended dignity appeared on the little round face. "Just one moment. Permit this old woman more nonsense. Some hours ago parrot drops from perch into vast eternity. Dead, like Cæsar."

"What of it?" said Eden wearily. "He died of old age. Don't let's argue about it, Charlie—"

"Who argues?" asked Chan. "I myself enjoy keen distaste for that pastime. Old woman though I am, I now deal with facts—undubitable facts." He spread a white sheet of paper on Holley's desk, and removing an envelope from his pocket, poured its contents on to the paper. "Examine," he directed. "What you see here are partial contents of food basin beside the perch of Tony. Kindly tell me what you look at."

"Hemp seed," said Eden. "A parrot's natural food."

"Ah, yes," agreed Chan. "Seed of the hemp. But that other—the fine, grayish-white powder that seem so plentiful."

"By gad," cried Holley.

"No argument here," continued Chan. "Before seek-

ing grocer I pause at drug emporium on corner. Wise
man about powders make most careful test for me. And
what does he say?"

"Arsenic," suggested Holley.

"Arsenic, indeed. Much sold to ranchers hereabouts
as rat killer. Parrot killer, too."

Eden and Holley looked at each other in amazement.

"Poor Tony very sick before he go on long journey."
Chan continued. "Very silent and very sick. In my time
I am on track of many murders, but I must come to this
peculiar mainland to ferret out parrot murder. Ah,
well—all my life I hear about wonders on this mainland."

"They poisoned him," Bob Eden cried. "Why?"

"Why not?" shrugged Chan. "Very true rumor says
'dead men tell no tales'! Dead parrots are in same fix, I
think. Tony speaks Chinese like me. Tony and me
never speak together again."

Eden put his head in his hands. "Well, I'm getting
dizzy," he said. "What, in heaven's name, is it all
about?"

"Reflect," urged Chan. "As I have said before, parrot not able to perpetrate original remarks. He repeats.
When Tony cry out in night 'help, murder, put down
gun' even old woman might be pardoned to think he
repeats something recently heard. He repeats because
words are recalled to him by—what?"

"Go on, Charlie," Eden said.

"Recalled by event, just preceding cry. What event?
I think deep—how is this? Recalled, maybe, by sudden
flashing on of lights in bedroom occupied by Martin
Thorn, the secretary."

"Charlie, what more do you know?" Eden asked.

"This morning I am about my old woman duties in bedroom of Thorn. I see on wall stained outline same size and shape as handsome picture of desert scene near by. I investigate. Picture has been moved, I note, and not so long ago. Why was picture moved? I lift it in my hands and underneath I see little hole that could only be made by flying bullet."

Eden gasped. "A bullet?"

"Precisely the fact. A bullet embedded deep in wall. One bullet that has gone astray and not found resting place in body of that unhappy man Tony heard cry for help some recent night."

Again Eden and Holley looked at each other. "Well," said the editor, "there was that gun, you know. Bill Hart's gun—the one that's gone from the living-room. We must tell Mr. Chan about that."

Chan shrugged. "Spare yourself trouble," he advised. "Already last night I have noted empty locality deserted by that weapon. I also found this, in waste-basket." He took a small crumpled card from his pocket, a typewritten card, which read: "Presented to P. J. Madden by William S. Hart. September 29, 1923." Will Holley nodded and handed it back. "All day," continued Chan, "I search for missing movie pistol. Without success— so far."

Will Holley rose, and warmly shook Chan's hand. "Mr. Chan," he said, "permit me to go on record here and now to the effect that you're all right." He turned to Bob Eden. "Don't ever come to me for advice again. You follow Mr. Chan."

Eden nodded. "I think I will," he said.

"Think more deeply," suggested Chan. "To follow an old woman. Where is the honor there?"

Eden laughed. "Oh, forget it, Charlie. I apologize with all my heart."

Chan beamed. "Thanks warmly. Then all is settled? We do not hand over pearls to-night, I think?"

"No, of course we don't," agreed Eden. "We're on the trail of something—heaven knows what. It's all up to you, Charlie, from now on. I follow where you lead."

"You were number one prophet, after all," said Chan. "Postman on vacation goes for long walk. Here on broad desert I can not forget profession. We return to Madden's ranch and find what we shall find. Some might say, Madden is there, give him necklace. Our duty as splendid American citizens does not permit. If we deliver necklace, we go away, truth is strangled, guilty escape. Necklace deal falls now into second place." He gathered up the evidence in the matter of Tony and restored it to his pocket. "Poor Tony. Only this morning he tell me I talk too much. Now like boom—boomerang, remark returns and smites him. It is my pressing duty to negotiate with food merchant. Meet me in fifteen minutes before hotel door."

When he had gone out, Holley and Eden were silent for a moment. "Well," said the editor at last, "I was wrong—all wrong. There's something doing out at Madden's ranch."

Eden nodded. "Sure there is. But what?"

"All day," continued Holley, "I've been wondering about that interview Madden gave me. For no apparent reason, he broke one of the strictest rules of his life. Why?"

"If you're asking me, save your breath," advised
Eden.

"I'm not asking you—I've got my own solution.
Quoting Charlie, I think deep about matter—how is this?
Madden knows that at any moment something may break
and this thing that has happened at his ranch be spread
all over the newspapers. Looking ahead, he sees he may
need friends among the reporters. So he's come down
from his high horse at last. Am I right?"

"Oh, it sounds logical," agreed Eden. "I'm glad
something does. You know, I told dad before I left San
Francisco that I was keen to get mixed up in a murder
mystery. But this—this is more than I bargained for.
No dead body, no weapon, no motive, no murder. Nothing. Why, we can't even prove anybody has been killed."
He stood up. "Well, I'd better be moving back to the
ranch. The ranch and—what? Whither am I drifting?"

"You stick to your Chinese pal," advised Holley.
"The boy's good. Something tells me he'll see you
through."

"I hope so," Eden replied.

"Keep your eyes open," added Holley. "And take
no chances. If you need help out there, don't forget Will
Holley."

"You bet I won't," Bob Eden answered. "So long.
Maybe I'll see you to-morrow."

He went out and stood on the curb before the Desert
Edge Hotel. It was Saturday evening, and Eldorado was
crowded with ranchers, lean, bronzed, work-stained men
in khaki riding breeches and gaudy lumber-jack blouses—
simple men to whom this was the city. Through the
window of the combined barber shop and pool room he

saw a group of them shaking dice. Others leaned against the trunks of the cottonwoods, talking of the roads, of crops, of politics. Bob Eden felt like a visitor from Mars.

Presently Chan passed, swung round in the street, and halted the little touring car opposite the boy. As Eden climbed in, he saw the detective's keen eyes fixed on the hotel doorway. Seating himself, he followed Chan's gaze.

A man had emerged from the Desert Edge Hotel—a man who looked strangely out of place among the roughly-clad ranchers. He wore an overcoat buttoned tightly about his throat, and a felt hat was low over his eyes, which were hidden by dark spectacles.

"See who's here," said Eden.

"Yes, indeed," answered Chan, as they moved down the street. "I think the Killarney Hotel has lost one very important guest. Their loss our gain—maybe."

They left the all-too-brief pavement of Main Street. and a look of satisfaction spread slowly over Charlie Chan's face.

"Much work to do," he said. "Deep mysteries to solve. How sweet, though far from home, to feel myself in company of old friend."

Surprised, Bob Eden looked at him. "An old friend," he repeated.

Chan smiled. "In garage on Punchbowl Hill lonesome car like this awaits my return. With flivver shuddering beneath me I can think myself on familiar Honolulu streets again."

They climbed between the mountains, and before them lay the soft glory of a desert sunset. Ignoring the rough road, Chan threw the throttle wide.

"Wow, Charlie," cried Eden, as his head nearly pierced the top. "What's the idea?"

"Pardon, please," said Chan, slowing a bit. "No good, I guess. For a minute I think maybe this little car can bounce the homesick feeling from my heart."

CHAPTER VIII

A FRIENDLY LITTLE GAME

FOR a time the little brother of the car on Punchbowl Hill plowed valiantly on, and neither the detective nor Bob Eden spoke. The yellow glare of the sun was cooling on the gray livery of the desert; the shadows cast by the occasional trees grew steadily longer. The far-off mountains purpled and the wind bestirred itself.

"Charlie," said Bob Eden. "What do you think of this country?"

"This desert land?" asked Charlie.

Eden nodded.

"Happy to have seen it. All my time I yearn to encounter change. Certainly have encountered that here."

"Yes, I guess you have. Not much like Hawaii, is it?"

"I will say so. Hawaii lie like handful of Phillimore pearls on heaving breast of ocean. Oahu little island with very wet neighborhood all about. Moisture hangs in air all time, rain called liquid sunshine, breath of ocean pretty damp. Here I climb round to other side of picture. Air is dry like last year's newspaper."

"They tell me you can love this country if you try."

Chan shrugged. "For my part, I reserve my efforts

112

in that line for other locality. Very much impressed by desert, thank you, but will move on at earliest opportunity."

"Here, too," Eden laughed. "Comes the night, and I long for lights about me that are bright. A little restaurant on O'Farrell Street, a few good fellows, a bottle of mineral water on the table. Human companionship, if it's not asking too much."

"Natural you feel that way," Chan agreed. "Youth is in your heart like a song. Because of you I am hoping we can soon leave Madden's ranch."

"Well, what do you think? What are we going to do now?"

"Watch and wait. Youth, I am thinking, does not like that business. But it must be. Speaking personally for myself, I am not having one happy fine time either. Act of cooking food not precisely my idea of merry vacation."

"Well, Charlie, I can stick it if you can," Eden said.

"Plenty fine sport you are," Chan replied. "Problems that we face are not without interest, for that matter. Most peculiar situation. At home I am called to look at crime, clear-cut like heathen idol's face. Somebody killed, maybe. Clues are plenty, I push little car down one path, I sway about, seeking another. Not so here. Starting forth to solve big mystery I must first ask myself, just what are this big mystery I am starting forth to solve?"

"You've said it," Eden laughed.

"Yet one big fact gleams clear like snow on distant mountain. On recent night, at Madden's ranch, unknown person was murdered. Who unknown was, why he was

killed, and who officiated at the homicide—these are
simple little matters remaining to be cleared."

"And what have we to go on?" Eden asked helplessly.

"A parrot's cry at night. The rude removal of that
unhappy bird. A bullet hole hiding back of picture
recently changed about. An aged pistol gone from dusty
wall. All the more honor for us if we unravel from such
puny clues."

"One thing I can't figure out—among others," said
Eden. "What about Madden? Does he know? Or is
that sly little Thorn pulling something off alone?"

"Important questions," Chan agreed. "In time we
learn the answers, maybe. Meanwhile best to make no
friend of Madden. You have told him nothing about San
Francisco, I hope. Shaky Phil Maydorf and his queer
behavior."

"No, oddly enough, I haven't. I was wondering
whether I hadn't better, now that Maydorf has shown
up in Eldorado."

"Why? Pearls are in no danger. Did I hear you
say in newspaper office you would greatly honor by
following me?"

"You certainly did."

"Then, for Madden, more of the hoo malimali. Nothing to be gained by other course, much maybe lost. You
tell him of Maydorf, and he might answer, deal is off
here, bring pearls to New York. What then? You go
away, he goes away, I go away. Mystery of recent event
at ranch house never solved."

"I guess you're right," said Eden. They sped on
through the gathering dusk, past the little office of the

Date City optimist, deserted now. "By the way," added the boy, "this thing you think has happened at the ranch—it may have occurred last Wednesday night?"

"You have fondly feeling for Wednesday night?" asked Chan. "Why?"

Briefly Bob Eden related Paula Wendell's story of that night—Thorn's obvious excitement when he met her at the door, his insistence that Madden could not speak to her, and most important of all, the little prospector with the black beard whom the girl saw in the yard. Chan listened with interest.

"Now you talk," he commented. "Here is one fine new clue for us. He may be most important, that black-bearded one. A desert rat, I think. The young woman goes much about this country? Am I correct?"

"Yes, she does."

"She can retain secrets, maybe?"

"You bet—this girl can."

"Don't trust her. We talk all over place we may get sorry, after while. However, venture so far as to ask please that she keep her pretty eyes open for that black-bearded rat. Who knows. Maybe he is vital link in our chain." They were approaching the little oasis Madden had set on the desert's dusty face. "Go in now," Chan continued, "and act innocent like very new baby. When you talk with father over telephone, you will find he is prepared. I have sent him telegraph."

"You have?" said Eden. "So did I. I sent him a couple of them."

"Then he is all prepared. Among other matters, I presumed to remind him voice coming over wire is often grasped by others in room as well as him who reclines at telephone."

"Say—that's a good idea. I guess you think of everything, Charlie."

The gate was open, and Chan turned the car into the
yard. "Guess I do," he sighed. "Now, with depressing
reluctance, I must think of dinner. Recall, we watch
and wait. And when we meet alone, the greatest care.
No one must pierce my identity. Only this noon I could
well have applied to myself resounding kick. That word
unevitable too luxurious for poor old Ah Kim. In future
I must pick over words like lettuce for salad. Good-by,
and splendid luck."

In the living-room a fire was already blazing in the
huge fireplace. Madden sat at a broad, flat-topped desk,
signing letters. He looked up as Bob Eden entered.

"Hello," he said. "Have a pleasant afternoon?"

"Quite," the boy replied. "I trust you had the same."

"I did not," Madden answered. "Even here I can't
get away from business. Been catching up with a three
days' accumulation of mail. There you are, Martin,"
he added, as the secretary entered. "I believe you'll
have time to take them in to the post-office before dinner.
And here are the telegrams—get them off, too. Take
the little car—it'll make better speed over these roads."

Thorn gathered up the letters, and with expert hands
began folding them and placing them in envelopes.
Madden rose, stretched, and came over to the fire. "Ah
Kim brought you back?" he inquired.

"He did," Bob Eden answered.

"Knows how to drive a car all right?" persisted Madden.

"Perfectly."

"An unusual boy, Ah Kim."

"Oh, not very," Eden said carelessly. "He told me he used to drive a vegetable truck in Los Angeles. I got that much out of him, but that's about all."

"Silent, eh?"

Eden nodded. "Silent as a lawyer from Northampton, Massachusetts," he remarked.

Madden laughed. "By the way," he said, as Thorn went out. "Your father didn't call."

"No? Well, he isn't likely to get home until evening. I'll try the house to-night, if you want me to."

"I wish you would," Madden said. "I don't want to seem inhospitable, my boy, but I'm very anxious to get away from here. Certain matters in the mail to-day— you understand—"

"Of course," Bob Eden answered. "I'll do all I can to help."

"That's mighty good of you," Madden told him, and the boy felt a bit guilty. "I think I'll take a nap before dinner. I find, nowadays, it's a great aid to digestion." The famous millionaire was more human than Bob Eden had yet seen him. He stood looking down at the boy, wistfully. "A matter you can't grasp, just yet," he added. "You're so damned young—I envy you."

He went out, leaving Bob Eden to a Los Angeles paper he had picked up in Eldorado. From time to time, as the boy read, the quaint little figure of Ah Kim passed noiselessly. He was setting the table for dinner.

An hour later, there on the lonely desert, they again sat down to Ah Kim's cooking. Very different from the restaurant of which Bob Eden thought with longing, but if the company was far from lively, the food was excellent, for the Chinese had negotiated well. When the servant came in with coffee, Madden said:

"Light the fire in the patio, Ah Kim. We'll sit out there a while."

The Chinese went to comply with this order, and Eden saw Madden regarding him expectantly. He smiled and rose.

"Well, dad ought to be struggling in from his hard day on the links any minute now," he said. "I'll put in that call."

Madden leaped up. "Let me do it," he suggested. "Just tell me the number."

The boy told him, and Madden spoke over the telephone in a voice to command respect.

"By the way," he said, when he had finished, "last night you intimated that certain things happened in San Francisco—things that made your father cautious. What —if you don't mind telling me?"

Bob Eden thought rapidly. "Oh, it may all have been a detective's pipe dream. I'm inclined to think now that it was. You see—"

"Detective? What detective?"

"Well, naturally dad has a tie-up with various private detective agencies. An operative of one of them reported that a famous crook had arrived in town and was showing an undue interest in our store. Of course, it may have meant nothing—"

"A famous crook, eh? Who?"

Never a good liar, Bob Eden hesitated. "I—I don't know that I remember the name. English, I believe— the Liverpool Kid, or something like that," he invented lamely.

Madden shrugged. "Well, if anything's leaked out about those pearls, it came from your side of the deal," he said. "My daughter, Thorn and I have certainly been discretion itself. However, I'm inclined to think it's all a pipe dream, as you say."

"Probably is," agreed Eden.

"Come outside," the millionaire invited. He led the way through the glass doors to the patio. There a huge fire roared in the outdoor fireplace, glowing red on the stone floor and on wicker chairs. "Sit down," suggested Madden. "A cigar—no, you prefer your cigarette, eh?" He lighted up, and leaning back in his chair, stared at the dark roof above—the far-off roof of the sky. "I like it out here best," he went on. "A bit chilly, maybe, but you get close to the desert. Ever notice how white the stars are in this country?"

Eden looked at him with surprise. "Sure—I've noticed," he said. "But I never dreamed you had, old boy," he added to himself.

Inside, Thorn was busy at the radio. A horrible medley of bedtime stories, violin solos, and lectures on health and beauty drifted out to them. And then the shrill voice of a woman, urging sinners to repent.

"Get Denver," Madden called loudly.

"I'm trying, Chief," answered Thorn.

"If I must listen to the confounded thing," Madden added to the boy, "I want what I hear to come from far away. Over the mountains and the plains—there's romance in that." The radio swept suddenly into a brisk band tune. "That's it," nodded Madden. "The orchestra at the Brown Palace in Denver—perhaps my girl is dancing to that very music at this moment. Poor kid—she'll wonder what's become of me. I promised to be there two days ago. Thorn!"

The secretary appeared at the door. "Yes, Chief?"
"Remind me to send Evelyn a wire in the morning."
"I'll do that, Chief," said Thorn, and vanished.

"And the band played on," remarked Madden. "All
the way from Denver, mile high amid the Rockies. I
tell you, man's getting too clever. He's riding for a fall.
Probably a sign of age, Mr. Eden, but I find myself longing for the older, simpler days. When I was a boy on
the farm, winter mornings, the little schoolhouse in the
valley. That sled I wanted—hard times, yes, but times
that made men. Oh well, I mustn't get started on that."

They listened on in silence, but presently a bedtime
story brought a bellow of rage from the millionaire and
Thorn, getting his cue, shut off the machine.

Madden stirred restlessly in his chair. "We haven't
enough for bridge," he remarked. "How about a little
poker to pass the time, my boy?"

"Why—that would be fine," Eden replied. "I'm
afraid you're pretty speedy company for me, however."

"Oh, that's all right—we'll put a limit on it."

Madden was on his feet, eager for action. "Come
along."

They went into the living-room and closed the doors.
A few moments later the three of them sat about a big
round table under a brilliant light.

"Jacks or better," Madden said. "Quarter limit, eh?"

"Well—" replied Eden, dubiously.

He had good reason to be dubious, for he was
instantly plunged into the poker game of his life. He
had played at college, and was even able to take care of
himself in newspaper circles in San Francisco, but all that
was child's play by comparison. Madden was no longer
the man who noticed how white the stars were. He

noticed how red, white and blue the chips were, and he caressed them with loving hands. He was Madden, the plunger, the gambler with railroads and steel mills and the fortunes of little nations abroad, the Madden who, after he had played all day in Wall Street, was wont to seek the roulette wheels on Forty-fourth Street at night.

"Aces," he cried. "Three of them. What have you got, Eden?"

"Apoplexy," remarked Eden, tossing aside his hand. "Right here and now I offer to sell my chances in this game for a canceled postage stamp, or what have you?"

"Good experience for you," Madden replied. "Martin—it's your deal."

A knock sounded suddenly on the door, loud and clear. Bob Eden felt a strange sinking of the heart. Out of the desert dark, out of the vast uninhabited wastes of the world, some one spoke and demanded to come in.

"Who can that be?" Madden frowned.

"Police," suggested Eden, hopefully. "The joint is pinched." No such luck, he reflected.

Thorn was dealing, and Madden himself went to the door and swung it open. From where he sat Eden had a clear view of the dark desert—and of the man who stood in the light. A thin man in an overcoat, a man he had seen first in a San Francisco pier-shed, and later in front of the Desert Edge Hotel. Shaky Phil Maydorf himself, but now without the dark glasses hiding his eyes.

"Good evening," said Maydorf, and his voice, too, was thin and cold. "This is Mr. Madden's ranch, I believe?"

"I'm Madden. What can I do for you?"

"I'm looking for an old friend of mine—your secretary, Martin Thorn."

Thorn rose and came round the table. "Oh, hello,"
he said, with slight enthusiasm.

"You remember me, don't you?" said the thin man.
"McCallum—Henry McCallum. I met you at a dinner
in New York a year ago."

"Yes, of course," answered Thorn. "Come in, won't
you? This is Mr. Madden."

"A great honor," said Shaky Phil.

"And Mr. Eden, of San Francisco."

Eden rose, and faced Shaky Phil Maydorf. The
man's eyes without the glasses were barbed and cruel,
like the desert foliage. For a long moment he stared
insolently at the boy. Did he realize, Eden wondered,
that his movements on the dock at San Francisco had not
gone unnoticed? If he did, his nerve was excellent.

"Glad to know you, Mr. Eden," he said.

"Mr. McCallum," returned the boy gravely.

Maydorf turned again to Madden. "I hope I'm not
intruding," he remarked with a wan smile. "Fact is, I'm
stopping down the road at Doctor Whitcomb's—bronchitis, that's my trouble. It's lonesome as the devil round
here, and when I heard Mr. Thorn was in the neighborhood, I couldn't resist the temptation to drop in."

"Glad you did," Madden said, but his tone belied the
words.

"Don't let me interrupt your game," Maydorf went
on. "Poker, eh? Is this a private scrap, or can anybody get into it?"

"Take off your coat," Madden responded sourly,
"and sit up. Martin, give the gentleman a stack of chips."

"This is living again," said the newcomer, accepting briskly. "Well, and how have you been, Thorn, old man?"

Thorn, with his usual lack of warmth, admitted that he had been pretty good, and the game was resumed. If Bob Eden had feared for his immediate future before, he now gave up all hope. Sitting in a poker game with Shaky Phil—well, he was certainly traveling and seeing the world.

"Gimme four cards," said Mr. Maydorf, through his teeth.

If it had been a bitter, brutal struggle before, it now became a battle to the death. New talent had come in— more than talent, positive genius. Maydorf held the cards close against his chest; his face was carved in stone. As though he realized what he was up against, Madden grew wary, but determined. These two fought it out, while Thorn and the boy trailed along, like non-combatants involved in a battle of the giants.

Presently Ah Kim entered with logs for the fire, and if the amazing picture on which his keen eyes lighted startled him, he gave no sign. Madden ordered him to bring highballs, and as he set the glasses on the table, Bob Eden noted with a secret thrill that the stomach of the detective was less than twelve inches from the long capable hands of Shaky Phil. If the redoubtable Mr. Maydorf only knew—

But Maydorf's thoughts were elsewhere than on the Phillimore pearls. "Dealer—one card," he demanded.

The telephone rang out sharply in the room. Bob Eden's heart missed a beat. He had forgotten that— and now— After the long wait he was finally to speak with his father—while Shaky Phil Maydorf sat only a few feet away! He saw Madden staring at him, and he rose.

"For me, I guess," he said carelessly. He tossed his cards on the table. "I'm out of it, anyhow." Crossing the room to the telephone, he took down the receiver. "Hello. Hello, dad. Is that you?"

"Aces and trays," said Maydorf. "All mine?" Madden laid down a hand without looking at his opponent's, and Shaky Phil gathered in another pot.

"Yes, dad—this is Bob," Eden was saying. "I arrived all right—stopping with Mr. Madden for a few days. Just wanted you to know where I was. Yes—that's all. Everything. I may call you in the morning. Have a good game? Too bad. Good-by!"

Madden was on his feet, his face purple. "Wait a minute," he cried.

"Just wanted dad to know where I am," Eden said brightly. He dropped back into his chair. "Whose deal is it, anyhow?"

Madden strangled a sentence in his throat, and once more the game was on. Eden was chuckling inwardly. More delay—and not his fault this time. The joke was on P. J. Madden.

His third stack was melting rapidly away, and he reflected with apprehension that the night was young, and time of no importance on the desert anyhow. "One more hand and I drop out," he said firmly.

"One more hand and we all drop out," barked Madden. Something seemed to have annoyed him.

"Let's make it a good one, then," said Maydorf. "The limit's off, gentlemen."

It was a good one, unexpectedly a contest between

Maydorf and Bob Eden. Drawing with the faint hope of completing two pairs, the boy was thrilled to encounter four nines in his hand. Perhaps he should have noted that Maydorf was dealing, but he didn't—he bet heavily, and was finally called. Laying down his hand, he saw an evil smile on Shaky Phil's face.

"Four queens," remarked Maydorf, spreading them out with an expert gesture. "Always was lucky with the ladies. I think you gentlemen pay me."

They did. Bob Eden contributed forty-seven dollars, reluctantly. All on the expense account, however, he reflected.

Mr. Maydorf was in a not unaccountable good humor. "A very pleasant evening," he remarked, as he put on his overcoat. "I'll drop in again, if I may."

"Good night," snapped Madden.

Thorn took a flashlight from the desk. "I'll see you to the gate," he announced. Bob Eden smiled. A flashlight—with a bright moon overhead.

"Mighty good of you," the outsider said. "Good night, gentlemen, and thank you very much." He was smiling grimly as he followed the secretary out.

Madden snatched up a cigar, and savagely bit the end from it. "Well?" he cried.

"Well," said Eden calmly.

"You made a lot of progress with your father, didn't you?"

The boy smiled. "What did you expect me to do? Spill the whole thing in front of that bird?"

"No—but you needn't have rung off so quick. I was going to get him out of the room. Now you can go over there and call your father again."

"Nothing of the sort," answered Eden. "He's gone to bed, and I won't disturb him till morning."

Madden's face purpled. "I insist. And my orders are usually obeyed."

"Is that so?" remarked Eden. "Well, this is one that won't be."

Madden glared at him. "You young—you—er—young—"

"I know," Eden said. "But this was all your fault. If you will insist on cluttering up the ranch with strangers, you must take the consequences."

"Who cluttered up the ranch?" Madden demanded. "I didn't invite that poor fool here. Where the devil did Thorn pick him up, anyhow? You know, the secretary of a man like me is always besieged by a lot of four-flushers—tip hunters and the like. And Thorn's an idiot, sometimes." The secretary entered and laid the flashlight on the desk. His employer regarded him with keen distaste. "Well, your little playmate certainly queered things," he said.

Thorn shrugged. "I know. I'm sorry, Chief. But I couldn't help it. You saw how he horned in."

"Your fault for knowing him. Who is he, anyhow?"

"Oh, he's a broker, or something like that. I give you my word, Chief, I never encouraged him. You know how those fellows are."

"Well, you go out to-morrow and tie a can to him. Tell him I'm busy here and don't want any visitors. Tell him for me that if he calls here again, I'll throw him out."

"All right. I'll go down to the doctor's in the morning and let him know—in a diplomatic way."

"Diplomatic nothing," snorted Madden. "Don't waste

diplomacy on a man like that. I won't, if I see him again."

"Well, gentlemen, I think I'll turn in," Eden remarked.

"Good night," said Madden, and the boy went out.

In his bedroom he found Ah Kim engaged in lighting the fire. He closed the door carefully behind him.

"Well, Charlie, I've just been in a poker game."

"A fact already noted by me," smiled Chan.

"Shaky Phil has made a start on us, anyhow. He got forty-seven precious iron men this quiet evening."

"Humbly suggest you be careful," advised Chan.

"Humbly believe you're right," laughed Eden. "I was hoping you were in the offing when Thorn and our friend went to the gate."

"Indeed I was," remarked Chan. "But moonlight so fierce, near approach was not possible."

"Well, I'm pretty sure of one thing, after to-night," Eden told him. "P. J. Madden never saw Shaky Phil before. Either that, or he's the finest actor since Edwin Booth."

"Thorn, however—"

"Oh, Thorn knew him all right. But he wasn't the least bit glad to see him. You know, Thorn's whole manner suggested to me that Shaky Phil has something on him."

"That might be possible," agreed Chan. "Especially come to think of my latest discovery."

"You've found something new, Charlie? What?"

"This evening, when Thorn haste to town in little car and I hear noisome snores of Madden who sleep on bed, I make explicit search in secretary's room."

"Yes—go on—quick. We might be interrupted."

"Under mountain of white shirts in Thorn's bureau reposes—what? Missing forty-five we call Bill Hart's gun."

"Good work! Thorn—the little rat—"

"Undubitably. Two chambers of that gun are quite unoccupied. Reflect on that."

"I'm reflecting. Two empty chambers."

"Humbly suggest you sleep now, gathering strength for what may be most excited to-morrow." The little detective paused at the door. "Two bullets gone who knows where," he said, in a low voice. "Answer is, we know where one went. Went crazy, landing in wall at spot now covered by desert picture."

"And the other?" said Bob Eden thoughtfully.

"Other hit mark, I think. What mark? We watch and wait, and maybe we discover. Good night, with plenty happy dreams."

CHAPTER IX

A RIDE IN THE DARK

ON SUNDAY morning Bob Eden rose at what was, for him, an amazingly early hour. Various factors conspired to induce this strange phenomenon—the desert sun, an extremely capable planet, filling his room with light, the roosters of P. J. Madden, loudly vocal in the dawn. At eight o'clock he was standing in the ranch house yard, ready for whatever the day might bring forth.

Whatever it brought, the day was superb. Now the desert was at its best, the chill of night still lingering in the magic air. He looked out over an opal sea, at changing colors of sand and cloud and mountaintop that shamed by their brilliance those glittering show-cases in the jewelry shop of Meek and Eden. Though it was the fashion of his age to pretend otherwise, he was not oblivious to beauty, and he set out for a stroll about the ranch with a feeling of awe in his heart.

Turning a rear corner of the barn, he came unexpectedly upon a jarring picture. Martin Thorn was busy beside a basket, digging a deep hole in the sand. In his dark clothes, with his pale face glistening from his unaccustomed exertion, he looked not unlike some prominent mortician.

"Hello," said Eden. "Who are you burying this fine morning?"

129

Thorn stopped. Beads of perspiration gleamed on his high white forehead.

"Somebody has to do it," he complained. "Tha new boy's too lazy. And if you let this refuse accumulate the place begins to look like a deserted picnic grounds."

He nodded toward the basket, filled with old tin cans.

"Wanted, private secretary to bury rubbish back of barn," smiled Eden. "A new sidelight on your profession, Thorn. Good idea to get them out of the way, at that," he added, leaning over and taking up a can. "Especially this one, which I perceive lately held arsenic."

"Arsenic?" repeated Thorn. He passed a dark coat sleeve across his brow. "Oh yes—we use a lot of that Rats, you know."

"Rats," remarked Eden, with an odd inflection, restoring the can to its place.

Thorn emptied the contents of the basket into the hole, and began to fill it in. Eden, playing well his rôle of innocent bystander, watched him idly.

"There—that's better," said the secretary, smoothing the sand over the recent excavation. "You know—I've always had a passion for neatness." He picked up the basket. "By the way," he added, "if you don't mind, I'd like to give you a little advice."

"Glad to have it," Eden replied, walking along beside him.

"I don't know how anxious you people are to sell that necklace. But I've been with the chief fifteen years, and I can tell you he's not the sort of man you can keep waiting with impunity. The first thing you know, young man, that deal for the pearls will be off."

"I'm doing my best," Eden told him. "Besides, Madden's getting a big bargain, and he must know it—if he stops to think—"

"Once P. J. Madden loses his temper," said Thorn, "he doesn't stop to think. I'm warning you, that's all."

"Mighty kind of you," answered Eden carelessly. Thorn dropped his spade and basket by the cookhouse, from which came the pleasant odor of bacon on the stocks. Walking slowly, the secretary moved on toward the patio. Ah Kim emerged from his work-room, his cheeks flushed from close juxtaposition to a cook-stove.

"Hello, boss," he said. "You takee look-see at sunlise thisee mawnin'?"

"Up pretty early, but not as early as that," the boy replied. He saw the secretary vanish into the house. "Just been watching our dear friend Thorn bury some rubbish back of the barn," he added. "Among other items, a can that lately contained arsenic."

Chan dropped the rôle of Ah Kim. "Mr. Thorn plenty busy man," he said. "Maybe he get more busy as time goes by. One wrong deed leads on to other wrong deeds, like unending chain. Chinese have saying that applies: 'He who rides on tiger can not dismount.'"

Madden appeared in the patio, full of pep and power. "Hey, Eden," he called. "Your father's on the wire."

"Dad's up early," remarked Eden, hurrying to join him.

"I called him," said Madden. "I've had enough delay."

Reaching the telephone, Bob Eden took up the receiver. "Hello, dad. I can talk freely this morning. I want to tell you everything's all right down here. Mr. Madden? Yes—he's fine—standing right beside me now And he's in a tearing hurry for that necklace."

"Very well—we'll get it to him at once," the elder Eden said. Bob Eden sighed with relief. His telegram had arrived.

"Ask him to get it off to-day," Madden commanded.

"Mr. Madden wants to know if it can start to-day," the boy said.

"Impossible," replied the jeweler. "I haven't got it."

"Not to-day," Bob Eden said to Madden. "He hasn't got—"

"I heard him," roared Madden. "Here—give me that phone. Look here, Eden—what do you mean you haven't got it?"

Bob Eden could hear his father's replies. "Ah—Mr. Madden—how are you? The pearls were in a quite disreputable condition—I couldn't possibly let them go as they were. So I'm having them cleaned—they're with another firm—"

"Just a minute, Eden," bellowed the millionaire. "I want to ask you something—can you understand the English language, or can't you? Keep still—I'll talk. I told you I wanted the pearls now—at once—pronto—what the devil language do you speak? I don't give a hang about having them cleaned. Good lord, I thought you understood."

"So sorry," responded Bob Eden's gentle father. "I'll get them in the morning, and they'll start to-morrow night."

"Yeah—that means Tuesday evening at the ranch. Eden, you make me sick. I've a good mind to call the whole thing off—" Madden paused, and Bob Eden held his breath. "However, if you promise the pearls will start to-morrow sure—"

"I give you my word," said the jeweler. "They will start to-morrow, at the very latest."

"All right. I'll have to wait, I suppose. But this is the last time I deal with you, my friend. I'll be on the lookout for your man on Tuesday. Good-by."

In a towering rage, Madden hung up. His ill-humor continued through breakfast, and Eden's gay attempts at conversation fell on barren ground. After the meal was finished, Thorn took the little car and disappeared down the road. Bob Eden loafed expectantly about the front yard.

Much sooner than he had dared to hope, his vigil was ended. Paula Wendell, fresh and lovely as the California morning, drove up in her smart roadster and waited outside the barbed-wire fence.

"Hello," she said. "Jump in. You act as though you were glad to see me."

"Glad! Lady, you're a life-saver. Relations are sort of strained this morning at the old homestead. You'll find it hard to believe, but P. J. Madden doesn't love me."

She stepped on the gas. "The man's mad," she laughed.

"I'll say he's mad. Ever eat breakfast with a rattlesnake that's had bad news?"

"Not yet. The company at the Oasis is mixed, but not so mixed as that. Well, what do you think of the view this morning? Ever see such coloring before?"

"Never. And it's not out of a drug store, either."

"I'm talking about the desert. Look at those snow-capped peaks."

"Lovely. But if you don't mind, I prefer to look closer. No doubt he's told you you're beautiful."

"Who?"

"Wilbur, your fiancé."

"His name is Jack. Don't jump on a good man when he's down."

"Of course he's a good man, or you wouldn't have picked him." They plowed along the sandy road. "But even so—look here, lady. Listen to a man of the world. Marriage is the last resort of feeble minds."

"Think so?"

"I know it. Oh, I've given the matter some thought. I've had to. There's my own case. Now and then I've met a girl whose eyes said, 'Well, I might.' But I've been cautious. Hold fast, my lad—that's my motto."

"And you've held fast?"

"You bet. Glad of it, too. I'm free. I'm having a swell time. When evening comes, and the air's full of zip and zowie, and the lights flicker round Union Square, I just reach for my hat. And who says, in a gentle patient voice, 'Where are you going, my dear? I'll go with you.' "

"Nobody."

"Not a living soul. It's grand. And you—your case is just like mine. Of course there are millions of girls who have nothing better to do than marriage. All right for them. But you—why—you've got a wonderful job. The desert, the hills, the cañons—and you're willing to give all that up for a gas-range in the rear room of an apartment."

"Perhaps we can afford a maid."

"Lots of people can—but where to get one nowadays? I'm warning you—think it over well. You're having a great time now—that will end with marriage. Mending Wilbur's socks—"

"I tell you his name is Jack."

"What of it? He'll be just as hard on the socks. I hate to think of a girl like you, tied down somewhere—"

"There's a lot in what you say," Paula Wendell admitted.

"I've only scratched the surface," Eden assured her.

The girl steered her car off the road through an open gate. Eden saw a huge, rambling ranch house surrounded by a group of tiny cottages. "Here we are at Doctor Whitcomb's," remarked Paula Wendell. "Wonderful person, the doctor. I want you two to meet."

She led the way through a screen door into a large living-room, not so beautifully furnished as Madden's, but bespeaking even greater comfort. A gray-haired woman was rocking contentedly near a window. Her face was kindly, her eyes calm and comforting. "Hello, Doctor," said the girl. "I've brought some one to call on you."

The woman rose, and her smile seemed to fill the room. "Hello, young man," she said, and took Bob Eden's hand.

"You—you're the doctor," he stammered.

"Sure am," the woman replied. "But you don't need me. You're all right."

"So are you," he answered. "I can see that."

"Fifty-five years old," returned the doctor, "but I can still get a kick out of that kind of talk from a nice young man. Sit down. The place is yours. Where are you staying?"

"I'm down the road, at Madden's."

"Oh yes—I heard he was here. Not much of a neighbor, this P. J. Madden. I've called on him occasionally, but he's never come to see me. Stand-offish—and that sort of thing doesn't go on the desert. We're all friends here."

"You've been a friend to a good many," said Paula Wendell.

"Why not?" shrugged Doctor Whitcomb. "What's life for, if not to help one another? I've done my best—I only wish it had been more."

Bob Eden felt suddenly humble in this woman's presence.

"Come on—I'll show you round my place," invited the doctor. "I've made the desert bloom—put that on my tombstone. You should have seen this neighborhood when I came. Just a rifle and a cat—that's all I had at first. And the cat wouldn't stay. My first house here I built with my own hands. Five miles to Eldorado—I walked in and back every day. Mr. Ford hadn't been heard of then."

She led the way into the yard, in and out among the little cottages. Tired faces brightened at her approach, weary eyes gleamed with sudden hope.

"They've come to her from all over the country," Paula Wendell said. "Broken-hearted, sick, discouraged. And she's given them new life—"

"Nonsense," cried the doctor. "I've just been friendly. It's a pretty hard world. Being friendly—that works wonders."

In the doorway of one of the cottages they came upon Martin Thorn, deep in converse with Shaky Phil Maydorf. Even Maydorf mellowed during a few words with the doctor.

Finally, when they reluctantly left, Doctor Whitcomb

followed them to the gate. "Come often," she said. "You will, won't you?"

"I hope to," answered Bob Eden. He held her great rough hand a moment. "You know—I'm beginning to sense the beauty of the desert," he added.

The doctor smiled. "The desert is old and weary and wise," she said. "There's beauty in that, if you can see it. Not everybody can. The latch-string's always out at Doctor Whitcomb's. Remember, boy."

Paula Wendell swung the car about, and in silence they headed home.

"I feel as though I'd been out to old Aunt Mary's," said Eden presently. "I sort of expected her to give me a cookie when I left."

"She's a wonderful woman," said the girl softly. "I ought to know. It was the light in her window I saw my first night on the desert. And the light in her eyes—I shall never forget. All the great people are not in the cities."

They rode on. About them the desert blazed stark and empty in the midday heat; a thin haze cloaked the distant dunes and the far-away slopes of the hills. Bob Eden's mind returned to the strange problems that confronted him. "You've never asked me why I'm here," he re-. marked.

"I know," the girl answered. "I felt that pretty soon you'd realize we're all friends on the desert—and tell me."

"I want to—some day. Just at present—well, I can't. But going back to that night you first visited Madden's ranch—you felt that something was wrong there?"

"I did."

"Well, I can tell you this much—you were probably

right." She glanced at him quickly. "And it's my job to find out if you were. That old prospector—I'd give a good deal to meet him. Isn't there a chance that you may run across him again?"

"Just a chance," she replied.

"Well, if you do, would you mind getting in touch with me at once. If it's not asking too much—"

"Not at all," she told him. "I'll be glad to. Of course, the old man may be clear over in Arizona by now. When I last saw him he was moving fast!"

"All the more reason for wanting to find him," Eden said. "I—I wish I could explain. It isn't that I don't trust you, you know. But—it's not altogether my secret."

She nodded. "I understand. I don't want to know."

"You grow more wonderful every minute," he told her.

The minutes passed. After a time the car halted before Madden's ranch, and Bob Eden alighted. He stood looking into the girl's eyes—somehow they were like the eyes of Doctor Whitcomb—restful and comforting and kind. He smiled.

"You know," he said, "I may as well confess it—I've been sort of disliking Wilbur. And now it comes to me suddenly—if I really mean all that about loving my freedom—then Wilbur has done me the greatest service possible. I ought not to dislike him any more. I ought to thank him from the bottom of my heart."

"What in the world are you talking about?"

"Don't you understand? I've just realized that I'm up against the big temptation of my life. But I don't have to fight it. Wilbur has saved me. Good old Wilbur. Give him my love when next you write."

She threw her car into gear. "Don't you worry," she
advised. "Even if there hadn't been a Wilbur, your freedom wouldn't have been in the slightest danger. I would
have seen to that."

"Somehow, I don't care for that remark," Eden said.
"It ought to reassure me, but as a matter of fact, I don't
like it at all. Well, I owe you for another buggy ride.
Sorry to see you go—it looks like a dull Sunday out here.
Would you mind if I drifted into town this afternoon?"

"I probably wouldn't even know it," said the girl.
"Good-by."

Bob Eden's prediction about Sunday proved true—it
was long and dull. At four in the afternoon he could
stand it no longer. The blazing heat was dying, a restless wind had risen, and with the permission of Madden,
who was still ill-humored and evidently restless too, he
took the little car and sped toward the excitement of
Eldorado.

Not much diversion there. In the window of the
Desert Edge Hotel the proprietor waded grimly through
an interminable Sunday paper. Main Street was hot and
deserted. Leaving the car before the hotel, the boy went
to Holley's office.

The editor came to the door to meet him. "Hello," he
said. "I was hoping you'd come along. Kind of lonesome in the great open spaces this afternoon. By the way,
there's a telegram here for you."

Eden took the yellow envelope and hurriedly tore it
open. The message was from his father:

"I don't understand what it's all about but I am most
disturbed. For the present I will follow your instructions.
I am trusting you two utterly but I must remind you that

it would be most embarrassing for me if sale fell through. Jordans are eager to consummate deal and Victor threatens to come down there any moment. Keep me advised."

"Huh," said Bob Eden. "That would be fine."

"What would?" asked Holley.

"Victor threatens to come—the son of the woman who owns the pearls. All we need here to wreck the works is that amiable bonehead and his spats."

"What's new?" asked Holley, as they sat down.

"Several things," Bob Eden replied. "To start with the big tragedy, I'm out forty-seven dollars." He told of the poker game. "In addition, Mr. Thorn has been observed burying a can that once held arsenic. Furthermore, Charlie has found that missing pistol in Thorn's bureau—with two chambers empty."

Holley whistled. "Has he really? You know, I believe your friend Chan is going to put Thorn back of the bars before he's through."

"Perhaps," admitted Eden. "Got a long way to go, though. You can't convict a man of murder without a body to show for it."

"Oh—Chan will dig that up."

Eden shrugged. "Well, if he does, he can have all the credit. And do all the digging. Somehow, it's not the sort of thing that appeals to me. I like excitement, but I like it nice and neat. Heard from your interview?"

"Yes. It's to be released in New York to-morrow." The tired eyes of Will Holley brightened. "I was sitting here getting a thrill out of the idea when you came in." He pointed to a big scrap-book on his desk. "Some of the stories I wrote on the old *Sun*," he explained. "Not bad, if I do say it myself."

Bob Eden picked up the book, and turned the pages with interest. "I've been thinking of getting a job on a newspaper myself," he said.

Holley looked at him quickly. "Think twice," he advised. "You, with a good business waiting for you—what has the newspaper game to offer you? Great while you're young, maybe—great even now when the old order is changing and the picture paper is making a monkey out of a grand profession. But when you're old—" He got up and laid a hand on the boy's shoulder. "When you're old—and you're old at forty—then what? The copy desk, and some day the owner comes in, and sees a streak of gray in your hair, and he says, 'Throw that doddering fool out. I want young men here.' No, my boy—not the newspaper game. You and I must have a long talk."

They had it. It was five by the little clock on Holley's desk when the editor finally stood up, and closed his scrap-book. "Come on," he said. "I'm taking you to the Oasis for dinner."

Eden went gladly. At one of the tables opposite the narrow counter, Paula Wendell sat alone.

"Hello," she greeted them. "Come over here. I felt in an expansive mood to-night—had to have the prestige of a table."

They sat down opposite her. "Did you find the day as dull as you expected?" inquired the girl of Eden.

"Very dull by contrast, after you left me," he answered.

"Try the chicken," she advised. "Born and raised right here at home, and the desert hen is no weak sister. Not so bad, however."

They accepted her suggestion. When the generously

filled platters were placed before them, Bob Eden squared away.

"Take to the lifeboats," he said. "I'm about to carve, and when I carve, it's a case of women and children first."

Holley stared down at his dinner. "Looks like the same old chicken," he sighed. "What wouldn't I give for a little home cooking."

"Ought to get married," smiled the girl. "Am I right, Mr. Eden?"

Eden shrugged. "I've known several poor fellows who got married hoping to enjoy a bit of home cooking. Now they're back in the restaurants, and the only difference is they've got the little woman along. Double the check and half the pleasure."

"Why all this cynicism?" asked Holley.

"Oh, Mr. Eden is very much opposed to marriage," the girl said. "He was telling me to-day."

"Just trying to save her," Eden explained. "By the way, do you know this Wilbur who's won her innocent, trusting heart?"

"Wilbur?" asked Holley blankly.

"He will persist in calling Jack out of his name," the girl said. "It's his disrespectful way of referring to my fiancé."

Holley glanced at the ring. "No, I don't know him," he announced. "I certainly congratulate him, though."

"So do I," Eden returned. "On his nerve. However, I oughtn't to knock Wilbur. As I was saying only this noon—"

"Never mind," put in the girl. "Wake up, Will. What are you thinking about?"

Holley started. "I was thinking of a dinner I had

ence at Mouquin's," he replied. "Closed up, now, I hear. Gone—like all the other old landmarks—the happy stations on the five o'clock cocktail route. You know, I wonder sometimes if I'd like New York to-day—"

He talked on of the old Manhattan he had known. In what seemed to Bob Eden no time at all, the dinner hour had passed. As they were standing at the cashier's desk, the boy noted for the first time a stranger lighting a cigar near by. He was, from his dress, no native—a small, studious-looking man with piercing eyes.

"Good evening, neighbor," Holley said.

"How are you," answered the stranger.

"Come down to look us over?" the editor asked, thinking of his next issue.

"Dropped in for a call on the kangaroo-rat," replied the man. "I understand there's a local variety whose tail measures three millimeters longer than any hitherto recorded."

"Oh," returned Holley. "One of those fellows, eh? We get them all—beetle men and butterfly men, mouse and gopher men. Drop round to the office of the *Times* some day and we'll have a chat."

"Delighted," said the little naturalist.

"Well, look who's here," cried Holley suddenly. Bob Eden turned, and saw entering the door of the Oasis a thin little Chinese who seemed as old as the desert. His face was the color of a beloved meerschaum pipe, his eyes beady and bright. "Louie Wong," Holley explained. "Back from San Francisco, eh, Louie?"

"Hello, boss," said Louie, in a high shrill voice. "My come back."

"Didn't you like it up there?" Holley persisted.

"San Flancisco no good," answered Louie. "All time lain dlop on nose. My like 'um heah."

"Going back to Madden's, eh?" Holley inquired. Louie nodded. "Well, here's a bit of luck for you, Louie. Mr. Eden is going out to the ranch presently, and you can ride with him."

"Of course," assented Eden.

"Catch 'um hot tea. You wait jus' litta time, boss," said Louie, sitting up to the counter.

"We'll be down in front of the hotel," Holley told him. The three of them went out. The little naturalist followed, and slipped by them, disappearing in the night.

Neither Holley nor Eden spoke. When they reached the hotel they stopped.

"I'm leaving you now," Paula Wendell said. "I have some letters to write."

"Ah, yes," Eden remarked. "Well—don't forget. My love to Wilbur."

"These are business letters," she answered, severely. "Good night."

The girl went inside. "So Louie's back," Eden said. "That makes a pretty situation."

"What's the matter?" Holley said. "Louie may have a lot to tell."

"Perhaps. But when he shows up at his old job— what about Charlie? He'll be kicked out, and I'll be alone on the big scene. Somehow, I don't feel I know my lines."

"I never thought of that," replied the editor. "However, there's plenty of work for two boys out there when Madden's in residence. I imagine he'll keep them both. And what a chance for Charlie to pump old Louie dry. You and I could ask him questions from now until doomsday and never learn a thing. But Charlie—that's another matter."

They waited, and presently Louie Wong came shuffling down the street, a cheap little suit-case in one hand and a full paper bag in the other.

"What you got there, Louie?" Holley asked. He examined the bag. "Bananas, eh?"

"Tony like 'um banana," the old man explained. "Pleasant foah Tony."

Eden and Holly looked at each other. "Louie," said the editor gently, "poor Tony's dead."

Any one who believes the Chinese face is always expressionless should have seen Louie's then. A look of mingled pain and anger contorted it, and he burst at once into a flood of language that needed no translator. It was profane and terrifying.

"Poor old Louie," Holley said. "He's reviling the street, as they say in China."

"Do you suppose he knows?" asked Eden. "That Tony was murdered, I mean."

"Search me," answered Holley. "It certainly looks that way, doesn't it?" Still loudly vocal, Louie Wong climbed on to the back seat of the flivver, and Bob Eden took his place at the wheel. "Watch your step, boy," advised Holley. "See you soon. Good night."

Bob Eden started the car, and with old Louie Wong set out on the strangest ride of his life.

The moon had not yet risen; the stars, wan and far-off and unfriendly, were devoid of light. They climbed between the mountains, and that mammoth doorway led seemingly to a black and threatening inferno that Eden could sense but could not see. Down the rocky road and on to the sandy floor of the desert they crept along; out of the dark beside the way gleamed little yellow eyes, flashing hatefully for a moment, then vanishing forever. Like the ugly ghosts of trees that had died the Joshuas writhed in agony, casting deformed, appealing arms aloft. And constantly as they rode on, muttered the weird voice of the old Chinese on the back seat, mourning the passing of his friend, the death of Tony.

Bob Eden's nerves were steady, but he was glad when the lights of Madden's ranch shone with a friendly glow ahead. He left the car in the road and went to open the gate. A stray twig was caught in the latch, but finally he got it open, and returning to the car, swung it into the yard. With a feeling of deep relief he swept up before the barn. Charlie Chan was waiting in the glow of the headlights.

"Hello, Ah, Kim," Eden called. "Got a little play-mate for you in the back seat. Louie Wong has come back to his desert." He leaped to the ground. All was silence in the rear of the car. "Come on, Louie," he cried. "Here we are."

He stopped, a sudden thrill of horror in his heart. In the dim light he saw that Louie had slipped to his knees, and that his head hung limply over the door at the left.

"My God!" cried Eden.

"Wait," said Charlie Chan. "I get flashlight."

He went, while Bob Eden stood fixed and frightened in his tracks. Quickly the efficient Charlie returned, and made a hasty examination with the light. Bob Eden saw a gash in the side of Louie's old coat—a gash that was bordered with something wet and dark.

"Stabbed in the side," said Charlie calmly. "Dead—like Tony."

"Dead—when?" gasped Eden. "In the minute I left the car at the gate. Why—it's impossible—"

Out of the shadows came Martin Thorn, his pale face gleaming in the dusk. "What's all this?" he asked. "Why—it's Louie. What's happened to Louie?"

He bent over the door of the car, and the busy flash-light in the hand of Charlie Chan shone for a moment on his back. Across the dark coat was a long tear—a tear such as might have been made in the coat of one climbing hurriedly through a barbed-wire fence.

"This is terrible," Thorn said. "Just a minute—I must get Mr. Madden."

He ran to the house, and Bob Eden stood with Charlie Chan by the body of Louie Wong.

"Charlie," whispered the boy huskily, "you saw that rip in Thorn's coat?"

"Most certainly," answered Chan. "I observed it. What did I quote to you this morning? Old saying of Chinese. He who rides a tiger can not dismount."

CHAPTER X

BLISS OF THE HOMICIDE SQUAD

IN ANOTHER moment Madden was with them there by the car, and they felt rather than saw a quivering, suppressed fury in every inch of the millionaire's huge frame. With an oath he snatched the flashlight from the hand of Charlie Chan and bent over the silent form in the back of the flivver. The glow from the lamp illuminated faintly his big red face, his searching eyes, and Bob Eden watched him with interest.

There in that dusty car lay the lifeless shape of one who had served Madden faithfully for many years. Yet no sign either of compassion or regret was apparent in the millionaire's face—nothing save a constantly growing anger. Yes, Bob Eden reflected, those who had reported Madden lacked a heart spoke nothing but the truth.

Madden straightened, and flashed the light into the pale face of his secretary.

"Fine business!" he snarled.

"Well, what are you staring at me for?" cried Thorn, his voice trembling.

"I'll stare at you if I choose—though God knows I'm sick of the sight of your silly face—"

"I've had about enough from you," warned Thorn, and the tremor in his voice was rage. For a moment they

148

regarded each other while Bob Eden watched them, amazed. For the first time he realized that under the mask of their daily relations these two were anything but friends.

Suddenly Madden turned the light on Charlie Chan. "Look here, Ah Kim—this was Louie Wong—the boy you replaced here—savvy? You've got to stay on the ranch now—after I've gone, too—how about it?"

"I think I stay, boss."

"Good. You're the only bit of luck I've had since I came to this accursed place. Bring Louie into the living-room—on the couch. I'll call Eldorado."

He stalked off through the patio to the house, and after a moment's hesitation Chan and the secretary picked up the frail body of Louie Wong. Slowly Bob Eden followed that odd procession. In the living-room, Madden was talking briskly on the telephone. Presently he hung up the receiver.

"Nothing to do but wait," he said. "There's a sort of constable in town—he'll be along pretty soon with the coroner. Oh, it's fine business. They'll overrun the place—and I came here for a rest."

"I suppose you want to know what happened," Eden began. "I met Louie Wong in town, at the Oasis Café. Mr. Holley pointed him out to me, and—"

Madden waved a great hand. "Oh, save all that for some half-witted cop. Fine business, this is."

He took to pacing the floor like a lion with the toothache. Eden dropped into a chair before the fire. Chan had gone out, and Thorn was sitting silently near by. Madden continued to pace. Bob Eden stared at the blazing logs. What sort of affair had he got into, anyhow?

What desperate game was afoot here on Madden's ranch, far out on the lonely desert? He began to wish himself out of it, back in town where the lights were bright and there was no constant undercurrent of hatred and suspicion and mystery.

He was still thinking in this vein when the clatter of a car sounded in the yard. Madden himself opened the door, and two of Eldorado's prominent citizens entered.

"Come in, gentlemen," Madden said, amiable with an effort. "Had a little accident out here."

One of the two, a lean man with a brown, weatherbeaten face, stepped forward.

"Howdy, Mr. Madden, I know you, but you don't know me. I'm Constable Brackett, and this is our coroner, Doctor Simms. A murder, you said on the phone."

"Well," replied Madden, "I suppose you could call it that. But fortunately no one was hurt. No white man, I mean. Just my old Chink, Louie Wong." Ah Kim had entered in time to hear this speech, and his eyes blazed for a moment as they rested on the callous face of the millionaire.

"Louie?" said the constable. He went over to the couch. "Why, poor old Louie. Harmless as they come, he was. Can't figure who'd have anything against old Louie."

The coroner, a brisk young man, also went to the couch and began an examination. Constable Brackett turned to Madden. "Now, we'll make just as little trouble as we can, Mr. Madden," he promised. Evidently he was much in awe of this great man. "But I don't like this. It reflects on me. I got to ask a few questions. You see that, don't you?"

"Of course," answered Madden. "Fire away. I'm sorry, but I can't tell you a thing. I was in my room when my secretary"—he indicated Thorn—"came in and said that Mr. Eden here had just driven into the yard with the dead body of Louie in the car."

The constable turned with interest to Eden. "Where'd you find him?" he inquired.

"He was perfectly all right when I picked him up," Eden explained. He launched into his story—the meeting with Louie at the Oasis, the ride across the desert, the stop at the gate, and finally the gruesome discovery in the yard. The constable shook his head.

"All sounds mighty mysterious to me," he admitted. "You say you think he was killed while you was openin' the gate. What makes you think so?"

"He was talking practically all the way out here," Eden replied. "Muttering to himself there in the back seat. I heard him when I got out to unfasten the gate."

"What was he sayin'?"

"He was talking in Chinese. I'm sorry, but I'm no sinologue."

"I ain't accused you of anything, have I?"

"A sinologue is a man who understands the Chinese language," Bob Eden smiled.

"Oh." The constable scratched his head. "This here secretary, now—"

Thorn came forward. He had been in his room, he said, when he heard a disturbance in the yard, and went outside. Absolutely nothing to offer. Bob Eden's glance fell on the tear across the back of Thorn's coat. He looked at Charlie Chan, but the detective shook his head. Say nothing, his eyes directed.

The constable turned to Madden. "Who else is on the place?" he wanted to know.

"Nobody but Ah Kim here. He's all right."

The officer shook his head. "Can't always tell," he averred. "All these tong wars, you know." He raised his voice to a terrific bellow. "Come here, you," he cried.

Ah Kim, lately Detective-Sergeant Chan of the Honolulu Police, came with expressionless face and stood before the constable. How often he had played the opposite rôle in such a scene—played it far better than this mainland officer ever would.

"Ever see this Louie Wong before?" thundered the constable.

"Me, boss? No, boss, I no see 'um."

"New round here, ain't you?"

"Come las' Fliday, boss."

"Where did you work before this?"

"All place, boss. Big town, litta town."

"I mean where'd you work last?"

"Lailload, I think, boss. Santa Fe lailload. Lay sticks on glound."

"Ah—er—well, doggone." The constable had run out of questions. "Ain't had much practise at this sort of thing," he apologized. "Been so busy confiscatin' licker these last few years I sort of lost the knack for police work. This is sheriff's stuff. I called him before we come out, an' he's sendin' Captain Bliss of the Homicide Squad down to-morrow mornin'. So we won't bother you no more to-night, Mr. Madden."

The coroner came forward. "We'll take the body in town, Mr. Madden," he said. "I'll have the inquest in there, but I may want to bring my jurors out here sometime to-morrow."

"Oh, sure," replied Madden. "Just attend to anything that comes up, and send all the bills to me. Believe me, I'm sorry this thing has happened."

"So am I," said the constable. "Louie was a good old scout."

"Yes—and—well, I don't like it. It's annoying."

"All mighty mysterious to me," the constable admitted again. "My wife told me I never ought to take this job. Well, so long, Mr. Madden—great pleasure to meet a man like you."

When Bob Eden retired to his room, Madden and Thorn were facing each other on the hearth. Something in the expression of each made him wish he could overhear the scene about to be enacted in that room.

Ah Kim was waiting beside a crackling fire. "I make 'um burn, boss," he said. Eden closed the door and sank into a chair.

"Charlie, in heaven's name, what's going on here?" he inquired helplessly.

Chan shrugged. "Plenty goes on," he said. "Two nights now gone since in this room I hint to you Chinese are psychic people. On your face then I see well-bred sneer."

"I apologize," Eden returned. "No sneering after this, even the well-bred kind. But I'm certainly stumped. This thing to-night—"

"Most unfortunate, this thing to-night," said Chan thoughtfully. "Humbly suggest you be very careful, or everything spoils. Local police come thumping on to scene, not dreaming in their slight brains that murder of Louie are of no importance in the least."

"Not important, you say?"

"No, indeed. Not when compared to other matters."

"Well, it was pretty important to Louie, I guess," said Eden.

"Guess so, too. But murder of Louie just like death of parrot—one more dark deed covering up very black deed occurring here before we arrive on mysterious scene. Before parrot go, before Louie make unexpected exit, unknown person dies screaming unanswered cries for help. Who? Maybe in time we learn."

"Then you think Louie was killed because he knew too much?"

"Just like Tony, yes. Poor Louie very foolish, does not stay in San Francisco when summoned there. Comes with sad blunder back to desert. Most bitterly unwelcome here. One thing puzzles me."

"Only one thing?" asked Eden.

"One at present. Other puzzles put aside for moment. Louie goes on Wednesday morning, probably before black deed was done. How then does he know? Did act have echo in San Francisco? I am most sad not to have talk with him. But there are other paths to follow."

"I hope so," sighed Bob Eden. "But I don't see them. This is too much for me."

"Plenty for me, too," agreed Chan. "Pretty quick I go home, lifelong yearning for travel forever quenched. Keep in mind, much better police do not find who killed Louie Wong. If they do, our fruit may be picked when not yet ripe. We should handle case. Officers of law must be encouraged off of ranch at earliest possible time, having found nothing."

"Well, the constable was easy enough," smiled Eden.

"All looked plenty mysterious to him," answered Chan, smiling, too.

"I sympathized with him in that," Eden admitted. "But this Captain Bliss probably won't be so simple. You watch your step, Charlie, or they'll lock you up."

Chan nodded. "New experiences crowd close on this mainland," he said. "Detective-Sergeant Chan a murder suspect. Maybe I laugh at that, when I get home again. Just now, laugh won't come. A warm good night—"

"Wait a minute," interrupted Eden. "How about Tuesday afternoon? Madden's expecting the messenger with the pearls then, and somehow, I haven't a stall left in me."

Chan shrugged. "Two days yet. Stop the worry. Much may manage to occur before Tuesday afternoon." He went out softly.

Just as they finished breakfast on Monday morning, a knock sounded on the door of the ranch house, and Thorn admitted Will Holley.

"Oh," said Madden sourly. His manner had not improved overnight. "So you're here again."

"Naturally," replied Holley. "Being a good newspaper man, I'm not overlooking the first murder we've had round here in years." He handed a newspaper to the millionaire. "By the way, here's a Los Angeles morning paper. Our interview is on the front page."

Madden took it without much interest. Over his shoulder Bob Eden caught a glimpse of the head-lines:

ERA OF PROSPERITY DUE, SAYS
FAMED MAGNATE
P. J. Madden, Interviewed on Desert
Ranch, Predicts Business Boom

Madden glanced idly through the story. When he had finished, he said: "In the New York papers, I suppose?"

"Of course," Holley answered. "All over the country this morning. You and I are famous, Mr. Madden. But what's this about poor old Louie?"

"Don't ask me," frowned Madden. "Some fool bumped him off. Your friend Eden can tell you more than I can." He got up and strode from the room.

Eden and Holley stared at each other for a moment, then went together into the yard.

"Pretty raw stuff," remarked Holley. "It makes me hot. Louie was a kindly old soul. Killed in the car, I understand."

Eden related what had happened. They moved farther away from the house.

"Well, who do you think?" Holley inquired.

"I think Thorn," Eden answered. "However, Charlie says Louie's passing was just a minor incident, and it will be better all round if his murderer isn't found just at present. Of course he's right."

"Of course he is. And there isn't much danger they'll catch the guilty man, at that. The constable is a helpless old fellow."

"How about this Captain Bliss?"

"Oh, he's a big noisy bluff with a fatal facility for getting the wrong man. The sheriff's a regular fellow, with brains, but he may not come round. Let's stroll out and look over the ground where you left the car last night. I've got something to slip you, a telegram—from your father, I imagine."

As they went through the gate, the telegram changed

hands. Holding it so it could not be seen from the house, Bob Eden read it through.

"Well, dad says he's going to put up the bluff to Madden that's he's sending Draycott with the pearls to-night."

"Draycott?" asked Holley.

"He's a private detective dad uses in San Francisco. As good a name as any, I suppose. When Draycott fails to arrive, dad's going to be very much upset." The boy considered for a moment. "I guess it's about the best he can do—but I hate all this deception. And I certainly don't like the job of keeping Madden cool. However, something may happen before then."

They examined the ground where Bob Eden had halted the car while he opened the gate the night before. The tracks of many cars passing in the road were evident—but no sign of any footsteps. "Even my footprints are gone," remarked Eden. "Do you suppose it was the wind, drifting the sand—"

Holley shrugged. "No," he said. "It was not. Somebody has been out here with a broom, my boy, and obliterated every trace of footsteps about that car."

Eden nodded. "You're right. Somebody—but who? Our old friend Thorn, of course."

They stepped aside as an automobile swung by them and entered Madden's yard.

"There's Bliss, now, with the constable," Holley remarked. "Well, they get no help from us, eh?"

"Not a bit," replied Eden. "Encourage them off the ranch at earliest possible moment. That's Charlie's suggestion."

They returned to the yard and waited. Inside the

living-room they heard Thorn and Madden talking with the two officers. After a time, Bliss came out, followed by the millionaire and Constable Brackett. He greeted Holley as an old friend, and the editor introduced Bob Eden.

"Oh, yes, Mr. Eden," said the captain. "Want to talk to you. What's your version of this funny busi- ness?"

Bob Eden looked at him with distaste. He was a big, flat-footed policeman of the usual type, and no great intelligence shone in his eyes. The boy gave him a care- fully edited story of the night before.

"Humph," said Bliss. "Sounds queer to me."

"Yes?" smiled Eden. "To me, too. But it happens to be the truth."

"Well, I'll have a look at the ground out there," remarked Bliss.

"You'll find nothing," said Holley. "Except the foot- prints of this young man and myself. We've just been taking a squint around."

"Oh, you have, have you?" replied Bliss grimly. He strode through the gate, the constable tagging after him. After a perfunctory examination the two returned.

"This is sure some puzzle," said Constable Brackett.

"Is that so?" Bliss sneered. "Well, get on to your- self. How about this Chink, Ah Kim? Had a good job here, didn't he? Louie Wong comes back. What does that mean? Ah Kim loses his job."

"Nonsense," protested Madden.

"Think so, do you?" remarked Bliss. "Well, I don't. I tell you I know these Chinks. They think nothing of sticking knives in each other. Nothing at all." Ah Kim emerged from around the side of the house. "Hey, you," cried Captain Bliss. Bob Eden began to worry.

Ah Kim came up. "You want'um me, boss?"

"You bet I want you. Going to lock you up."

"Why foah, boss?"

"For knifing Louie Wong. You can't get away with that stuff round here."

The Chinese regarded this crude practitioner of his own arts with a lifeless eye. "You clazy, boss," he said.

"Is that so?" Bliss's face hardened. "I'll show you just how crazy I am. Better tell me the whole story now. It'll go a lot easier with you if you do."

"What stoahy, boss?"

"How you sneaked out and put a knife in Louie last night."

"Maybe you catch 'um knife, hey, boss?" asked Ah Kim, maliciously.

"Never mind about that!"

"Poah old Ah Kim's fingah plints on knife, hey, boss?"

"Oh, shut up," said Bliss.

"Maybe you takee look-see, find velvet slippah plints in sand, hey, boss?" Bliss glared at him in silence. "What I tell you—you clazy cop, hey, boss?"

Holley and Eden looked at each other with keen enjoyment. Madden broke in, "Oh, come now, Captain, you haven't got a thing against him, and you know it. You take my cook away from me without any evidence, and I'll make you sweat for it."

"Well—I—" Bliss hesitated. "I know he did it, and I'll prove it later." His eyes lighted. "How'd you get into this country?" he demanded.

"Melican citizen, boss. Boahn San Flancisce. Foahty-flive yeah old now."

"Born here, eh? Is that so? Then you've got your chock-gee, I suppose. Let me see it."

Bob Eden's heart sank to his boots. Though many Chinese were without chock-gees, he knew that the lack of one would be sufficient excuse for this stupid police-man to arrest Chan at once. Another moment, and they'd all be done for—

"Come on," bellowed Bliss.

"What you say, boss?" parried Ah Kim.

"You know what I said. Your chock-gee—certifi-cate—hand it over or by heaven I'll lock you up so quick—"

"Oh, boss—ce'tiflicate—allight, boss." And before Eden's startled gaze the Chinese took from his blouse a worn slip of paper about the size of a bank-note, and handed it to Bliss.

The Captain read it sourly and handed it back. "All right—but I ain't through with you yet," he said.

"Thanks, boss," returned Ah Kim, brightening. "You plenty clazy, boss. Thasaw. Goo'by." And he shuffled away.

"I told you it looked terrible mysterious to me," com-mented the constable.

"Oh, for Pete's sake, shut up," cried Bliss. "Mr. Madden, I'll have to admit I'm stumped for the time being. But that condition don't last long with me. I'll get to the bottom of this yet. You'll see me again."

"Run out any time," Madden invited with deep insin-cerity. "If I happen on anything, I'll call Constable Brackett."

Bliss and the constable got into their car and rode away. Madden returned to the house.

"Oh, excellent Chan," said Will Holley softly. "Where in Sam Hill did he get that chock-gee?"

"It looked as though we were done for," Eden admitted. "But good old Charlie thinks of everything."

Holley climbed into his car. "Well, I guess Madden isn't going to invite me to lunch. I'll go along. You know, I'm keener than ever to get the answer to this puzzle. Louie was my friend. It's a rotten shame."

"I don't know where we're going, but we're on our way," Eden answered. "I'd feel pretty helpless if I didn't have Charlie with me."

"Oh, you've got a few brains, too." Holley assured him.

"You're clazy, boss," Eden laughed, as the editor drove away.

Returning to his room, he found Ah Kim calmly making the bed.

"Charlie, you're a peach," said the boy, closing the door. "I thought we were sunk without warning. Whose chock-gee did you have, anyhow?"

"Ah Kim's chock-gee, to be sure," smiled Chan.

"Who's Ah Kim?"

"Ah Kim humble vegetable merchant who drive me amidst other garden truck from Barstow to Eldorado. I make simple arrangement to rent chock-gee short while. Happy to note long wear in pockets make photograph look like image of anybody. Came to me in bright flash Madden might ask for identification certificate before engaging me for honorable tasks. Madden did not do so, but thing fit in plenty neat all the same."

"It certainly did," Eden agreed. "You're a brick to do all this for the Jordans—and for dad. I hope they pay you handsomely."

Chan shook his head. "What you say in car riding to ferry? Postman on holiday itches to try long stretch of road. All this sincere pleasure for me. When I untie knots and find answer, that will be fine reward." He bowed and departed.

Some hours later, while they waited for lunch, Bob Eden and Madden sat talking in the big living-room. The millionaire was reiterating his desire to return east at the earliest possible moment. He was sitting facing the door. Suddenly on his big red face appeared a look of displeasure so intense it startled the boy. Turning about, Eden saw standing in the doorway the slight figure of a man, a stooped, studious-looking man who carried a suit-case in one hand. The little naturalist of the Oasis Café.

"Mr. Madden?" inquired the newcomer.

"I'm Madden," said the millionaire. "What is it?"

"Ah, yes." The stranger came into the room, and set down his bag. "My name, sir, is Gamble, Thaddeus Gamble, and I am keenly interested in certain fauna surrounding your desert home. I have here a letter from an old friend of yours, the president of a college that has received many benefactions at your hands. If you will be so kind as to look it over—"

He offered the letter and Madden took it, glaring at him in a most unfriendly manner. When the millionaire had read the brief epistle, he tore it into bits and, rising, tossed them into the fireplace.

"You want to stop here a few days?" he said.

It would be most convenient if I could," answered Gamble. "Of course, I should like to pay for my accommodations—"

Madden waved his hand. Ah Kim came in, headed for the luncheon table. "Another place, Ah Kim," ordered Madden. "And show Mr. Gamble to the room in the left wing—the one next to Mr. Eden's."

"Very kind of you, I'm sure," remarked Gamble suavely. "I shall try to make as little trouble as may be. Luncheon impends, I take it. Not unwelcome, either. This—er—this desert air, sir—er—I'll return in a moment."

He followed Ah Kim out. Madden glared after him, his face purple. Bob Eden realized that a new puzzle had arrived.

"The devil with him," cried Madden. "But I had to be polite. That letter." He shrugged. "Gad, I hope I get out of here soon."

Bob Eden continued to wonder. Who was Mr. Gamble? What did he want at Madden's ranch?

CHAPTER XI

WHATEVER Mr. Gamble's mission at the ranch, Bob Eden reflected during lunch, it was obviouly a peaceful one. Seldom had he encountered a more mild-mannered little chap. All through the meal the new-comer talked volubly and well, with the gentle, cultivated accent of a scholar. Madden was sour and unrespon-sive; evidently he still resented the intrusion of this stranger. Thorn as usual sat silent and aloof, a depress-ing figure in the black suit he had to-day donned to replace the one torn so mysteriously the night before. It fell to Bob Eden to come to Mr. Gamble's aid and keep the conversation going.

The luncheon over, Gamble rose and went to the door. For a moment he stood staring out across the blazing sand toward the cool white tops of the mountains, far away.

"Magnificent," he commented. "I wonder, Mr. Mad-den, if you realize the true grandeur of this setting for your ranch house? The desert, the broad lonely desert, that has from time immemorial cast its weird spell on the souls of men. Some find it bleak and disquieting, but as for myself—"

"Be here long?" cut in Madden.

164

"Ah, that depends. I sincerely hope so. I want to see this country after the spring rains—the verbena and the primroses in bloom. The thought enchants me. What says the prophet Isaiah? 'And the desert shall rejoice and blossom as the rose. And the parched ground shall become a pool, and the thirsty land springs of water.' You know Isaiah, Mr. Madden?"

"No, I don't. I know too many people now," responded Madden grimly.

"I believe you said you were interested in the fauna round here, Professor?" Bob Eden remarked.

Gamble looked at him quickly. "You give me my title," he said. "You are an observant young man. Yes, there are certain researches I intend to pursue—the tail of the kangaroo-rat, which attains here a phenomenal length. The maxillary arch in the short-nosed pocket-mouse, I understand, has also reached in this neighborhood an eccentric development."

The telephone rang, and Madden himself answered it. Listening carefully, Bob Eden heard: "Telegram for Mr. Madden." At this point the millionaire pressed the receiver close to his ear, and the rest of the message was an indistinct blur.

Eden was sorry for that, for he perceived that as Madden listened an expression of keen distress came over his face. When finally he put the receiver slowly back on to its hook, he sat for a long time looking straight before him, obviously very much perplexed.

"What do you grow here in this sandy soil, Mr. Madden?" Professor Gamble inquired.

"Er—er—" Madden came gradually back to the scene. "What do I grow? A lot of things. You'd be

surprised, and so would Isaiah." Gamble was smiling at
him in a kindly way, and the millionaire warmed a bit.
"Come out, since you're interested, and I'll show you
round."

"Very good of you, sir," replied Gamble, and meekly
followed into the patio. Thorn rose and joined them.
Quickly Eden went to the telephone and got Will Holley
on the wire.

"Look here," he said in a low voice, "Madden has
just taken a telegram over the phone, and it seemed to
worry him considerably. I couldn't make out what it
was, but I'd like to know at once. Do you stand well
enough with the operator to find out—without rousing
suspicion, of course?"

"Sure," Holley replied. "That kid will tell me anything. Are you alone there? Can I call you back in a
few minutes?"

"I'm alone just now," Eden responded. "If I
shouldn't be when you call back, I'll pretend you want
Madden and turn you over to him. You can fake something to say. But if you hurry, that may not be necessary. Speed, brother, speed!"

As he turned away, Ah Kim came in to gather up the
luncheon things.

"Well, Charlie," Eden remarked. "Another guest at
our little hotel, eh?"

Chan shrugged. "Such news comes plenty quick to
cookhouse," he said.

Eden smiled. "You're the one who wanted to watch
and wait," he reminded the detective. "If you're threat-
ened with housemaid's knee, don't blame me."

"This Gamble," mused Chan. "Seems harmless like
May morning, I think."

"Oh, very. A Bible student. And it strikes me there's a fair opening for a good Bible student round here."

"Undangerous and mild," continued Chan. "Yet hidden in his scant luggage is one pretty new pistol completely loaded."

"Going to shoot the tails off the rats, most likely," Eden smiled. "Now, don't get suspicious of him, Charlie. He's probably just a tenderfoot who believes the movies and so came to this wild country armed to defend himself. By the way, Madden just got a telegram over the phone, and it was, judging by appearances, another bit of unwelcome news for our dear old friend. Holley's looking it up for me. If the telephone rings, go into the patio and be ready to tip me off in case any one is coming."

Silently Ah Kim resumed his work at the table. In a few moments, loud and clear, came the ring of Holley on the wire. Running to the telephone, Eden put his hand over the bell, muffling it. Chan stepped into the patio.

"Hello, Holley," said the boy softly. "Yes. Yes. O. K. Shoot. Um. . . . Say, that's interesting, isn't it? Coming to-night, eh? Thanks, old man."

He hung up, and Charlie returned. "A bit of news," said Eden, rising. "That telegram was from Miss Evelyn Madden. Got tired of waiting in Denver, I guess. The message was sent from Barstow. The lady arrives to-night at Eldorado on the six-forty. Looks as though I may have to give up my room and check out."

"Miss Evelyn Madden?" repeated Chan.

"That's right—you don't know, do you? She's Madden's only child. A proud beauty, too—I met her in San

Francisco. Well, it's no wonder Madden was perplexed, is it?"

"Certainly not," agreed Chan. "Murderous ranch like this no place for refined young woman."

Eden sighed. "Just one more complication," he said. "Things move, but we don't seem to get anywhere."

"Once more," returned Chan, "I call to your attention that much unused virtue, patience. Aspect will be brighter here now. A woman's touch—"

"This woman's touch means frost-bite," smiled Eden. "Charlie, I'll bet you a million—not even the desert will thaw out Evelyn Madden."

Chan departed to his duties in the cookhouse. Madden and Thorn drifted in after a time; Gamble, it appeared, had retired to his room. The long hot afternoon dragged by, baking hours of deathly calm during which the desert lived up to its reputation. Madden disappeared and presently his "noisome" snores filled the air. A good idea, Bob Eden decided.

In a recumbent position on his bed, he found that time passed more swiftly. In fact, he didn't know it was passing. Toward evening he awoke, hot and muddled of mind, but a cold shower made him feel human again.

At six o'clock he crossed the patio to the living-room. In the yard before the barn he saw Madden's big car standing ready for action, and remembered. The millionaire was no doubt about to meet his daughter in town, and the haughty Evelyn was not to be affronted with the flivver.

But when he reached the living-room, Eden saw that it was evidently Thorn who had been selected for the trip to Eldorado. The secretary stood there in his gloomy clothes, a black slouch hat accentuating the paleness of his face. As Eden entered, what was obviously a serious conversation between Thorn and the millionaire came to a sudden halt.

"Ah, good evening," said Eden. "Not leaving us, Mr. Thorn?"

"Business in town," returned Thorn. "Well, Chief, I'll go along."

Again the telephone rang. Madden leaped to it. For a moment he listened and history repeated itself on his face. "Bad news all the time," Eden thought.

Madden put his great hand over the mouthpiece, and spoke to his secretary. "It's that old bore down the road, Doctor Whitcomb," he announced, and Eden felt a flash of hot resentment at this characterization. "She wants to see me this evening—says she has something very important to tell me."

"Say you're busy," suggested Thorn.

"I'm sorry, Doctor," Madden began over the phone, "but I am very much occupied—"

He stopped, evidently interrupted by a flood of conversation. Again he put his hand over the transmitter. "She insists, confound it," he complained.

"Well, you'll have to see her then," said Thorn.

"All right, Doctor," Madden capitulated. "Come about eight."

Thorn went out, and the big car roared off toward the road and Evelyn Madden's train. Mr. Gamble entered, refreshed and ready with a few apt quotations. Eden amused himself with the radio.

At the usual hour, much to Eden's surprise, they

dined. Thorn's chair was empty and there was, oddly enough, no place for Evelyn; nor did the millionaire make any arrangements regarding a room for his daughter. Strange, Eden thought.

After dinner, Madden led them to the patio. Again he had arranged for a fire out there, and the blaze glowed red on the stone floor, on the adobe walls of the house, and on the near-by perch of Tony, now empty and forlorn.

"This is living," remarked Gamble, when they had sat down and he had lighted one of Madden's cigars. "The poor fools cooped up in cities—they don't know what they're missing. I could stay here forever."

His final sentence made no hit with the host, and silence fell. At a little past eight they heard the sound of a car entering the yard. Thorn and the girl, perhaps— but evidently Madden didn't think so, for he said:

"That's the doctor. Ah Kim!" The servant appeared. "Show the lady out here."

"Well, she doesn't want to see me," Gamble said, getting up. "I'll go in and find a book."

Madden looked at Bob Eden, but the boy remained where he was. "The doctor's a friend of mine," he explained.

"Is that so?" growled Madden.

"Yes—I met her yesterday morning. A wonderful woman."

Doctor Whitcomb appeared. "Well, Mr. Madden?" She shook hands. "It's a great pleasure to have you with us again."

"Thanks," said Madden coolly. "You know Mr. Eden, I believe?"

"Oh, hello," smiled the woman. "Glad to see you. Not very pleased with you, however. You didn't drop in to-day."

"Rather busy," Eden replied. "Won't you sit down, please."

He brought forward a chair; it seemed that Madden needed a hint or two on hospitality. The guest sank into it. Madden, his manner very haughty and aloof, sat down some distance away, and waited.

"Mr. Madden," said Doctor Whitcomb, "I'm sorry if I seem to intrude—I know that you are here to rest, and that you don't welcome visitors. But this is not a social call. I came here about—about this terrible thing that has happened on your place."

For a moment Madden did not reply. "You— mean—" he said slowly.

"I mean the murder of poor Louie Wong," the woman answered.

"Oh." Was there relief in Madden's voice? "Yes— of course."

"Louie was my friend—he often came to see me. I was so sorry, when I heard. And you—he served you faithfully, Mr. Madden. Naturally you're doing everything possible to run down his murderer."

"Everything," replied Madden carelessly.

"Whether what I have to tell has any connection with the killing of Louie—that's for policemen to decide," went on the doctor. "You can hand my story on to them —if you will."

"Gladly," replied Madden. "What is your story, Doctor?"

"On Saturday evening a man arrived at my place who

said his name was McCallum, Henry McCallum," began
Doctor Whitcomb, "and that he came from New York.
He told me he suffered from bronchitis, though I must
say I saw no symptoms of it. He took one of my cabins
and settled down for a stay—so I thought."

"Yes," nodded Madden. "Go on."

"At dark Sunday night—a short time before the hour
when poor Louie was killed—some one drove up in a big
car before my place and blew the horn. One of my boys
went out, and the stranger asked for McCallum. McCallum came, talked with the man in the car for a moment,
then got in and rode off with him—in this direction. That
was the last I've seen of Mr. McCallum. He left a suit-
case filled with clothes in his cabin, but he has not
returned."

"And you think he killed Louie?" asked Madden, with
a note of polite incredulity in his voice.

"I don't think anything about it. How should I
know? I simply regard it as a matter that should be called
to the attention of the police. As you are much closer
to the investigation than I am, I'm asking you to tell
them about it. They can come down and examine McCallum's property, if they wish."

"All right," said Madden, rising pointedly. "I'll tell
them. Though if you're asking my opinion, I don't
think—"

"Thank you," smiled the doctor. "I wasn't asking
your opinion, Mr. Madden." She too stood. "Our interview, I see, is ended. I'm sorry if I've intruded—"

"Why, you didn't intrude," protested Madden.
"That's all right. Maybe your information is valuable.
Who knows?"

"Very good of you to say so," returned the doctor, with gentle sarcasm. She glanced toward the parrot's perch. "How's Tony? He, at least, must miss Louie a lot."

"Tony's dead," said Madden bruskly.

"What! Tony, too!" The doctor was silent for a moment. "A rather memorable visit, this one of yours," she said slowly. "Please give my regards to your daughter. She is not with you?"

"No," returned Madden. "She is not with me." That was all.

"A great pity," Doctor Whitcomb replied. "I thought her a charming girl."

"Thank you," Madden said. "Just a moment. My boy will show you to your car."

"Don't trouble," put in Bob Eden. "I'll attend to that." He led the way through the bright living-room, past Mr. Gamble deep in a huge book. In the yard the doctor turned to him.

"What a man!" she said. "As hard as granite. I don't believe the death of Louie means a thing to him."

"Very little, I'm afraid," Eden agreed.

"Well, I rely on you. If he doesn't repeat my story to the sheriff, you must."

The boy hesitated. "I'll tell you something—in confidence," he said. "Everything possible is being done to find the murderer of Louie. Not by Madden—but by—others."

The doctor sat silent for a moment in the dark car under the dark, star-spangled sky. "I think I understand," she said softly. "With all my heart, I wish you luck, my boy."

Eden took her hand. "If I shouldn't see you again, Doctor—I want you to know. Just meeting you has been a privilege."

"I'll remember that," she answered. "Good night."

The boy watched her back the car through the open gate. When he returned to the living-room, Madden and Gamble were together there. "Confounded old busy-body," Madden said.

"Wait a minute," Eden said hotly. "That woman with just her two hands has done more good in the world than you with all your money. And don't you forget it."

"Does that give her a license to butt into my affairs?" demanded Madden.

Further warm words were on the tip of the boy's tongue, but he restrained himself. However, he reflected that he was about fed up with this arrogant, callous millionaire.

He looked toward the clock. A quarter to nine, and still no sign of Thorn and Evelyn Madden. Was the girl's train late? Hardly likely.

Though he did not feel particularly welcome in the room, he waited on. He would see this latest development through. At ten o'clock Mr. Gamble rose, and commenting favorably on the desert air, went to his room.

At five minutes past ten the roar of the big car in the yard broke the intense stillness. Bob Eden sat erect, his eager eyes straying from one door to another. Presently the glass doors leading to the patio opened. Martin Thorn came in alone.

Without a word to his chief, the secretary threw down his hat and dropped wearily into a chair. The silence became oppressive.

"Got your business attended to, eh?" suggested Eden cheerfully.

"Yes," said Thorn—no more. Eden rose.

"Well, I guess I'll turn in," he said, and went to his room. As he entered he heard the splash of Mr. Gamble in the bath that lay between his apartment and that occupied by the professor. His seclusion was ended. Have to be more careful in the future.

Shortly after his lights were on, Ah Kim appeared at the door. Eden, finger on lips, indicated the bath. The Chinese nodded. They stepped to the far side of the bedroom and spoke in low tones.

"Well, where's little Evelyn?" asked the boy.

Chan shrugged. "More mystery," he whispered.

"Just what has our friend Thorn been doing for the past four hours?" Eden wondered.

"Enjoying moonlit ride on desert, I think," Chan returned. "When big car go out, I note speedometer. Twelve thousand eight hundred and forty miles. Four miles necessary to travel to town, and four to return with. But when big car arrives home, speedometer announces quietly twelve thousand eight hundred and seventy-nine miles."

"Charlie, you think of everything," Eden said admiringly.

"Strange place this Thorn has been," Charlie added. "Much red clay on ground." He exhibited a fragment of earth. "Scraped off on accelerator," he explained. "Maybe you have seen such place round here?"

"Nothing like it," replied Eden. "You don't suppose he's harmed the gal—but no, Madden seems to be in on it, and she's his darling."

"Just one more little problem rising up," said Chan.

Eden nodded. "Lord, I haven't met so many problems since I gave up algebra. And by the way, to-morrow's Tuesday. The pearls are coming, hurrah, hurrah. At least, old P. J. thinks they are. He's going to be hard to handle to-morrow."

A faint knock sounded on the door to the patio, and Chan had just time to get to the fireplace and busy himself there when it was opened and Madden, oddly noiseless for him, entered.

"Why, hello—" began Eden.

"Hush!" said Madden. He looked toward the bathroom. "Go easy, will you. Ah Kim, get out of here."

"Allight, boss," said Ah Kim, and went.

Madden stepped to the bathroom door and listened. He tried it gently; it opened at his touch. He went in, locked the door leading into the room occupied by Gamble, and returned, shutting the door behind him.

"Now," he began, "I want to see you. Keep your voice down. I've finally got hold of your father on the telephone, and he tells me a man named Draycott will arrive with the pearls at Barstow to-morrow noon."

Eden's heart sank. "Ah—er—that ought to bring him here to-morrow night—"

Madden leaned close, and spoke in a hoarse undertone. "Whatever happens," he said, "I don't want that fellow to come to the ranch."

Eden stared at him in amazement. "Well, Mr. Madden, I'll be—"

"Hush! Leave my name out of it."

"But after all our preparation—"

"I tell you I've changed my mind. I don't want the

pearls brought to the ranch at all. I want you to go to Barstow to-morrow, meet this Draycott, and order him to go on to Pasadena. I'm going down there on Wednesday. Tell him to meet me at the door of the Garfield National Bank in Pasadena at noon, sharp, Wednesday. I'll take the pearls then—and I'll put them where they'll be safe."

Bob Eden smiled. "All right," he agreed. "You're the boss."

"Good," said Madden. "I'll have Ah Kim drive you into town in the morning, and you can catch the Barstow train. But remember—this is between you and me. Not a word to anybody. Not to Gamble—of course. Not even to Thorn."

"I get you," Eden answered.

"Fine! Then it's set. Good night."

Madden went softly out. For a long time Eden stared after him, more puzzled than ever.

"Well, anyhow," he said at last, "it means another day of grace. For this relief, much thanks."

CHAPTER XII

A NEW day dawned, and over the stunted, bizarre shapes of that land of drought the sun resumed its merciless vigil. Bob Eden was early abroad; it was getting to be a habit with him. Before breakfast was served he had a full hour for reflection, and it could not be denied that he had much upon which to reflect. One by one he recalled the queer things that had happened since he came to the ranch. Foremost in his thoughts was the problem of Evelyn Madden. Where was that haughty lady now? No morning mists on the landscape here, but in his mind a constantly increasing fog. If only something definite would occur, something they could understand.

After breakfast he rose from the table and lighted a cigarette. He knew that Madden was eagerly waiting for him to speak.

"Mr. Madden," he said, "I find that I must go to Barstow this morning on rather important business. It's an imposition, I know. But if Ah Kim could drive me to town in time for the ten-fifteen train—"

Thorn's green eyes popped with sudden interest. Madden looked at the boy with ill-concealed approval.

"Why, that's all right," he replied. "I'll be glad to

178

arrange it for you. Ah Kim—you drive Mr. Eden in town in half an hour. Savvy?"

"All time moah job," complained Ah Kim. "Gettum up sunlise woik woik till sun him dlop. You want 'um taxi dliver why you no say so?"

"What's that?" cried Madden.

Ah Kim shrugged. "Allight, boss. I dlive 'um."

When, later on, Eden sat in the car beside the Chinese and the ranch was well behind them, Chan regarded him questioningly.

"Now you produce big mystery," he said. "Barstow on business has somewhat unexpected sound to me."

Eden laughed. "Orders from the big chief," he replied. "I'm to go down there and meet Al Draycott—and the pearls."

For a moment Chan's free hand rested on his waist and the "undigestible" burden that still lay there.

"Madden changes fickle mind again?" he inquired.

"That's just what he's done." Eden related the purport of the millionaire's call on him the night before.

"What you know concerning that!" exclaimed Chan wonderingly.

"Well, I know this much," Eden answered. "It gives us one more day for the good old hoo malimali. Outside of that, it's just another problem for us to puzzle over. By the way, I didn't tell you why Doctor Whitcomb came to see us last night."

"No necessity," Chan replied. "I am loafing idle inside door close by and hear it all."

"Oh, you were? Then you know it may have been Shaky Phil, and not Thorn, who killed Louie?"

"Shaky Phil—or maybe stranger in car who drive up

and call him into road. Must admit that stranger interests me very deep. Who was he? Was it maybe him
who carried news of Louie's approach out on to dreary
desert?"

"Well, if you're starting to ask me questions," replied
Eden, "then the big mystery is over and we may as well
wash up and go home. For I haven't got an answer in
me." Eldorado lay before them, its roofs gleaming under
the morning sun. "By the way, let's drop in and see Holley. The train isn't due yet—I suppose I'd better take it,
somebody might be watching. In the interval, Holley
may have news."

The editor was busy at his desk. "Hello, you're up
and around pretty early this morning," he said. He pushed
aside his typewriter. "Just dashing off poor old Louie's
obit. What's new out at Mystery Ranch?"

Bob Eden told him of Doctor Whitcomb's call, also of
Madden's latest switch regarding the pearls, and his own
imminent wild goose chase to Barstow.

Holley smiled. "Cheer up—a little travel will broaden
you," he remarked. "What did you think of Miss Evelyn?
But then, I believe you had met her before."

"Think of Miss Evelyn? What do you mean?" asked
Eden, surprised.

"Why, she came last night, didn't she?"

"Not so anybody could notice it. No sign of her at
the ranch."

Holley rose and walked up and down for a moment.
"That's odd. That's very odd. She certainly arrived on
the six-forty train."

"You're sure of that?" Eden asked.

"Of course I am. I saw her." Holley sat down

again. "I wasn't very much occupied last night—it was one of my free nights—I have three hundred and sixty-five of them every year. So I strolled over to the station and met the six-forty. Thorn was there, too. A tall handsome girl got off the train, and I heard Thorn address her as Miss Evelyn. 'How's dad?' she asked. 'Get in,' said Thorn, 'and I'll tell you about him. He wasn't able to come to meet you himself.' The girl entered the car, and they drove away. Naturally, I thought she was brightening your life long before this."

Eden shook his head. "Funny business," he commented. "Thorn got back to the ranch a little after ten, and when he came he was alone. Charlie here discovered, with his usual acumen, that the car had traveled some thirty-nine miles."

"Also clinging to accelerator, as though scraped off from shoe of Thorn, small fragment of red clay," added Chan. "You are accustomed round here, Mr. Holley. Maybe you can mention home of red clay."

"Not offhand," replied Holley. "There are several places— But say, this thing gets deeper and deeper. Oh— I was forgetting—there's a letter here for you, Eden."

He handed over a neat missive addressed in an old-fashioned hand. Eden inspected it with interest. It was from Madame Jordan, a rather touching appeal not to let the deal for the pearls fall through. He went back and began to read it aloud. Mrs. Jordan could not understand. Madden was there, he had bought the pearls— why the delay? The loss of that money would be serious for her.

When he had finished, Eden looked accusingly at Chan, then tore the letter to bits and threw them into a waste-paper basket. "I'm about through," he said. "That woman is one of the dearest old souls that ever lived, and it strikes me we're treating her shamefully. After all, what's happening out at Madden's ranch is none of our business. Our duty to Madame Jordan—"

"Pardon me," broke in Chan, "but coming to that, I have sense of duty most acute myself. Loyalty blooms in my heart forever—"

"Well, and what do you think we ought to do?" demanded Eden.

"Watch and wait."

"But good lord—we've done that. I was thinking about it this morning. One inexplicable event after another, and never anything definite, anything we can get our teeth into. Such a state of affairs may go on forever. I tell you, I'm fed up."

"Patience," said Chan, "are a very lovely virtue. Through long centuries Chinese cultivate patience like kind gardener tending flowers. White men leap about similar to bug in bottle. Which are better method, I inquire?"

"But listen, Charlie. All this stuff we've discovered out at the ranch—that's for the police."

"For stupid Captain Bliss, maybe. He with the feet of large extensiveness."

"I can't help the size of his feet. What's that got to do with it? No, sir—I can't see why we don't give Madden the pearls, get his receipt, and then send for the sheriff and tell him the whole story. After that, he can worry about who was killed at Madden's ranch."

"He would solve the problem," scoffed Chan. "Great mind, no doubt, like Captain Bliss. Your thought has, from me, nothing but hot opposition."

"Well, but I'm considering Madame Jordan. I've got her interests at heart."

Chan patted him on the back. "Who can question that? You fine young fellow, loyal and kind. But listen now to older heads. Mr. Holley, you have inclination to intrude your oar?"

"I certainly have," smiled Holley. "I'm all on the side of Chan, Eden. It would be a pity to drop this thing now. The sheriff's a good sort, but all this would be too deep for him. No, wait just a little while—"

"All right," sighed Eden. "I'll wait. Provided you tell me one thing. What are we waiting for?"

"Madden goes to Pasadena to-morrow," Chan suggested. "No doubt Thorn will accompany, and we quench this Gamble somehow. Great time for us. All our search at ranch up to now hasty and breathless, like man pursuing trolley-car. To-morrow we dig deep."

"You can do it," replied Eden. "I'm not eager to dig for the sort of prize you want." He paused. "At that, I must admit I'm pretty curious myself. Charlie, you're an old friend of the Jordans, and you can take the responsibility for this delay."

"Right here on shoulders," Chan agreed, "responsibility reclines. Same way necklace reposes on stomach. Seem to coddle there now, those Phillimore pearls, happy and content. Humbly suggest you take this aimless journey to Barstow."

Eden looked at his watch. "I suppose I might as well. Bit of city life never did anybody any harm. But I warn you that when I come back, I want a little light. If any more dark, mysterious things happen at that ranch, I certainly will run right out into the middle of the desert and scream."

Taking the train proved an excellent plan, for on the station platform he met Paula Wendell, who evidently had the same idea. She was trim and charming in riding togs, and her eyes sparkled with life.

"Hello," she said. "Where are you bound?"

"Going to Barstow, on business," Eden explained.

"Is it important?"

"Naturally. Wouldn't squander my vast talents on any other kind."

A dinky little train wandered in, and they found a seat together in one of its two cars.

"Sorry to hear you're needed in Barstow," remarked the girl, "I'm getting off a few stations down. Going to rent a horse and take a long ride up into Lonely Cañon. It wouldn't have been so lonely if you could have come along."

Eden smiled happily. Certainly one had few opportunities to look into eyes like hers. "What station do we get off at?" he inquired.

"We? I thought you said—"

"The truth isn't in me, these days. Barstow doesn't need my presence any more than you need a beauty doctor. Lonely Cañon, after to-day, will have to change its name."

"Good," she answered. "We get off at Seven Palms. The old rancher who rents me a horse will find one for you, I'm sure."

"I'm not precisely dressed for the rôle," admitted Eden. "But I trust it will be all the same to the horse."

The horse didn't appear to mind. His rather dejected manner suggested that he had expected something like this. They left the tiny settlement known as Seven Palms and cantered off across the desert.

"For to admire and for to see, for to behold this world so wide," said Eden. "Never realized how very wide it was until I came down here."

"Beginning to like the desert?" the girl inquired.

"Well, there's something about it," he admitted. "It grows on you, that's a fact. I don't know that I could put the feeling into words."

"I'm sure I can't," she answered. "Oh, I envy you, coming here for the first time. If only I could look at this country again with a fresh, disinterested eye. But it's just location to me. I see all about me the cowboys, the cavalcades, the caballeros of Hollywood. Tragedies and feats of daring, rescues and escapes. I tell you, these dunes and cañons have seen more movies than Will Hays."

"Hunting locations to-day?" Eden asked.

"Always hunting," she sighed. "They've just sent me a new script—as new as those mountains over there. All about the rough cowpuncher and the millionaire's dainty daughter from the East—you know."

"I certainly do. Girl's fed up on those society orgies, isn't she?"

"Who wouldn't be? However, the orgies are given in full, with the swimming pool working overtime, as always. But that part doesn't concern me. It's after she comes out here, sort of hungering to meet a real man, that I must start worrying. Need I add, she meets him? Her horse runs away over the desert, and tosses her off amid the sage-brush. In the nick of time, the cowpuncher finds her. Despite their different stations, love blossoms here in the waste land. Sometimes I'm almost glad that mine is beginning to be an obsolete profession."

"Is it? How come?"

"Oh, the movies move. A few years back the location finder was a rather important person. To-day most of this country has been explored and charted, and every studio is equipped with big albums full of pictures. So every time a new efficiency expert comes along—which is about once a week—and starts lopping off heads, it's the people in my line who are the first to go. In a little while we'll be as extinct as the dodo."

"You may be extinct," Eden answered. "But there the similarity between you and the dodo will stop abruptly."

The girl halted her horse. "Just a minute. I want to take a few pictures here. It looks to me like a bit of desert we haven't used yet. Just the sort of thing to thrill the shopgirls and the bookkeepers back there where the East hangs out." When she had swung again into the saddle, she added: "It isn't strange they love it, those tired people in the cities. Each one thinks—oh, if only I could go there."

"Yes, and if they got here once, they'd die of loneliness the first night," Bob Eden said. "Just pass out in agony moaning for the subway and the comics in the evening paper."

"I know they would," the girl replied. "But fortunately they'll never come."

They rode on, and the girl began to point out the various unfriendly-looking plants of the desert, naming them one by one. Arrow-weed, bitter-brush, mesquite, desert plantain, catclaw, thistle-sage.

"That's a cholla," she announced. "Another variety of cactus. There are seventeen thousand in all."

"All right," Eden replied. "I'll take your word for it. You needn't name them." His head was beginning to ache with all this learning.

Presently sumac and Canterbury bell proclaimed their nearness to the cañon, and they cantered out of the desert heat into the cathedral-like coolness of the hills. In and out over almost hidden trails the horses went. Wild plum glowed on the slopes, and far below under native palms a narrow stream tinkled invitingly.

Life seemed very simple and pleasant there in Lonely Cañon, and Bob Eden felt suddenly close indeed to this lively girl with the eager eyes. All a lie that there were crowded cities. The world was new, unsullied and unspoiled, and they were alone in it.

They descended by way of a rather treacherous path and in the shelter of the palms that fringed the tiny stream, dismounted for a lunch which Paula Wendell claimed to have concealed in her knapsack.

"Wonderfully restful here," Bob Eden said.

"But you said the other day you weren't tired," the girl reminded him.

"Well, I'm not. But somehow I like this anyhow. However, I guess it isn't all a matter of geography. It's not so much the place you're in—it's who you're with. After which highly original remark, I hasten to add that I really can't eat a thing."

"You were right," she laughed. "The truth isn't in you. I know what you're thinking—I didn't bring enough for two. But these Oasis sandwiches are meant for ranchers, and one is my limit. There are four of them—I must have had a premonition. We'll divide the milk equally."

"But look here,—it's your lunch. I should have thought to get something at Seven Palms."

"There's a roast beef sandwich. Try that, and maybe you won't feel so talkative."

"Well, I—um—gumph—"

"What did I tell you? Oh, the Oasis aims to fill. Milk?"

"Ashamed of myself," mumbled Eden. But he was easily persuaded.

"You haven't eaten a thing," he said finally,

"Oh, yes I have. More than I usually do. I'm one of those dainty eaters."

"Good news for Wilbur," replied Eden. "The upkeep won't be high. Though if he has any sense, he'll know that whatever the upkeep on a girl like you, it will be worth it."

"I sent him your love," said the girl.

"Is that so? Well, I'm sorry you did, in a way. I'm no hypocrite, and try as I may, I can't discover any lurking fondness for Wilbur. Oddly enough, the boy begins to annoy me."

"But you said—"

"I know. But isn't it just possible that I've overrated this freedom stuff? I'm young, and the young are often mistaken. Stop me if you've heard this one, but the more I see of you—"

"Stop. I've heard it."

"I'll bet you have. Many times."

"And my suggestion is that we get back to business. If we don't that horse of yours is going to eat too much Bermuda grass."

Through the long afternoon, amid the hot yellow

dunes, the wind-blown foothills of that sandy waste, they rode back to Seven Palms by a roundabout route. The sun was sinking, the rose and gold wonder of the skies reflected on snow and glistening sand, when finally they headed for the village.

"If only I could find a novel setting for the final love scene," sighed the girl.

"Whose final love scene?"

"The cowpuncher's and the poor little rich girl's. So many times they've just wandered off into the sunset, hand in hand. Really need a little more kick in it than that."

Eden heard a clank as of a horse's hoofs on steel. His mount stumbled, and he reined it in sharply.

"What in Sam Hill's that?" he asked.

"Oh—that! It's one of the half-buried rails of the old branch road—a memento of a dream that never came true. Years ago they started to build a town over there under those cottonwoods, and the railroad laid down fifteen miles of track from the main line. A busy metropolis of the desert—that's what they meant it to be—and there's just one little old ruined house standing to-day. But that was the time of Great Expectations. They brought out crowds of people, and sold six hundred lots one hectic afternoon."

"And the railroad?"

"Ran just one train—and stopped. All they had was an engine and two old street-cars brought down from San Francisco. One of the cars has been demolished and the timber carried away, but the wreck of the other is still standing not far from here."

Presently they mounted a ridge, and Bob Eden cried, ' What do you know about that?"

There before them on the lonely desert, partly buried in the drifting sand, stood the remnant of a trolley-car. It was tilted rakishly to one side, its windows were yellow with dust, but on the front, faintly decipherable still, was the legend "Market Street."

At that familiar sight, Bob Eden felt a keen pang of nostalgia. He reined in his horse and sat staring at this symbol of the desert's triumph over the proud schemes of man. Man had thought he could conquer, he had come with his engines and his dreams, and now an old battered trolley stood alone as a warning and a threat.

"There's your setting," he said. "They drive out together and sit there on the steps, your lovers. What a background—a car that once trundled from Twin Peaks to the Ferry, standing lonely and forlorn amid the cactus plants."

"Fine," the girl answered. "I'm going to hire you to help me after this."

They rode close to the car and dismounted. The girl unlimbered her camera and held it steady. "Don't you want me in the picture?" Eden asked. "Just as a sample lover, you know."

"No samples needed," she laughed. The camera clicked. As it did so the two young people stood rooted to the desert in amazement. An old man had stepped suddenly from the interior of the car—a bent old man with a coal-black beard.

Eden's eyes sought those of the girl. "Last Wednesday night at Madden's?" he inquired in a low voice.

She nodded. "The old prospector," she replied.

The black-bearded one did not speak, but stood with a startled air on the front platform of that lost trolley, under the caption "Market Street."

CHAPTER XIII

WHAT MR. CHERRY SAW

BOB EDEN stepped forward. "Good evening," he said. "I hope we haven't disturbed you."

Moving with some difficulty, the old man descended from the platform to the sandy floor of the desert. "How do," he said gravely, shaking hands. He also shook hands with Paula Wendell. "How do, miss. No, you didn't disturb me none. Just takin' my forty winks—I ain't so spry as I used to be."

"We happened to be passing—" Eden began.

"Ain't many pass this way," returned the old man. "Cherry's my name—William I. Cherry. Make yourselves to home. Parlor chairs is kind o' scarce, miss."

"Of course," said the girl.

"We'll stop a minute, if we may," suggested Eden.

"It's comin' on supper time," the old man replied hospitably. "How about grub? There's a can o' beans, an' a mite o' bacon—"

"Couldn't think of it," Eden told him. "You're mighty kind, but we'll be back in Seven Palms shortly." Paula Wendell sat down on the car steps, and Eden took a seat on the warm sand. The old man went to the rear of the trolley and returned with an empty soap-box.

191

After an unsuccessful attempt to persuade Eden to accept it as a chair, he put it to that use himself.

"Pretty nice home you've picked out for yourself,"
Eden remarked.

"Home?" The old man surveyed the trolley-car criti-
cally. "Home, boy? I ain't had no home these thirty
years. Temporary quarters, you might say."

"Been here long?" asked Eden.

"Three, four days. Rheumatism's been actin' up.
But I'm movin' on to-morrey."

"Moving on? Where?"

"Why—over yonder."

"Just where is that?" Eden smiled.

"Where it's allus been. Over yonder. Somewhere
else."

"Just looking, eh?"

"Jest lookin'. You've hit it. Goin' on over yonder
an' jest lookin'." His tired old eyes were on the moun-
taintops.

"What do you expect to find?" inquired Paula Wendell.

"Struck a vein o' copper once, miss," Mr. Cherry
said. "But they got her away from me. Howsomever,
I'm lookin' still."

"Been on the desert a long time?" Eden asked.

"Twenty, twenty-five years. One desert or another."

"And before that?"

"Prospected in West Australia from Hannans to
Hall's Creek—through the Territory into Queensland.
Drove cattle from the gulf country into New South
Wales. Then I worked in the stoke hole on ocean
liners."

"Born in Australia, eh?" Eden suggested.

"Who—me?" Mr. Cherry shook his head. "Born in South Africa—English descent. Been all up and down the Congo an' Zambesi—all through British Central Africa."

"How in the world did you get to Australia?" Eden wondered.

"Oh, I don't know, boy. I was filibusterin' down along the South American continent fer a while, an' then I drifted into a Mexican campaign. Seems like there was somethin' I wanted in Australia—anyhow, I got there. Jest the way I got here. It was over yonder, an' I went."

Eden shook his head. "Ye gods, I'll bet you've seen a lot!"

"I guess I have, boy. Doctor over in Redlands was tellin' me t'other day—you need spectacles, he says. 'Hell, Doc,' I says, 'what fer? I've seen everything,' I says, and I come away.

Silence fell. Bob Eden wasn't exactly sure how to go about this business; he wished he had Chan at his elbow. But his duty was clear.

"You—er—you've been here for three or four days, you say?"

" 'Bout that, I reckon."

"Do you happen to recall where you were last Wednesday night?"

The old man's eyes were keen enough as he glanced sharply at the boy. "What if I do?"

"I was only going to say that if you don't, I can refresh your memory. You were at Madden's ranch house, over near Eldorado."

Slowly Mr. Cherry removed his slouch hat. With

gnarled bent fingers he extracted a toothpick from the
band. He stuck it defiantly in his mouth. "Maybe I
was. What then?"

"Well—I'd like to have a little talk with you about
that night."

Cherry surveyed him closely. "You're a new one on
me," he said. "An' I thought I knew every sheriff an'
deputy west o' the Rockies."

"Then you'll admit something happened at Madden's
that might interest a sheriff?" returned Eden quickly.

"I ain't admittin' nothin'," answered the old prospector.

"You have information regarding last Wednesday
night at Madden's," Eden persisted. "Vital information.
I must have it."

"Nothin' to say," replied Cherry stubbornly

Eden took another tack. "Just what was your business at Madden's ranch?"

Mr. Cherry rolled the aged toothpick in his mouth.
"No business at all. I jest dropped in. Been wanderin'
the desert a long time, like I said, an' now an' ag'in I
drifted in at Madden's. Me an' the old caretaker, Louie
Wong, was friends. When I'd come along he'd stake
me to a bit o' grub, an' a bed in the barn. Sort o' company fer him, I was. He was lonesome-like at the
ranch—only a Chink, but lonesome-like, same as if he'd
been white."

"A kindly old soul, Louie," suggested Eden.

"One o' the best, boy, an' that's no lie."

Eden spoke slowly. "Louie Wong has been murdered," he said.

"What's that?"

"Stabbed in the side last Sunday night near the ranch gate. Stabbed—by some unknown person."

"Some dirty dog," said Mr. Cherry indignantly.

"That's just how I feel about it. I'm not a policeman, but I'm doing my best to find the guilty man. The thing you saw that night at the ranch, Mr. Cherry, no doubt has a decided bearing on the killing of Louie. I need your help. Now, will you talk?"

Mr. Cherry removed the toothpick from his mouth and, holding it before him, regarded it thoughtfully. "Yes," he said, "I will. I was hopin' to keep out o' this. Judges an' courts an' all that truck ain't fer me. I give 'em a wide berth. But I'm a decent man, an' I ain't got nothin' to hide. I'll talk, but I don't hardly know how to begin."

"I'll help you," Eden answered, delighted. "The other night when you were at Madden's ranch perhaps you heard a man cry, 'Help! Help! Murder! Put down that gun. Help.' Something like that, eh?"

"I ain't got nothin' to hide. That's jest what I heard."

Eden's heart leaped. "And after that—you saw something—"

The old man nodded. "I saw plenty, boy. Louie Wong wasn't the first to be killed at Madden's ranch. I saw murder done."

Eden gasped inwardly. He saw Paula Wendell's eyes wide and startled. "Of course you did," he said. "Now go on and tell me all about it."

Mr. Cherry restored the toothpick to its predestined place in his mouth, but it interfered in no way with his speech.

"Life's funny," he began. "Full o' queer twists an'

turns. I thought this was jest one more secret fer me an' the desert together. Nobody knows about you, I says. Nobody ain't goin' to question you. But I was wrong, I see, an' I might as well speak up. It's nothin' to me, one way or t'other, though I would like to keep out o' court-rooms—"

"Well, maybe I can help you," Eden suggested. "Go on. You say you saw murder—"

"Jest hold yer horses, boy," Mr. Cherry advised. "As I was sayin', last Wednesday night after dark I drifts in at Madden's as usual. But the minute I comes into the yard, I see there's something doin' there. The boss has come. Lights in most o' the windows, an' a big car in the barn, longside Louie's old flivver. Howsomever, I'm tired, an' I figures I'll jest wait round fer Louie, keepin' out o' sight o' the big fellow. A little supper an' a bed, maybe, kin be negotiated without gettin' too conspicuous.

"So I puts my pack down in the barn, an' steps over to the cookhouse. Louie ain't there. Jest as I'm comin' out o' the place, I hears a cry from the house—a man's voice, loud an' clear. 'Help,' he says. 'Put down that gun. I know your game. Help. Help.' Jest as you said. Well, I ain't lookin' fer no trouble, an' I stands there a minute, uncertain. An' then the cry comes again, almost the same words—but not the man this time. It's Tony, the Chinese parrot, on his perch in the patio, an' from him the words is shrill an' piercin'—more terrible, somehow. An' then I hears a sharp report—the gun is workin'. The racket seems to come from a lighted room in one ell—a window is open. I creeps closer, an' there goes the gun ag'in. There's a sort of groan. It's hit, sure enough. I goes up to the window an' looks in."

He paused. "Then what?" Bob Eden asked breath-
lessly.

"Well, it's a bedroom, an' he's standin' there with the
smokin' gun in his hand, lookin' fierce but frightened-
like. An' there's somebody on the floor, t'other side o'
the bed—all I kin see is his shoes. He turns toward the
window, the gun still in his hand—"

"Who?" cried Bob Eden. "Who was it with the gun
in his hand? You're talking about Martin Thorn?"

"Thorn? You mean that little sneakin' secretary?
No—I ain't speakin' o' Thorn. I'm speakin' o' him—"

"Who?"

"The big boss. Madden. P. J. Madden himself."

There was a moment of tense silence. "Good lord,"
gasped Eden. "Madden? You mean to say that Madden— Why, it's impossible. How did you know? Are you
sure?"

"O' course I'm sure. I know Madden well enough.
I seen him three years ago at the ranch. A big man, red-
faced, thin gray hair—I couldn't make no mistake about
Madden. There he was standin', the gun in his hand, an'
he looks toward the window. I ducks back. An' at that
minute this Thorn you're speakin' of—he comes tearin'
into the room. 'What have you done now?' he says. 'I've
killed him,' says Madden, 'that's what I've done.' 'You
poor fool,' says Thorn. 'It wasn't necessary.' Madden
throws down the gun. 'Why not?' he wants to know.
'I was afraid of him.' Thorn sneers. 'You was always
afraid o' him,' he says. 'You dirty coward. That time
in New York—' Madden gives him a look. 'Shut up,' he
says. 'Shut up an' fergit it. I was afraid o' him an' I
killed him. Now git busy an' think what we better do.'"

The old prospector paused, and regarded his wide-eyed audience. "Well, mister," he continued. "An' miss—I come away. What else was there to be done? It was no affair o' mine, an' I wasn't hungerin' fer no court-room an' all that. Jest slip away into the night, I tells myself, the good old night that's been yer friend these many years. Slip away an' let others worry. I runs to the barn an' gits my pack, an' when I comes out, a car is drivin' into the yard. I crawls through the fence an' moseys down the road. I thought I was out o' it an' safe, an' how you got on to me is a mystery. But I'm decent, an' I ain't hidin' anything. That's my story— the truth, s'help me."

Bob Eden rose and paced the sand. "Man alive," he said, "this is serious business."

"Think so?" inquired the old prospector.

"Think so! You know who Madden is, don't you? One of the biggest men in America—"

"Sure he is. An' what does that mean? You'll never git him fer what he done. He'll slide out o' it some way. Self-defense—"

"Oh, no, he won't. Not if you tell your story. You've got to go back with me to Eldorado—"

"Wait a minute," cut in Cherry. "That's something I don't aim to do—go an' stifle in no city. Leastways, not till it's absolutely necessary. I've told my story, an' I'll tell it ag'in, any time I'm asked. But I ain't goin' back to Eldorado—bank on that, boy."

"But listen—"

"Listen to me. How much more information you got? Know who that man was, layin' behind the bed? Found his body yet?"

"No, we haven't, but—"

"I thought so. Well, you're jest startin' on this job. What's my word ag'in' the word o' P. J. Madden—an' no other evidence to show? You got to dig some up."

"Well, perhaps you're right."

"Sure I am. I've done you a favor—now you do one fer me. Take this here information an' go back an' make the most o' it. Leave me out entirely if you kin. If you can't—well, I'll keep in touch. Be down round Needles in about a week—goin' to make a stop there with my old friend, Slim Jones. Porter J. Jones, Real Estate—you kin git me there. I'm makin' you a fair proposition— don't you say so, miss?"

The girl smiled at him. "Seems fair to me," she admitted.

"It's hardly according to Hoyle," said Eden. "But you have been mighty kind. I don't want to see you stifle in a city—though I find it hard to believe you and I are talking about the same Eldorado. However, we're going to part friends, Mr. Cherry. I'll take your suggestion—I'll go back with what you've told me—it's certainly very enlightening. And I'll keep you out of it— if I can."

The old man got painfully to his feet. "Shake," he said. "You're a white man, an' no mistake. I ain't tryin' to save Madden—I'll go on the stand if I have to. But with what I've told you, maybe you can land him without me figurin' in it."

"We'll have to go along," Eden told him. He laughed. "I don't care what the book of etiquette says— Mr. Cherry, I'm very pleased to have met you."

"Same here," returned Cherry. "Like a talk now an

then with a good listener. An' the chance to look at a pretty gal—well, say, I don't need no specs to enjoy that.''

They said good-by, and left the lonely old man standing by the trolley-car there on the barren desert. For a long moment they rode in silence.

"Well," said Eden finally, "you've heard something, lady."

"I certainly have. Something I find it difficult to believe."

"Perhaps you won't find it so difficult if I go back and tell you a few things. You've been drawn into the big mystery at Madden's at last, and there's no reason why you shouldn't know as much as I do about it. So I'm going to talk."

"I'm keen to hear," she admitted.

"Naturally, after to-day. Well, I came down here to transact a bit of business with P. J.—I needn't go into that, it has no particular bearing. The first night I was on the ranch—" He proceeded to detail one by one the mysterious sequence of events that began with the scream of the parrot from the dark. "Now you know. Some one had been killed, that was evident. Some one before Louie. But who? We don't know yet. And by whom? To-day gave us that answer, anyhow."

"It seems incredible."

"You don't believe Cherry's story?" he suggested.

"Well—these old boys who wander the desert get queer sometimes. And there was that about his eyes— the doctor at Redlands, you know—"

"I know. But all the same, I think Cherry told the truth. After a few days with Madden, I consider him capable of anything. He's a hard man, and if any one stood in his way—good night. Some poor devil stood there—but not for long. Who? We'll find out. We must."

"We?"

"Yes—you're in on this thing, too. Have to be, after this, whether you like it or not."

"I think I'm going to like it," Paula Wendell said.

They returned their tired horses to the stable at Seven Palms, and after a sketchy dinner at the local hotel, caught the Eldorado train. When they alighted, Charlie and Will Holley were waiting.

"Hello," said the editor. "Why, hello, Paula—where you been? Eden, here's Ah Kim. Madden sent him in for you."

"Hello, gentlemen," cried Eden gaily. "Before Ah Kim and I head for the ranch, we're all going over to the office of that grand old sheet, the *Eldorado Times*. I have something to impart."

When they reached the newspaper office—which Ah Kim entered with obvious reluctance—Eden closed the door and faced them. "Well, folks," he announced, "the clouds are breaking. I've finally got hold of something definite. But before I go any further—Miss Wendell, may I present Ah Kim? So we sometimes call him, after our quaint fashion. In reality, you are now enjoying the priceless opportunity of meeting Detective-Sergeant Charlie Chan, of the Honolulu police."

Chan bowed. "I'm so glad to know you, Sergeant," said the girl, and took up her favorite perch on Holley's typewriter table.

"Don't look at me like that, Charlie," laughed Eden. "You're breaking my heart. We can rely on Miss Wendell, absolutely. And you can't freeze her out any longer, because she now knows more about your case than you do. As they say on the stage—won't you—sit down?"

Puzzled and wondering, Chan and Will Holley found chairs. "I said this morning I wanted a little light," Eden continued. "I've got it already—how's that for service? Aimless trip to Barstow, Charlie, proved to be all aim. Miss Wendell and I turned aside for a canter over the desert, and we have met and interviewed that little black-bearded one—our desert rat."

"Boy—now you're talking," cried Holley.

Chan's eyes lighted.

"Chinese are psychic people, Charlie," Eden went on. "I'll tell the world. You were right. Before we arrived at Madden's ranch, some one staged a little murder there. And I know who did it."

"Thorn," suggested Holley.

"Thorn nothing! No piker like Thorn. No, gentlemen, it was the big chief—Madden himself—the great P. J. Last Wednesday night at his ranch Madden killed a man. Add favorite pastimes of big millionaires."

"Nonsense," objected Holley.

"You think so, eh? Listen." Eden repeated the story Cherry had told.

Chan and Holley heard him out in amazed silence.

"And what are present whereabouts of old prospector?" inquired Chan when he had finished.

"I know, Charlie," answered Eden. "That's the flaw in my armor. I let him go. He's on his way—over yonder. But I know where he's going and we can get hold of him when we need him. We've got other matters to look after first."

"We certainly have," agreed Holley. "Madden! I can hardly believe it."

Chan considered. "Most peculiar case ever shoved on my attention," he admitted. "It marches now, but look how it marches backwards. Mostly murder means dead body on the rug, and from clues surrounding, I must find who did it. Not so here. I sense something wrong, after long pause light breaks and I hear name of guilty man who killed. But who was killed? The reason, please? There is work to be done—much work."

"You don't think," suggested Eden, "that we ought to call in the sheriff—"

"What then?" frowned Chan. "Captain Bliss arrives on extensive feet, committing blunder with every step. Sheriff faces strange situation, all unprepared. Madden awes them with greatness, and escapes Scotch-free. None of the sheriff, please—unless maybe you lose faith in Detective-Sergeant Chan."

"Never for a minute, Charlie," Eden answered. "Wipe out that suggestion. The case is yours."

Chan bowed. "You're pretty good, thanks. Such a tipsy-turvy puzzle rouses professional pride. I will get to bottom of it or lose entire face. Be good enough to watch me."

"I'll be watching," Eden answered. "Well, shall we go along?"

In front of the Desert Edge Hotel Bob Eden held out his hand to the girl. "The end of a perfect day," he said. "Except for one thing."

"Yes? What thing?"

"Wilbur. I'm beginning to find the thought of him intolerable."

"Poor Jack. You're so hard on him. Good night—and—"

"And what?"

"Be careful, won't you? Out at the ranch, I mean."

"Always careful—on ranches—everywhere. Good night."

As they sped over the dark road to Madden's, Chan was thoughtfully silent. He and Eden parted in the yard. When the boy entered the patio, he saw Madden sitting alone, wrapped in an overcoat, before a dying fire.

The millionaire leaped to his feet. "Hello," he said. "Well?"

"Well?" replied Eden. He had completely forgotten his mission to Barstow.

"You saw Draycott?" Madden whispered.

"Oh!" The boy remembered with a start. More deception—would it ever end? "To-morrow at the door of the bank in Pasadena," he said softly. "Noon sharp."

"Good," answered Madden. "I'll be off before you're up. Not turning in already?"

"I think I will," responded Eden. "I've had a busy day."

"Is that so?" said Madden carelessly, and strode into the living-room. Bob Eden stood staring after the big broad shoulders, the huge frame of this powerful man. A man who seemed to have the world in his grasp, but who had killed because he was afraid.

CHAPTER XIV

THE THIRD MAN

A S SOON as he was fully awake the following morning, Bob Eden's active brain returned to the problem with which it had been concerned when he dropped off to sleep. Madden had killed a man. Cool, confident and self-possessed though he always seemed, the millionaire had lost his head for once. Ignoring the possible effect of such an act on his fame, his high position, he had with murderous intent pulled the trigger on the gun Bill Hart had given him. His plight must have been desperate indeed.

Whom had he killed? That was something yet to be discovered. Why had he done it? By his own confession, because he was afraid. Madden, whose very name struck terror to many and into whose presence lesser men came with awe and trembling, had himself known the emotion of fear. Ridiculous, but "you were always afraid of him," Thorn had said.

Some hidden door in the millionaire's past must be found and opened. First of all, the identity of the man who had gone west last Wednesday night on this lonely ranch must be ascertained. Well, at least the mystery was beginning to clear, the long sequence of inexplicable, maddening events since they came to the desert was broken for a moment by a tangible bit of explanation. Here was a start, something into which they could get their teeth. From this they must push on to—what?

Chan was waiting in the patio when Bob Eden came out. His face was decorated with a broad grin.

"Breakfast reposes on table," he announced. "Consume it speedily. Before us stretches splendid day for investigation with no prying eyes."

"What's that?" asked Eden. "Nobody here? How about Gamble?"

Chan led the way to the living-room, and held Bob Eden's chair. "Oh, cut that, Charlie," the boy said. "You're not Ah Kim to-day. Do you mean to say that Gamble has also left us?"

Chan nodded. "Gamble develops keen yearning to visit Pasadena," he replied. "On which journey he is welcome as one of his long-tailed rats."

Eden quaffed his orange juice. "Madden didn't want him, eh?"

"Not much," Chan answered. "I rise before day breaks and prepare breakfast, which are last night's orders. Madden and Thorn arrive, brushing persistent sleep out of eyes. Suddenly enters this Professor Gamble, plentifully awake and singing happy praise for desert sunrise. 'You are up early,' says Madden, growling like dissatisfied dog. 'Decided to take little journey to Pasadena along with you,' announces Gamble. Madden purples like distant hills when evening comes, but regards me and quenches his reply. When he and Thorn enter big car, behold Mr. Gamble climbing into rear seat. If looks could assassinate Madden would then and there have rendered him extinct, but such are not the case.

Car rolls off on to sunny road with Professor Gamble
smiling pleasantly in back. Welcome as long-tailed rat
but not going to worry about it, thank you."

Eden chuckled. "Well, it's a good thing from our
standpoint, Charlie. I was wondering what we were going to do with Gamble nosing round. Big load off our
shoulders right away."

"Very true," agreed Chan. "Alone here, we relax
all over place and find what is to find. How you like
oatmeal, boy? Not so lumpy, if I may be permitted the
immodesty."

"Charlie, the world lost a great chef when you became a policeman. But—the devil! Who's that driving
in?"

Chan went to the door. "No alarm necessary," he
remarked. "Only Mr. Holley."

The editor appeared. "Here I am, up with the lark
and ready for action," he announced. "Want to be in on
the big hunt, if you don't mind."

"Certainly don't," said Eden. "Glad to have you.
We've had a bit of luck already." He explained about
Gamble's departure.

Holley nodded wisely. "Of course Gamble went to
Pasadena," he remarked. "He's not going to let Madden
out of his sight. You know, I've had some flashes of in-
spiration about this matter out here."

"Good for you," replied Eden. "For instance—"

"Oh, just wait a while. I'll dazzle you with them at
the proper moment. You see, I used to do a lot of police
reporting. Little bright eyes, I was often called."

"Pretty name," laughed Eden.

"Little bright eyes is here to look about," Holley continued. "First of all, we ought to decide what we're looking for."

"I guess we know that, don't we?" Eden asked.

"Oh, in a general way, but let's be explicit. To go back and start at the beginning—that's the proper method, isn't it, Chan?"

Charlie shrugged. "Always done—in books," he said. "In real life, not so much so."

Holley smiled. "That's right—dampen my young enthusiasm. However, I am now going to recall a few facts. We needn't stress the side issues at present—the pearls, the activities of Shaky Phil in San Francisco, the murder of Louie, the disappearance of Madden's daughter—all these will be explained when we get the big answer. We are concerned to-day chiefly with the story of the old prospector."

"Who may have been lying, or mistaken," Eden suggested.

"Yes—his tale seems unbelievable, I admit. Without any evidence to back it up, I wouldn't pay much attention to it. However, we have that evidence. Don't forget Tony's impassioned remarks, and his subsequent taking off. More important still, there is Bill Hart's gun, with two empty chambers. Also the bullet hole in the wall. What more do you want?"

"Oh, it seems to be well substantiated," Eden agreed.

"It is. No doubt about it—somebody was shot at this place Wednesday night. We thought at first Thorn was the killer, now we switch to Madden. Madden lured somebody to Thorn's room, or cornered him there, and killed him. Why? Because he was afraid of him? We think hard about Wednesday night—and what do we want to know? We want to know—who was the third man?"

"The third man?" Eden repeated.

"Precisely. Ignore the prospector—who was at the ranch? Madden and Thorn—yes. And one other. A man who, seeing his life in danger, called loudly for help. A man who, a moment later, lay on the floor beyond the bed, and whose shoes alone were visible from where the prospector stood. Who was he? Where did he come from? When did he arrive? What was his business? Why was Madden afraid of him? These are the questions to which we must now seek answers. Am I right, Sergeant Chan?"

"Undubitably," Charlie replied. "And how shall we find those answers? By searching, perhaps. Humbly suggest we search."

"Every nook and corner of this ranch," agreed Holley. "We'll begin with Madden's desk. Some stray bit of correspondence may throw unexpected light. It's locked, of course. But I've brought along a pocketful of old keys— got them from a locksmith in town."

"You act like number one detective," Chan remarked.

"Thanks," answered Holley. He went over to the big flat-topped desk belonging to the millionaire and began to experiment with various keys. In a few moments he found the proper one and all the drawers stood open.

"Splendid work," said Chan.

"Not much here, though," Holley declared. He removed the papers from the top left-hand drawer and laid them on the blotting pad. Bob Eden lighted a cigarette and strolled away. Somehow this idea of inspecting Madden's mail did not appeal to him.

The representatives of the police and the press, however, were not so delicately minded. For more than half an hour Chan and the editor studied the contents of Madden's desk. They found nothing, save harmless and understandable data of business deals, not a solitary scrap that could by the widest stretch of the imagination throw any light on the identity or meaning of the third man. Finally, perspiring and baffled, they gave up and the drawers were relocked.

"Well," said Holley, "not so good, eh? Mark the desk off our list and let's move on."

"With your permission," Chan remarked, "we divide the labors. For you gentlemen the inside of the house. I myself have fondly feeling for outdoors." He disappeared.

One by one, Holley and Eden searched the rooms. In the bedroom occupied by the secretary they saw for themselves the bullet hole in the wall. An investigation of the bureau, however, revealed the fact that Bill Hart's pistol was no longer there. This was their sole discovery of any interest.

"We're up against it," admitted Holley, his cheerful manner waning. "Madden's a clever man, and he didn't leave a warm trail, of course. But somehow—somewhere—"

They returned to the living-room. Chan, hot and puffing, appeared suddenly at the door. He dropped into a chair.

"What luck, Charlie?" Eden inquired.

"None whatever," admitted Chan gloomily. "Heavy disappointment causes my heart to sag. No gambler myself, but would have offered huge wager something buried on this ranch. When Madden, having shot, remarked, 'Shut up and forget. I was afraid and I killed. Now think quick what we had better do,' I would expect first thought is—burial. How else to dispose of dead? So just now I have examined every inch of ground, with highest hope. No good. If burial made, it was not here. I see by your faces you have similar bafflement to report."

"Haven't found a thing," Eden replied.

Chan sighed. "I drag the announcement forth in pain," he said. "But I now gaze solemnly at stone wall."

They sat in helpless silence. "Well, let's not give up yet," Bob Eden remarked. He leaned back in his chair and blew a ring of smoke toward the paneled ceiling. "By the way, has it ever occurred to you that there must be some sort of attic above this room?"

Chan was instantly on his feet. "Clever suggestion," he cried. "Attic, yes, but how to ascend?" He stood staring at the ceiling a moment, then went quickly to a large closet in the rear of the room. "Somewhat humiliated situation for me," he announced. Crowding close beside him in the dim closet, the other two looked aloft at an unmistakable trap-door.

Bob Eden was selected for the climb, and with the aid of a stepladder Chan brought from the barn, he managed it easily. Holley and the detective waited below. For a moment Eden stood in the attic, his head bent low, cobwebs caressing his face, while he sought to accustom his eyes to the faint light.

"Nothing here, I'm afraid," he called. "Oh, yes, there is. Wait a minute."

They heard him walking gingerly above, and clouds of dust descended on their heads. Presently he was lowering a bulky object through the narrow trap—a battered old Gladstone bag.

"Seems to be something in it," Eden announced.

They took it with eager hands, and set it on the desk in the sunny living-room. Bob Eden joined them.

"By gad," the boy said, "not much dust on it, is there? Must have been put there recently. Holley, here's where your keys come in handy."

It proved a simple matter for Holley to master the lock. The three men crowded close.

Chan lifted out a cheap toilet case, with the usual articles—a comb and brush, razors, shaving cream, tooth paste, then a few shirts, socks and handkerchiefs. He examined the laundry mark.

"D—thirty-four," he announced.

"Meaning nothing," Eden said.

Chan was lifting a brown suit of clothes from the bottom of the bag.

"Made to order by tailor in New York," he said, after an inspection of the inner coat pocket. "Name of purchaser, however, is blotted out by too much wearing." He took from the side pockets a box of matches and a half-empty packet of inexpensive cigarettes. "Finishing the coat," he added.

He turned his attention to the vest and luck smiled upon him. From the lower right-hand pocket he removed an old-fashioned watch, attached to a heavy chain. The timepiece was silent; evidently it had been unwound for some time. Quickly he pried open the back case, and a little grunt of satisfaction escaped him. He passed the watch to Bob Eden.

"Presented to Jerry Delaney by his Old Friend, Honest Jack McGuire," read Eden in a voice of triumph. "And the date—August twenty-sixth, 1913."

"Jerry Delaney!" cried Holley. "By heaven, we're getting on now. The name of the third man was Jerry Delaney."

"Yet to be proved he was the third man," Chan cautioned. "This, however, may help."

He produced a soiled bit of colored paper—a passenger's receipt for a Pullman compartment. "Compartment B—car 198," he read. "Chicago to Barstow." He turned it over. "Date when used, February eighth, present year."

Bob Eden turned to a calendar. "Great stuff," he cried. "Jerry Delaney left Chicago on February eighth— a week ago Sunday night. That got him into Barstow last Wednesday morning, February eleventh—the morning of the day he was killed. Some detectives, we are."

Chan was still busy with the vest. He brought forth a key ring with a few keys, then a worn newspaper clipping. The latter he handed to Eden.

"Read it, please?" he suggested.

Bob Eden read:

"Theater-goers of Los Angeles will be delighted to know that in the cast of *One Night in June,* the musical comedy opening at the Mason next Monday night, will be Miss Norma Fitzgerald. She has the rôle of Marcia, which calls for a rich soprano voice, and her vast army of admirers hereabouts know in advance how well she will acquit herself in such a part. Miss Fitzgerald has been on the stage twenty years—she went on as a mere child— and has appeared in such productions as *The Love Cure.*" Eden paused. "There's a long list." He resumed reading: "Matinées of *One Night in June* will be on Wednesdays and Saturdays, and for this engagement a special scale of prices has been inaugurated."

Eden put the clipping down on the table. "Well, that's one more fact about Jerry Delaney. He was interested in a soprano. So many men are—but still, it may lead somewhere."

"Poor Jerry," said Holley, looking down at the rather pitiful pile of the man's possessions. "He won't need a hair-brush, or a razor, or a gold watch where he's gone." He took up the watch and regarded it thoughtfully. "Honest Jack McGuire. I seem to have heard that name somewhere."

Chan was investigating the trousers pockets. He turned them out one by one, but found nothing.

"Search is now complete," he announced. "Humbly suggest we put all back as we found it. We have made delightful progress."

"I'll say we have," cried Eden, with enthusiasm. "More progress than I ever thought possible. Last night we knew only that Madden had killed a man. To-day we know the name of the man." He paused. "I don't suppose there can be any doubt about it?" he inquired.

"Hardly," Holley replied. "A man doesn't part with such personal possessions as a hair-brush and a razor as long as he has any further use for them. If he's through with them, he's through with life. Poor devil!"

"Let's go over it all again before we put these things away," said Eden. "We've learned that the man Madden feared, the man he killed, was Jerry Delaney. What do we know of Delaney? He was not in very affluent circumstances, though he did have his clothes made by a tailor. Not a smart tailor, judging by the address. He smoked Corsican cigarettes. Honest Jack McGuire, whoever he may be, was an old friend of his, and thought so

highly of him he gave Jerry a watch. What else? Delaney was interested in an actress named Norma Fitzgerald. A week ago last Sunday he left Chicago at eight
P. M.—the Limited—for Barstow, riding in Compartment B, car 198. And that, I guess, about sums up what
we know of Jerry Delaney."

Charlie Chan smiled. "Very good," he said. "A
splendid list, rich with promise. But one fact you have
missed complete."

"What's that?" inquired Eden.

"One very easy fact," continued Chan. "Take this
vest once on Jerry Delaney. Examine close—what do
you discover?"

Carefully Eden looked over the vest, then with a
puzzled air handed it to Holley, who did the same. Holley
shook his head.

"Nothing?" asked Chan, laughing silently. "Can it be
you are not such able detectives as I thought? Here—
place hand in pocket—"

Bob Eden thrust his fingers into the pocket indicated
by Chan. "It's chamois-lined," he said. "The watch
pocket, that's all."

"True enough," answered Chan. "And on the left, I
presume."

Eden looked foolish. "Oh," he admitted, "I get you.
The watch pocket is on the right."

"And why," persisted Charlie. "With coat buttoned,
certain man can not reach watch easily when it reposes at
left. Therefore he instructs tailor, make pocket for watch
on right, please." He began to fold up the clothes in order
to return them to the bag. "One other fact we know
about Jerry Delaney, and it may be used in tracing his

movements the day he came to this ranch. Jerry Delaney had peculiarity to be left-handed."

"Great Scott!" cried Holley suddenly. They turned to him. He had picked up the watch again and was staring at it. "Honest Jack McGuire—I remember now."

"You know this McGuire?" inquired Chan quickly.

"I met him, long ago," Holley replied. "The first night I brought Mr. Eden out here to the ranch, he asked me if I'd ever seen P. J. Madden before. I said that twelve years ago I saw Madden in a gambling house on East Forty-fourth Street, New York, dolled up like a prince and betting his head off. Madden himself remembered the occasion when I spoke to him about it."

"But McGuire?" Chan wanted to know.

"I recall now that the name of the man who ran that gambling house was Jack McGuire. Honest Jack, he had the nerve to call himself. It was a queer joint—that was later proved. But Jack McGuire was Delaney's old friend—he gave Jerry a watch as a token of their friendship. Gentlemen, this is interesting. McGuire's gambling house on Forty-fourth Street comes back into the life of P. J. Madden."

CHAPTER XV

WILL HOLLEY'S THEORY

WHEN the bag was completely repacked and again securely locked, Bob Eden climbed with it to the dusty attic. He reappeared, the trap-door was closed and the stepladder removed. The three men faced one another, pleased with their morning's work.

"It's after twelve," said Holley. "I must hurry back to town."

"About to make heartfelt suggestion you remain at lunch," remarked Chan.

Holley shook his head. "That's kind of you, Charlie, but I wouldn't think of it. You must be about fed-up on this cooking proposition, and I won't spoil your first chance for a little vacation. You take my advice, and make Eden rustle his own grub to-day."

Chan nodded. "True enough that I was planning a modest repast," he returned. "Cooking business begins to get tiresome like the company of a Japanese. However, fitting punishment for a postman who walks another man's beat. If Mr. Eden will pardon, I relax to the extent of sandwiches and tea this noon."

"Sure," said Eden. "We'll dig up something together. Holley, you'd better change your mind."

"No," replied Holley. "I'm going to town and make

217

a few inquiries. Just by way of substantiating what we found here to-day. If Jerry Delaney came out here last Wednesday, he must have left some sort of trail through the town. Some one may have seen him. Was he alone? I'll speak to the boys at the gas station, the hotel proprietor—"

"Humbly suggest utmost discretion," said Chan.

"Oh, I understand the need of that. But there's really no danger. Madden has no connection whatever with the life of the town. He won't hear of it. Just the same, I'll be discretion itself. Trust me. I'll come out here again later in the day."

When he had gone, Chan and Eden ate a cold lunch in the cookhouse, and resumed their search. Nothing of any moment rewarded their efforts, however. At four that afternoon Holley drove into the yard. With him was a lean, sad-looking youth whom Eden recognized as the real-estate salesman of Date City.

As they entered the room, Chan withdrew, leaving Eden to greet them. Holley introduced the youth as Mr. DeLisle.

"I've met DeLisle," smiled Bob Eden. "He tried to sell me a corner lot on the desert."

"Yeah," said Mr. DeLisle. "And some day, when the United Cigar Stores and Woolworth are fighting for that stuff, you'll kick yourself up and down every hill in Frisco. However, that's your funeral."

"I brought Mr. DeLisle along," explained Holley, "because I want you to hear the story he's just told me. About last Wednesday night."

"Mr. DeLisle understands that this is confidential—" began Eden.

"Oh, sure," said the young man. "Will's explained all that. You needn't worry. Madden and I ain't exactly pals—not after the way he talked to me."

"You saw him last Wednesday night?" Eden suggested.

"No, not that night. It was somebody else I saw then. I was out here at the development until after dark, waiting for a prospect—he never showed up, the lowlife. Anyhow, along about seven o'clock, just as I was closing up the office, a big sedan stopped out in front. I went out. There was a little guy driving and another man in the back seat. 'Good evening,' said the little fellow. 'Can you tell me, please, if we're on the road to Madden's ranch?' I said sure, to keep right on straight. The man in the back spoke up. 'How far is it?' he wants to know. 'Shut up, Jerry,' says the little guy. 'I'll attend to this.' He shifted the gears, and then he got kind of literary. 'And an highway shall be there and a way,' he says. 'Not any too clearly defined, Isaiah.' And he drove off. Now why do you suppose he called me Isaiah?"

Eden smiled. "Did you get a good look at him?"

"Pretty good, considering the dark. A thin pale man with sort of grayish lips—no color in them at all. Talked kind of slow and precise—awful neat English, like he was a professor or something."

"And the man in the back seat?"

"Couldn't see him very well."

"Ah, yes. And when did you meet Madden?"

"I'll come to that. After I got home I began to think— Madden was out at the ranch, it seemed. And I got a big idea. Things ain't been going so well here lately— Florida's been nabbing all the easy—all the good prospects—and I said to myself, how about Madden? There's big money. Why not try and interest Madden in Date City? Get him behind it. Worth a shot anyhow. So bright and early Thursday morning, I came out to the ranch."

"About what time?"

"Oh, it must have been a little after eight. I'm full of pep at that hour of the day, and I knew I'd need it. I knocked at the front door, but nobody answered. I tried it—it was locked. I came around to the back and the place was deserted. Not a soul in sight."

"Nobody here," repeated Eden, wonderingly.

"Not a living thing but the chickens and the turkeys. And the Chinese parrot, Tony. He was sitting on his perch. 'Hello, Tony,' I said. 'You're a damn crook,' he answers. Now I ask you, is that any way to greet a hardworking, honest real-estate man? Wait a minute—don't try to be funny."

"I won't," Eden laughed. "But Madden—"

"Well, just then Madden drove into the yard with that secretary of his. I knew the old man right away from his pictures. He looked tired and ugly, and he needed a shave. 'What are you doing here?' he wanted to know. 'Mr. Madden,' I said, 'have you ever stopped to consider the possibilities of this land round here?' And I waltzed right into my selling talk. But I didn't get far. He stopped me, and then he started. Say—the things he called me. I'm not used to that sort of thing—abuse by an expert, and that's what it was. I saw his psychology was all wrong, so I walked out on him. That's the best way— when the old psychology ain't working."

"And that's all?" Eden inquired.

"That's my story, and I'll stick to it," replied Mr. De-Lisle.

"I'm very much obliged," Eden said. "Of course, this is all between ourselves. And I may add that if I ever do decide to buy a lot on the desert—"

"You'll consider my stuff, won't you?"

"I certainly will. Just at present, the desert doesn't look very good to me."

Mr. DeLisle leaned close. "Whisper it not in Eldorado," he said. "I sometimes wish I was back in good old Chi myself. If I ever hit the Loop again, I'm going to nail myself down there."

"If you'll wait outside a few minutes, DeLisle—" Holley began.

"I get you. I'll just mosey down to the development and see if the fountain's working. You can pick me up there."

The young man went out. Chan came quickly from behind a near-by door.

"Get all that, Charlie?" Eden inquired.

"Yes, indeed. Most interesting."

"We move right on," said Holley. "Jerry Delaney came out to the ranch about seven o'clock Wednesday night, and he didn't come alone. For the first time a fourth man enters the picture. Who? Sounded to me very much like Professor Gamble."

"No doubt about that," replied Eden. "He's an old friend of the prophet Isaiah's—he admitted it here Monday after lunch."

"Fine," commented Holley. "We begin to place Mr. Gamble. Here's another thing—some one drove up to the doctor's Sunday night and carried Shaky Phil away.

Couldn't that have been Gamble, too? What do you say, Charlie?"

Chan nodded. "Possible. That person knew of Louie's return. If we could only discover—"

"By George," Eden cried. "Gamble was at the desk of the Oasis when Louie came in. You remember, Holley?"

The editor smiled. "All fits in very neatly. Gamble sped out here like some sinister version of Paul Revere with the news of Louie's arrival. He and Shaky Phil were at the gate when you drove up."

"But Thorn. That tear in Thorn's coat?"

"We must have been on the wrong trail there. This new theory sounds too good. What else have we learned from DeLisle? After the misadventure with Delaney, Madden and Thorn were out all night. Where?"

Chan sighed. "Not such good news, that. Body of Delaney was carried far from this spot."

"I'm afraid it was," admitted Holley. "We'll never find it without help from somebody who knows. There are a hundred lonely cañons round here where poor Delaney could have been tossed aside and nobody any the wiser. We'll have to go ahead and perfect our case without the vital bit of evidence—the body of Delaney. But there are a lot of people in on this, and before we get through, somebody is going to squeal."

Chan was sitting at Madden's desk, idly toying with the big blotting pad that lay on top. Suddenly his eyes lighted, and he began to separate the sheets of blotting paper.

"What is this?" he said.

They looked, and saw in the detective's pudgy hand a

large sheet of paper, partly filled with writing. Chan perused the missive carefully, and handed it to Eden. The letter was written in a man's strong hand. "It's dated last Wednesday night," Eden remarked to Holley. He read:

"Dear Evelyn:
"I want you to know of certain developments here at the ranch. As I've told you before, Martin Thorn and I have been on very bad terms for the past year. This afternoon the big blow-off finally arrived, and I dismissed him from my service. To-morrow morning I'm going with him to Pasadena, and when we get there, we part for all time. Of course he knows a lot of things I wish he didn't—otherwise I'd have scrapped him a year ago. He may make trouble, and I am warning you in case he shows up in Denver. I'm going to take this letter in town myself and mail it to-night, as I don't want Thorn to know anything about it—"

The letter stopped abruptly at that point.

"Better and better," said Holley. "Another sidelight on what happened here last Wednesday night. We can picture the scene for ourselves. Madden is sitting at his desk, writing that letter to his daughter. The door opens— some one comes in. Say it's Delaney—Delaney, the man P. J.'s feared for years. Madden hastily slips the letter between the leaves of the blotter. He gets to his feet, knowing that he's in for it now. A quarrel ensues, and by the time it's over, they've got into Thorn's room somehow and Delaney is dead on the floor. Then—the problem of what to do with the body, not solved until morning. Madden comes back to the ranch tired and worn, realizing that he can't dismiss Thorn now. He must make his peace with the secretary. Thorn knows too much. How about it, Charlie?"

"It has plenty logic," Chan admitted.

"I said this morning I had some ideas on this affair out here," the editor continued, "and everything that has happened to-day has tended to confirm them. I'm ready to spring my theory now—that is, if you care to listen."

"Shoot," said Eden.

"To me, it's all as clear as a desert sunrise," Holley went on. "Just let me go over it for you. Reconstruct it, as the French do. To begin with, Madden is afraid of Delaney. Why? Why is a rich man afraid of anybody? Blackmail, of course. Delaney has something on him—maybe something that dates back to that gambling house in New York. Thorn can't be depended on—they've been rowing and he hates his employer. Perhaps he has even gone so far as to link up with Delaney and his friends. Madden buys the pearls, and the gang hears of it and decides to spring. What better place than way out here on the desert? Shaky Phil goes to San Francisco; Delaney and the professor come south. Louie, the faithful old retainer, is lured away by Shaky Phil. The stage is set. Delaney arrives with his threat. He demands the pearls, money, both. An argument follows, and in the end Delaney, the blackmailer, is killed by Madden. Am I right so far?"

"Sounds plausible," Eden admitted.

"Well, imagine what followed. When Madden killed Delaney, he probably thought Jerry had come alone. Now he discovers there are others in the gang. They have not only the information with which Delaney was threatening him, but they have something else on him too. Murder! The pack is on him—he must buy them off. They clamor for money—and the pearls. They force Madden to call up and order the Phillimore necklace sent down here at once. When did he do that, Eden?"

"Last Thursday morning," Eden replied.

"See—what did I tell you? Last Thursday morning, when he got back from his grisly midnight trip. They were on him then—they were blackmailing him to the limit. That's the answer to our puzzle. They're blackmailing him now. At first Madden was just as eager as they were for the necklace—he wanted to settle the thing and get away. It isn't pleasant to linger round the spot where you've done murder. The past few days his courage has begun to return, he's temporizing, seeking a way out. I'm a little sorry for him, I really am." Holley paused. "Well, that's my idea. What do you think, Charlie? Am I right?"

Chan sat turning Madden's unfinished letter slowly in his hand.

"Sounds good," admitted the detective. "However, here and there objections arise."

"For example?" Holley demanded.

"Madden is big man. Delaney and these others nobody much. He could announce he killed blackmailer in self-defense."

"So he could—if Thorn were friendly and would back him up. But the secretary is hostile and might threaten to tell a different story. Besides, remember it isn't only the killing of Delaney they have against him. There's the information Delaney has been holding over his head."

Chan nodded. "So very true. One other fact, and then I cease my brutal faultfinding. Louie, long in confidence of Chinese parrot, is killed. Yet Louie depart for San Francisco on Wednesday morning, twelve hours be-

fore tragic night. Is not his murder then a useless ges-
turing?"

Holley considered. "Well, that is a point. But he
was Madden's friend, which was a pretty good reason for
not wanting him here. They preferred their victim alone
and helpless. A rather weak explanation, perhaps. Otherwise I'm strong for my theory. You're not so keen on it."

Chan shook his head. "For one reason only. Long
experience has taught fatal consequence may follow if I
get too addicted to a theory. Then I try and see, can I
make everything fit. I can, and first thing I know theory
explodes in my countenance with loud bang. Much better I have found to keep mind free and open."

"Then you haven't any idea on all this to set up against
mine?" Holley asked.

"No solitary one. Frankly speaking, I am completely
in the dark." He glanced at the letter in his hand. "Or
nearly so," he added. "We watch and wait, and maybe
I clutch something soon."

"That's all right," said Eden, "but I have a feeling we
don't watch and wait much longer at Madden's ranch.
Remember, I promised that Draycott would meet him to-
day in Pasadena. He'll be back soon, asking how come?"

"Unfortunate incident," shrugged Chan. "Draycott
and he have failed to connect. Many times that has happened when two strangers make appointment. It can
happen again."

Eden sighed. "I suppose so. But I hope P. J. Madden's feeling good-natured when he comes home from
Pasadena to-night. There's a chance that he's toting Bill
Hart's gun again, and I don't like the idea of lying behind
a bed with nothing showing but my shoes. I haven't had
a shine for a week."

CHAPTER XVI

"THE MOVIES ARE IN TOWN"

THE sun set behind far peaks of snow; the desert purpled under a sprinkling of stars. In the thermometer
that hung on a patio wall the mercury began its quick
relentless fall, a sharp wind swept over the desolate waste,
and loneliness settled on the world.

"Warm food needed now," remarked Chan. "With
your permission I will open numerous cans."

"Anything but the arsenic," Eden told him. He departed for the cookhouse.

Holley had long since gone, and Bob Eden sat alone
by the window, looking out at a vast silence. Lots of
room left in America yet, he reflected. Did they think of
that, those throngs of people packed into subways at this
hour, seeking tables in noisy restaurants, waiting at
jammed corners for the traffic signal, climbing weary and
worn at last to the pigeon-holes they called home? Elbow
room on the desert; room to expand the chest. But a
feeling of disquiet, too, a haunting realization of one
man's ridiculous unimportance in the scheme of things.

Chan entered with a tray on which the dishes were
piled high. He set down on the table two steaming plates
of soup.

227

"Deign to join me," he suggested. "First course is now served with the kind assistance of the can-opener."

"Aged in the tin, eh, Charlie?" smiled Eden, drawing up. "Well, I'll bet it's good, at that. You're a bit of a magician in the kitchen." They began to eat. "Charlie, I've been thinking," the boy continued. "I know now why I have this sense of unrest on the desert. It's because I feel so blamed small. Look at me, and then look out the window, and tell me where I get off to strut like a somebody through the world."

"Not bad feeling for the white man to experience," Chan assured him. "Chinese has it all time. Chinese knows he is one minute grain of sand on seashore of eternity. With what result? He is calm and quiet and humble. No nerves, like hopping, skipping Caucasian. Life for him not so much ordeal."

"Yes, and he's happier, too," said Eden.

"Sure," replied Chan. He produced a platter of canned salmon. "All time in San Francisco I behold white men hot and excited. Life like a fever, always getting worse. What for? Where does it end? Same place as Chinese life, I think."

When they had finished Eden attempted to help with the dishes, but was politely restrained. He sat down and turned on the radio. The strong voice of a leather-lunged announcer rang out in the quiet room.

"Now, folks, we got a real treat for you this balmy, typical California evening. Miss Norma Fitzgerald, of the *One Night in June* company now playing at the Mason, is going to sing—er—what are you going to sing, Norma? Norma says wait and find out."

At mention of the girl's name, Bob Eden called to the

detective, who entered and stood expectantly. "Hello, folks," came Miss Fitzgerald's greeting. "I certainly am glad to be back in good old L. A."

"Hello, Norma," Eden said, "never mind the songs. Two gentlemen out on the desert would like a word with you. Tell us about Jerry Delaney."

She couldn't have heard him, for she began to sing in a clear, beautiful soprano voice. Chan and the boy listened in silence.

"More of the white man's mysteries," Charlie remarked when she had finished. "So near to her, and yet so far away. Seems to me that we must visit this lady soon."

"Ah yes—but how?" inquired Eden.

"It will be arranged," Chan said, and vanished.

Eden tried a book. An hour later he was interrupted by the peal of the telephone bell, and a cheery voice answered his hello.

"Still pining for the bright lights?"

"I sure am," he replied.

"Well, the movies are in town," said Paula Wendell. "Come on in."

He hurried to his room. Chan had built a fire in the patio, and was sitting before it, the warm light flickering on his chubby impassive face. When Eden returned with his hat, he paused beside the detective.

"Getting some new ideas?" he asked.

"About our puzzle?" Chan shook his head. "No. At this moment I am far from Madden's ranch. I am in Honolulu where nights are soft and sweet, not like chilly desert dark. Must admit my heart is weighed a little with homesick qualms. I picture my humble house on Punchbowl Hill, where lanterns glow and my ten children are gathered round."

"Ten!" cried Eden. "Great Scott—you *are* a father."

"Very proud one," assented Chan. "You are going from here?"

"I'm running in town for a while. Miss Wendell called up—it seems the picture people have arrived. By the way, I just remembered—to-morrow is the day Madden promised they could come out here. I bet the old man's clean forgot it."

"Most likely. Better not to tell him, he might refuse permission. I have unlimited yearning to see movies in throes of being born. Should I go home and report that experience to my eldest daughter, who is all time sunk in movie magazines, ancestor worship breaks out plenty strong at my house."

Eden laughed. "Well then, let's hope you get the chance. I'll be back early."

A few minutes later he was again in the flivver, under the platinum stars. He thought fleetingly of Louie Wong, buried now in the bleak little graveyard back of Eldorado, but his mind turned quickly to happier things. With a lively feeling of anticipation he climbed between the twin hills at the gateway, and the yellow lights of the desert town were winking at him.

The moment he crossed the threshold of the Desert Edge Hotel, he knew this was no ordinary night in Eldorado. From the parlor at the left came the strains of giddy, inharmonious music, laughter, and a medley of voices. Paula Wendell met him and led him in.

The stuffy little room, dated by heavy mission furniture and bits of broken plaster hanging crazily from the

ceiling, was renewing its youth in pleasant company. Bob
Eden met the movies in their hours of ease, child-like,
happy people, seemingly without a care in the world. A
very pretty girl gave him a hand which recalled his
father's jewelry shop, and then restored it to the ukulele
she was playing. A tall young man designated as Rannie,
whose clothes were perfection and whose collar and shirt
shamed the blue of California's sky, desisted briefly from
his torture of a saxophone.

"Hello, old-timer," he remarked. "I hope you brought
your harp." And instantly ran amuck on the saxophone
again.

A middle-aged actor with a bronzed, rather hard face
was officiating at the piano. In a far corner a grand dame
and an old man with snow-white hair sat apart from the
crowd, and Eden dropped down beside them.

"What was the name?" asked the old man, his hand
behind his ear. "Ah, yes, I'm glad to meet any friend of
Paula's. We're a little clamorous here to-night, Mr. Eden.
It's like the early days when I was trouping—how we
used to skylark on station platforms! We were happy
then—no movies. Eh, my dear?" he added to the woman.

She bent a bit. "Yes—but I never trouped much.
Thank heaven I was usually able to steer clear of those
terrible towns where Main Street is up-stairs. Mr.
Belasco rarely asked me to leave New York." She turned
to Eden. "I was in Belasco companies fifteen years," she
explained.

"Wonderful experience, no doubt," the boy replied.

"Greatest school in the world," she said. "Mr. Belasco
thought very highly of my work. I remember once at a
dress rehearsal he told me he could never have put on the

piece without me, and he gave me a big red apple. You know that was Mr. Belasco's way of—"

The din had momentarily stopped, and the leading man cried:

"Suffering cats! She's telling him about the apple, and the poor guy only just got here. Go on, Fanny, spring the one about the time you played Portia. What Charlie Frohman said—as soon as he came to, I mean."

"Humph," shrugged Fanny. "If you young people in this profession had a few traditions like us, the pictures wouldn't be such a joke. I thank my stars—"

"Hush, everybody," put in Paula Wendell. "Introducing Miss Diane Day on Hollywood's favorite instrument, the ukulele."

The girl she referred to smiled and, amid a sudden silence, launched into a London music-hall song. Like most of its genre, its import was not such as to recommend it for a church social, but she did it well, with a note of haunting sweetness in her voice. After another of the same sort she switched suddenly into *Way Down upon the Suwanee River* and there were tears in her voice now, a poignant sadness in the room. It was too solemn for Rannie.

"Mr. Eddie Boston at the piano, Mr. Randolph Renault handling the saxophone," he shouted, "will now offer for your approval that touching ballad, *So's Your Old Mandarin*. Let her go, Professor."

"Don't think they're always like this," Paula Wendell said to Eden above the racket. "It's only when they have a hotel to themselves, as they usually have here."

They had it indeed to themselves, save for the lads of the village, who suddenly found pressing business in the lobby, and passed and repassed the parlor door, open-mouthed with wonder.

The approval shown the instrumental duet was scant indeed, due, Mr. Renault suggested, to professional jealousy.

"The next number on our very generous program," he announced, "will follow immediately. It's called *Let's Talk about My Sweetie Now*. On your mark—Eddie."

"Nothing doing," cried the girl known as Diane. "I haven't had my Charleston lesson to-day, and it's getting late. Eddie—kindly oblige."

Eddie obliged. In another moment every one save the two old people in the corner had leaped into action. The framed, autographed portraits that other film celebrities had bestowed on the proprietor of the Desert Edge rattled on the walls. The windows shook. Suddenly in the doorway appeared a bald man with a gloomy eye.

"Good lord," he shouted. "How do you expect me to get my rest?"

"Hello, Mike," said Rannie. "What is it you want to rest from?"

"You direct a gang like this for a while, and you'll know," replied Mike sourly. "It's ten o'clock. If you'll take my advice for once, you'll turn in. Everybody's to report in costume here in the lobby to-morrow morning at eight-thirty."

This news was greeted with a chorus of low moans. "Nine-thirty, you say?" Rannie inquired.

"Eight-thirty. You heard me. And anybody who's late pays a good stiff fine. Now please go to bed and let decent people sleep."

"Decent people?" repeated Rannie softly, as the director vanished. "He's flattering himself again." But the party was over, and the company moved reluctantly up the stairs to the second floor. Mr. Renault returned the saxophone to the desk.

"Say, landlord, there's a sour note in this thing," he complained. "Have it fixed before I come again."

"Sure will, Mr. Renault," promised the proprietor.

"Too early for bed, no matter what Mike says," remarked Eden, piloting Paula Wendell to the street. "Let's take a walk. Eldorado doesn't look much like Union Square, but night air is night air wherever you find it."

"Lucky for me it isn't Union Square," said the girl. "I wouldn't be tagging along, if it was."

"Is that so?"

They strolled down Main Street, white and empty in the moonlight. In a lighted window of the Spot Cash Store hung a brilliant patchwork quilt.

"To be raffled off by the ladies of the Orange Blossom Club for the benefit of the Orphans' Home," Eden read. "Think I'll take a chance on that to-morrow."

"Better not get mixed up with any Orange Blossom Club," suggested Paula Wendell.

"Oh, I can take care of myself. And it's the orphans I'm thinking of, you know."

"That's your kind heart," she answered. They climbed a narrow sandy road. Yellow lamplight in the front window of a bungalow was suddenly blotted out.

"Look at that moon," said Eden. "Like a slice of honeydew melon just off the ice."

"Fond of food, aren't you," remarked the girl. "I'll always think of you wrestling with that steak."

"A man must eat. And if it hadn't been for the steak, we might never have met."

"What if we hadn't?" she asked.

"Pretty lonesome for me down here in that event."
They turned about in silence. "You know, I've been
thinking," Eden continued. "We're bound to come to the
end of things at the ranch presently. And I'll have to go
back—"

"Back to your freedom. That will be nice."

"You bet it will. All the same, I don't want you to
forget me after I've gone. I want to go on being your—
er—your friend. Or what have you?"

"Splendid. One always needs friends."

"Write to me occasionally. I'll want to know how
Wilbur is. You never can tell—is he careful crossing the
streets?"

"Wilbur will always be fine, I'm sure." They stopped
before the hotel. "Good night," said the girl.

"Just a minute. If there hadn't been a Wilbur—"

"But there was. Don't commit yourself. I'm afraid
it's the moon, looking so much like a slice of melon—"

"It's not the moon. It's you."

The proprietor of the Desert Edge came to the door.
Dim lights burned in the interior of the hotel.

"Lord, Miss Wendell," he said. "I nearly locked you
out."

"I'm coming," returned the girl. "See you at the
ranch to-morrow, Mr. Eden."

"Fine," answered Eden. He nodded to the landlord,
and the front door of the hotel banged shut in his face.

As he drove out across the lonely desert, he began to
wonder what he was going to say to the restless P. J.
Madden when he reached the ranch. The millionaire
would be home from Pasadena now; he had expected to

meet Draycott there. And Draycott was in San Francisco, little dreaming of the part his name was playing in the drama of the Phillimore pearls. P. J. would be furious; he would demand an explanation.

But nothing like that happened. The ranch house was in darkness and only Ah Kim was in evidence about the place.

"Madden and others in bed now," explained the Chinese. "Came home tired and very much dusted and at once retired to rooms."

"Well, I've got it on good authority that to-morrow is another day," replied Eden. "I'll turn in, too."

When he reached the breakfast table on Thursday morning, the three men were there before him. "Everything run off smoothly in Pasadena yesterday?" he inquired brightly.

Thorn and Gamble stared at him, and Madden frowned. "Yes, yes, of course," he said. He added a look which clearly meant: "Shut up."

After breakfast Madden joined the boy in the yard. "Keep that matter of Draycott to yourself," he ordered.

"You saw him, I suppose?" Eden inquired.

"I did not."

"What! Why, that's too bad. But not knowing each other I suppose—"

"No sign of anybody that looked like your man to me. You know, I'm beginning to wonder about you—"

"But Mr. Madden. I told him to be there."

"Well, as a matter of fact, I didn't care especially. Things didn't work out as I expected. I think now you'd better get hold of him and tell him to come to Eldorado. Did he call you up?"

"He may have. I was in town last night. At any
rate, he's sure to call soon."

"Well, if he doesn't, you'd better go over to Pasadena
and get hold of him—"

A truck filled with motion-picture camera men, props,
and actors in weird costumes stopped before the ranch.
Two other cars followed. Some one alighted to open the
gate.

"What's this?" cried Madden.

"This is Thursday," answered Eden. "Have you forgotten—"

"Forgot it completely," said Madden. "Thorn!
Where's Thorn?"

The secretary emerged from the house. "It's the
movies, Chief. This was the day—"

"Damnation!" growled Madden. "Well, we'll have to
go through with it. Martin, you look after things." He
went inside.

The movies were all business this morning, in contrast
to the careless gaiety of the night before. The cameras
were set up in the open end of the patio. The actors, in
Spanish costume, stood ready. Bob Eden went over to
Paula Wendell.

"Good morning," she said. "I came along in case
Madden tried to renig on his promise. You see, I know
so much about him now—"

The director passed. "This will be O. K.," he remarked to the girl.

"Pleased him for once," she smiled to Eden. "That
ought to get into the papers."

The script was a story of old California, and presently
they were grinding away at a big scene in the patio.

"No, no, no," wailed the director. "What ails you this morning, Rannie? You're saying good-by to the girl—you love her, love her, love her. You'll probably never see her again."

"The hell I won't," replied the actor. "Then the thing's a flop right now."

"You know what I mean—you think you'll never see her again. Her father has just kicked you out of the house forever. A bit of a critic, the father. But come on—this is the big farewell. Your heart is broken. Broken, my boy—what are you grinning about?"

"Come on, Diane," said the actor. "I'm never going to see you again, and I'm supposed to be sorry about it. Ye gods, the things these script-writers imagine. However, here goes. My art's equal to anything."

Eden strolled over to where the white-haired patriarch and Eddie Boston were sitting together on a pile of lumber beside the barn. Near at hand, Ah Kim hovered, all eyes for these queer antics of the white men.

Boston leaned back and lighted a pipe. "Speaking of Madden," he remarked, "makes me think of Jerry Delaney. Ever know Jerry, Pop?"

Startled, Eden moved nearer. The old man put his hand behind his ear.

"Who's that?" he inquired.

"Delaney," shouted Boston. Chan also edged closer. "Jerry Delaney. There was one smooth worker in his line, pop. I hope I get a chance—I'm going to ask Madden if he remembers—"

A loud outcry for Mr. Boston arose in the patio, and he laid down his pipe and fled. Chan and Bob Eden looked at each other.

The company worked steadily until the lunch hour arrived. Then, scattered about the yard and the patio, they busied themselves with the generous sandwiches of the Oasis and with coffee served from thermos bottles. Suddenly Madden appeared in the doorway of the living-room. He was in a genial mood.

"Just a word of welcome," he said. "Make your-selves at home." He shook hands with the director and, moving about, spoke a few moments with each member of the company in turn. The girl named Diane held his attention for some time.

Presently he came to Eddie Boston. Casually Eden managed it so that he was near by during that interview.

"Boston's the name," said the actor. His hard face lighted. "I was hoping to meet you, Mr. Madden. I wanted to ask if you remember an old friend of mine—Jerry Delaney, of New York?"

Madden's eyes narrowed, but the poker face triumphed.

"Delaney?" he repeated, vacantly.

"Yes—Jerry Delaney, who used to hang out at Jack McGuire's place on Forty-fourth Street," Boston per-sisted. "You know, he—"

"I don't recall him," said Madden. He was moving away. "I meet so many people."

"Maybe you don't want to recall him," said Boston, and there was an odd note in his voice. "I can't say I blame you either, sir. No, I guess you wouldn't care much for Delaney. It was a crime what he did to you—"

Madden looked anxiously about. "What do you know about Delaney?" he asked in a low tone.

"I know a lot about him," Boston replied. He came close, and Bob Eden could barely distinguish the words. "I know all about Delaney, Mr. Madden."

For a moment they stood staring at each other.

"Come inside, Mr. Boston," Madden suggested, and Eden watched them disappear through the door into the living-room.

Ah Kim came into the patio with a tray on which were cigars and cigarettes, the offering of the host. As he paused before the director, that gentleman looked at him keenly. "By gad, here's a type," he cried. "Say, John—how'd you like to act in the pictures?"

"You clazy, boss," grinned Ah Kim.

"No, I'm not. We could use you in Hollywood."

"Him lookee like you make 'um big joke."

"Nothing of the kind. You think it over. Here." He wrote on a card. "You change your mind, you come and see me. Savvy?"

"Maybe nuddah day, boss. Plenty happly heah now." He moved along with his tray.

Bob Eden sat down beside Paula Wendell. He was, for all his outward calm, in a very perturbed state of mind.

"Look here," he began, "something has happened, and you can help us again." He explained about Jerry Delaney, and repeated the conversation he had just overheard between Madden and Eddie Boston. The girl's eyes were wide. "It wouldn't do for Chan or me to make any inquiries," he added. "What sort of fellow is this Boston?"

"Rather unpleasant person," she said. "I've neve" liked him."

"Well, suppose you ask him a few questions, the first chance you have. I presume that won't come until you get back to town. Find out all he knows about Jerry Delaney, but do it in a way that won't rouse his suspicions, if you can."

"I'll certainly try," she answered. "I'm not very clever—"

"Who says you're not? You're mighty clever—and kind, too. Call me up as soon as you've talked with him, and I'll hurry in town."

The director was on his feet. "Come on—let's get this thing finished. Is everybody here? Eddie! Where's Eddie?"

Mr. Boston emerged from the living-room, his face a mask, telling nothing. Not going to be an easy matter, Bob Eden reflected, to pump Eddie Boston.

An hour later the movies vanished down the road in a cloud of dust, with Paula Wendell's roadster trailing. Bob Eden sought out Charlie Chan. In the seclusion behind the cookhouse, he again went over Boston's surprising remarks to Madden. The detective's little black eyes shone.

"We march again," he said. "Eddie Boston becomes with sudden flash our one best wager. He must be made to talk. But how?"

"Paula Wendell's going to have a try at it," Eden replied.

Chan nodded. "Fine idea, I think. In presence of pretty girl, what man keeps silent? We pin our eager hopes on that."

CHAPTER XVII

IN · MADDEN'S FOOTSTEPS

AN HOUR later Bob Eden answered a ring on the telephone. Happily the living-room was deserted. Paula Wendell was on the wire.

"What luck?" asked the boy in a low voice.

"Not so good," she answered. "Eddie was in a terrific rush when we got back to town. He packed his things, paid his bill, and was running out of the hotel when I caught him. 'Listen, Eddie—I want to ask you—' I began, but that was as far as I got. He pointed to the station. 'Can't talk now, Paula,' he said. 'Catching the Los Angeles train.' And he managed to swing aboard it just as it was pulling out."

Eden was silent for a moment. "That's odd. He'd naturally have gone back with the company, wouldn't he? By automobile?"

"Of course. He came that way. Well, I'm awfully sorry, Chief. I've fallen down on the job. I guess there's nothing for me to do but turn in my shield and nightstick—"

"Nothing of the sort. You did your best."

"But it wasn't good enough. I'm sorry. I'm forced to start for Hollywood in my car in about an hour. Shall you be here when I come back?"

Eden sighed. "Me? It begins to look as though I'd be here forever."

"How terrible."

"What sort of speech is that?"

"For you, I mean."

"Oh! Well, thank you very much. I'll hope to see you soon."

He hung up and went into the yard. Ah Kim was loitering near the cookhouse. Together they strolled into the barn.

"We pinned our eager hopes on empty air," said Eden. He repeated his conversation with Paula Wendell.

Chan nodded, unperturbed. "I would have made fat wager same would happen. Eddie Boston knows all about Delaney, and admits the fact to Madden. What the use we try to see Boston then? Madden has seen him first."

Bob Eden dropped down on a battered old settee that had been exiled from the house. He put his head in his hands.

"Well, I'm discouraged," he admitted. "We're up against a stone wall, Charlie."

"Many times in my life I find myself in that precise locality," returned the detective. "What happens? I batter old head until it feels sore, and then a splendid idea assails me. I go around."

"What do you suggest?"

"Possibilities of ranch now exhausted and drooping. We must look elsewhere. Names of three cities gallop into mind—Pasadena, Los Angeles, Hollywood."

"All very fine—but how to get there? By gad—I think I can manage it at that. Madden was saying this

morning I ought to go to Pasadena and look up Draycott.
It seems that for some strange reason they didn't meet
yesterday."

Chan smiled. "Did he display peevish feeling as result?"

"No, oddly enough, he didn't. I don't think he wanted
to meet Draycott, with the professor tagging along. Paula
Wendell's going over that way shortly in her car. If I
hurry, I may be able to ride with her."

"Which, to my thinking, would be joyful traveling,"
agreed Chan. "Hasten along. We have more talk when
I act part of taxi-driver and carry you to Eldorado."

Bob Eden went at once to Madden's bedroom. The
door was open and he saw the huge figure of the millionaire stretched on the bed, his snores shattering the calm
afternoon. He hammered loudly on the panel of the
door.

Madden leaped from the bed with startling sudden-
ness, his eyes instantly wide and staring. He seemed like
one expecting trouble. For a moment, Eden pitied the
great man. Beyond all question Madden was caught in
some inexplicable net; he was harassed and worn, but
fighting still. Not a happy figure, for all his millions.

"I'm awfully sorry to disturb you, sir," Eden said.
"But the fact is I have a chance to ride over to Pasadena
with some of the movie people, and I think I'd better go.
Draycott hasn't called, and—"

"Hush," said Madden sharply. He closed the door.
"The matter of Draycott is between you and me. I suppose you wonder what it's all about, but I can't tell you—
except to say that this fellow Gamble doesn't strike me as
being what he pretends. And—"

"Yes, sir," said Eden hopefully, as the millionaire paused.

"Well, I won't go into that. You locate Draycott and tell him to come to Eldorado. Tell him to put up at the Desert Edge and keep his mouth shut. I'll get in touch with him shortly. Until I do he's to lie low. Is that understood?"

"Perfectly, Mr. Madden. I'm sorry this thing has dragged out as it has—"

"Oh, that's all right. You go and tell Ah Kim I said he was to drive you to Eldorado—unless your movie friends are coming out here for you."

"No—I shall have to enlist Ah Kim again. Thank you, sir. I'll be back soon."

"Good luck," answered Madden.

Hastily Eden threw a few things into his suit-case, and waited in the yard for Ah Kim and the flivver. Gamble appeared.

"Not leaving us, Mr. Eden?" he inquired in his mild way.

"No such luck—for you," the boy replied. "Just a short trip."

"On business, perhaps?" persisted the professor gently.

"Perhaps," smiled Eden, and the car with its Chinese chauffeur appearing at that moment, he leaped in.

Again he and Chan were abroad in the yellow glory of a desert sunset. "Well, Charlie," Eden said, "I'm a little new at this detective business. What am I to do first?"

"Toss all worry out of mind. I shall hover round your elbow, doing prompt work."

"You? How are you going to get away?"

"Easy thing. To-morrow morning I announce I take day off to visit sick brother in Los Angeles. Very ancient plea of all Chinese servants. Madden will be angry, but he will not suspect. Train leaves Eldorado at seven in the morning, going to Pasadena. I am aboard, reaching there at eleven. You will, I hope, condescend to meet me at station?"

"With the greatest pleasure We take Pasadena first, eh?"

"So I would plan it. We ascertain Madden's movements there on Wednesday. What happened at bank? Did he visit home? Then Hollywood, and maybe Eddie Boston. After that, we ask the lady soprano to desist from singing and talk a little time."

"All right, but we're going to be a fine pair," Eden replied, "with no authority to question anybody. You may be a policeman in Honolulu, but that isn't likely to go very big in Southern California."

Chan shrugged. "Ways will open. Paths will clear."

"I hope so," the boy answered. "And here's another thing. Aren't we taking a big chance? Suppose Madden hears of our antics? Risky, isn't it?"

"Risky pretty good word for it," agreed Chan. "But we are desperate now. We take long gambles."

"I'll say we're desperate," sighed Eden. "Me, I'm getting desperater every minute. I may as well tell you that if we come back from this trip with no definite light on things, I'll be strongly tempted to lift a big burden from your stomach—and my mind."

"Patience very nice virtue," smiled Chan.

"Well, you ought to know," Eden said. "You've got a bigger supply on hand than any man I ever met."

When they reached the Desert Edge Hotel, Eden was relieved to see Paula Wendell's car parked in front. They waited by the little roadster, and while they did so, Will Holley came along. They told him of their plans.

"I can help you a bit," said the editor. "Madden has a caretaker at his Pasadena house—a fine old chap named Peter Fogg. He's been down here several times, and I know him rather well." He wrote on a card. "Give him that, and tell him I sent you."

"Thanks," said Eden. "We'll need it, or I'm much mistaken."

Paula Wendell appeared.

"Great news for you," Eden announced. "I'm riding with you as far as Pasadena."

"Fine," she replied. "Jump in."

Eden climbed into the roadster. "See you boys later," he called, and the car started.

"You ought to get a regular taxi, with a meter," Eden suggested.

"Nonsense. I'm glad to have you."

"Are you really?"

"Certainly am. Your weight will help to keep the car on the road."

"Lady, you surely can flatter," he told her. "I'll drive, if you like."

"No, thanks—I guess I'd better. I know the roads."

"You're always so efficient, you make me nervous," he commented.

"I wasn't so efficient when it came to Eddie Boston. I'm sorry about that."

"Don't you worry. Eddie's a tough bird. Chan and I will try him presently."

"Where does the big mystery stand now?" asked the girl.

"It stands there leering at us," the boy replied. "Just as it always has." For a time they speculated on Madden's unexplained murder of Delaney. Meanwhile they were climbing between the hills, while the night gathered about them. Presently they dropped down into a green fertile valley, fragrant with the scent of blossoms.

"Um," sighed Eden, breathing deep. "Smells pretty. What is it?"

The girl glanced at him. "You poor, benighted soul. Orange blossoms."

"Oh! Well, naturally I couldn't be expected to know that."

"Of course not."

"The condemned man gets a rather pleasant whiff in his last moments, doesn't he? I suppose it acts like ether—and when he comes to, he's married." A reckless driver raced toward them on the wrong side of the road. "Look out!"

"I saw him coming," said the girl. "You're safe with me. How many times must I tell you that?"

They had dinner and a dance or two at an inn in Riverside, and all too soon, it seemed to Eden, arrived at Pasadena. The girl drove up before the Maryland Hotel, prepared to drop him.

"But look here," he protested. "I'll see you safely to Hollywood, of course."

"No need of that," she smiled. "I'm like you. I can take care of myself."

"Is that so?"

"Want to see me to-morrow?"

"Always want to see you to-morrow. Chan and I are coming over your way. Where can we find you?"

She told him she would be at the picture studio at one o'clock, and with a gay good-by, disappeared down the brightly-lighted stretch of Colorado Street. Eden went in to a quiet night at the hotel.

After breakfast in the morning he recalled that an old college friend named Spike Bristol was reported in the class histories as living now in Pasadena. The telephone directory furnished Bristol's address, and Eden set out to find him. His friend turned out to be one of the more decorative features of a bond office.

"Bond salesman, eh?" said Eden, when the greetings were over.

"Yes—it was either that or real estate," replied Bristol. "I was undecided for some time. Finally I picked this."

"Of course," laughed Eden. "As any class history proves, gentlemen prefer bonds. How are you getting on?"

"Fine. All my old friends are buying from me."

"Ah, now I know why you were so glad to see me."

"Sure was. We have some very pretty first mortgage sixes—"

"I'll bet you have—and you can keep them. I'm here on business, Spike—private business. Keep what I say under your hat."

"Never wear one," answered Spike brightly. "That's the beauty of this climate—"

"You can't sell me the climate, either. Spike, you know P. J. Madden, don't you?"

"Well—we're not very chummy. He hasn't asked

me to dinner. But of course all us big financiers are acquainted. As for Madden, I did him a service only a couple of days ago."

"Elucidate."

"This is just between us. Madden came in here Wednesday morning with a hundred and ten thousand dollars' worth of negotiable bonds—mostly Liberties—and we sold them for him the same day. Paid him in cash, too."

"Precisely what I wanted to know. Spike, I'd like to talk with somebody at Madden's bank about his actions there Wednesday."

"Who are you—Sherlock Holmes?"

"Well—" Eden thought of Chan. "I am connected with the police, temporarily." Spike whistled. "I may go so far as to say—and for heaven's sake keep it to yourself—that Madden is in trouble. At the present moment I'm stopping at his ranch on the desert, and I have every reason to believe he's being blackmailed."

Spike looked at him. "What if he is? That ought to be his business."

"It ought to be, but it isn't. A certain transaction with my father is involved. Do you know anybody at the Garfield Bank?"

"One of my best friends is cashier there. But you know these bankers—hard-boiled eggs. However, we'll have a try."

They went together to the marble precincts of the Garfield Bank. Spike held a long and earnest conversation with his friend. Presently he called Eden over and introduced him.

"How do you do," said the banker. "You realize that what Spike here suggests is quite irregular. But if he vouches for you, I suppose— What is it you want to know?"

"Madden was here on Wednesday. Just what happened?"

"Yes, Mr. Madden came in on Wednesday. We hadn't seen him for two years, and his coming caused quite a stir. He visited the safe deposit vaults and spent some time going through his box."

"Was he alone?"

"No, he wasn't," the banker replied. "His secretary, Thorn, who is well known to us, was with him. Also a little, middle-aged man whom I don't recall very clearly."

"Ah, yes. He examined his safety deposit box. Was that all?"

The banker hesitated. "No. He had wired his office in New York to deposit a rather large sum of money to our credit with the Federal Reserve Bank—but I'd really rather not say any more."

"You paid over to him that large sum of money?"

"I'm not saying we did. I'm afraid I've said too much already."

"You've been very kind," Eden replied. "I promise you won't regret it. Thank you very much."

He and Bristol returned to the street. "Thanks for your help, Spike," Eden remarked. "I'm leaving you here."

"Cast off like an old coat," complained Bristol. "How about lunch?"

"Sorry. Some other time. I must run along now. The station's down here, isn't it? I leave you to your climate."

"Sour grapes," returned Spike. "Don't go home and get lost in the fog. So long."

From the eleven o'clock train a quite different Charlie Chan alighted. He was dressed as Eden had seen him in San Francisco.

"Hello, Dapper Dan," the boy said.

Chan smiled. "Feel respected again," he explained. "Visited Barstow and rescued proper clothes. No cooking to-day, which makes life very pretty."

"Madden put up a fight when you left?"

"How could he do so? I leave before his awakening, dropping quaintly worded note at door. No doubt now his heart is heavy, thinking I have deserted forever. Happy surprise for him when Ah Kim returns to home nest."

"Well, Charlie, I've been busy," said Eden. He went over his activities of the morning. "When the old boy came back to the ranch the other night, he must have been oozing cash at every pore. I tell you, Holley's right. He's being blackmailed."

"Seems that way," agreed Chan. "Here is another thought. Madden has killed a man, and fears discovery. He gets huge sum together so if necessity arouses he can flee with plenty cash until affair blows overhead. How is that?"

"By George—it's possible," admitted Eden.

"To be considered," replied Chan. "Suggest now we visit caretaker at local home."

A yellow taxi carried them to Orange Grove Avenue. Chan's black eyes sparkled as they drove through the cheerful handsome city. When they turned off under the shade of the pepper trees lining the favorite street of the millionaires, the detective regarded the big houses with awe.

"Impressive sight for one born in thatched hut by side of muddy river," he announced. "Rich men here live like emperors. Does it bring content?"

"Charlie," said Eden, "I'm worried about this caretaker business. Suppose he reports our call to Madden. We're sunk."

"Without bubble showing. But what did I say—we accept long chance and hope for happy luck."

"Is it really necessary to see him?"

"Important to see everybody knowing Madden. This caretaker may turn out useful find."

"What shall we say to him?"

"The thing that appears to be true. Madden in much trouble—blackmail. We are police on trail of crime."

"Fine. And how can you prove that?"

"Quick flash of Honolulu badge, which I have pinned to vest. All police badges much alike, unless person has suspicion to read close."

"Well, you're the doctor, Charlie. I follow on."

The taxi halted before the largest house on the street—or in the world, it seemed. Chan and Eden walked up the broad driveway to find a man engaged in training roses on a pergola. He was a scholarly-looking man even in his overalls, with keen eyes and a pleasant smile.

"Mr. Fogg?" inquired Eden.

"That's my name," the man said. Bob Eden offered Holley's card, and Fogg's smile broadened.

"Glad to meet any friend of Holley's," he remarked. "Come over to the side veranda and sit down. What can I do for you?"

"We're going to ask a few questions, Mr. Fogg," Eden began. "They may seem odd—you can answer

them or not, as you prefer. In the first place, Mr. Madden was in Pasadena last Wednesday?"

"Why yes—of course he was."

"You saw him then?"

"For a few minutes—yes. He drove up to the door
in that Requa car he uses out here. That was about six
o'clock. I talked with him for a while, but he didn't get
out of the car."

"What did he say?"

"Just asked me if everything was all right, and added
that he might be back shortly for a brief stay here—with
his daughter."

"With his daughter, eh?"

"Yes."

"Did you make any inquiries about the daughter?"

"Why, yes—the usual polite hope that she was well.
He said she was quite well, and anxious to get here."

"Was Madden alone in the car?"

"No. Thorn was with him—as always. And another
man whom I had never seen before."

"They didn't go into the house?"

"No. I had the feeling Mr. Madden intended to,
but changed his mind."

Bob Eden looked at Charlie Chan, "Mr. Fogg—did
you notice anything about Madden's manner? Was he
just as always?"

Fogg's brow wrinkled. "Well, I got to thinking about
it after he left. He did act extremely nervous and sort
of—er—harassed."

"I'm going to tell you something, Mr. Fogg, and I
rely entirely on your discretion. You know that if we
weren't all right, Will Holley would not have sent us.

Mr. Madden is nervous—he is harassed. We have every reason to believe that he is the victim of a gang of black-mailers. Mr. Chan—" Chan opened his coat for a brief second, and the celebrated California sun flashed on a silver badge.

Peter Fogg nodded. "I'm not surprised," he said seriously. "But I'm sorry to hear it, just the same. I've always liked Madden. Not many people do—but he has certainly been a friend to me. As you may imagine, this work I'm doing here is hardly in my line. I was a lawyer back east. Then my health broke, and I had to come out here. It was a case of taking anything I could get. Yes, sir, Madden has been kind to me, and I'll help you any way I can."

"You say you're not surprised. Have you any reason for that statement?"

"No particular reason—but a man as famous as Mad-den—and as rich—well, it seems to me inevitable."

For the first time Charlie Chan spoke. "One more question, sir. Is it possible you have idea why Mr. Mad-den should fear a certain man. A man named—Jerry Delaney."

Fogg looked at him quickly, but did not speak.

"Jerry Delaney," repeated Bob Eden. "You've heard that name, Mr. Fogg?"

"I can tell you this," answered Fogg. "The chief is rather friendly at times. Some years ago he had this house gone over and a complete set of burglar-alarms installed. I met him in the hall while the men were busy at the windows. 'I guess that'll give us plenty of notice if anybody tries to break in,' he said. 'I imagine a big man like you has plenty of enemies, Chief,' said I. He looked at me kind of funny. 'There's only one man in the world I'm afraid of, Fogg,' he answered. 'Just one.' I got sort of nervy. 'Who's that, Chief?' I asked. 'His name is Jerry Delaney,' he said. 'Remember that, if anything happens.' I told him I would. He was moving off. 'And why are you afraid of this Delaney, Chief?' I asked him. It was a cheeky thing to say, and he didn't answer at first."

"But he did answer?" suggested Bob Eden.

"Yes. He looked at me for a minute, and he said: 'Jerry Delaney follows one of the queer professions, Fogg. And he's too damn good at it.' Then he walked away into the library, and I knew better than to ask him anything more."

CHAPTER XVIII

A FEW moments later they left Peter Fogg standing on the neatly manicured lawn beside P. J. Madden's empty palace. In silence they rode down the avenue, then turned toward the more lively business district.

"Well, what did we get out of that?" Bob Eden wanted to know. "Not much, if you ask me."

Chan shrugged. "Trifles, mostly. But trifles sometimes blossom big. Detective business consist of one unsignificant detail placed beside other of the same. Then with sudden dazzle, light begins to dawn."

"Bring on your dazzle," said Eden. "We've learned that Madden visited his house here on Wednesday, but did not go inside. When questioned about his daughter, he replied that she was well and would be along soon. What else? A thing we knew before—that Madden was afraid of Delaney."

"Also that Delaney followed queer profession."

"What profession? Be more explicit."

Chan frowned. "If only I could boast expert knowledge of mainland ways. How about you? Please do a little speculating."

Eden shook his head. "Promised my father I'd never speculate. Just as well, too, for in this case I'd get nowhere. My brain—if you'll pardon the mention of one

257

more insignificant detail—is numb. Too many puzzles make Jack a dull boy."

The taxi landed them at the station whence hourly buses ran to Hollywood, and they were just in time to connect with the twelve o'clock run. Back up the hill and over the bridge spanning the Arroyo they sped. A cheery world lay about them, tiny stucco bungalows tinted pink or green, or gleaming white, innumerable service stations. In time they came to the outskirts of the film city, where gaily colored mansions perched tipsily on miniature hills. Then down a long street that seemed to stretch off into eternity, into the maelstrom of Hollywood's business district.

Expensive cars honked deliriously about the corner where they alighted, and on the sidewalk milled a busy throng, most of them living examples of what the well-dressed man or woman will wear if not carefully watched. They crossed the street.

"Watch your step, Charlie," Eden advised. "You're in the auto salesman's paradise." He gazed curiously about him. "The most picturesque factory town in the world. Everything is here except the smoking chimneys."

Paula Wendell was waiting for them in the reception-room of the studio with which she was connected. "Come along," she said. "I'll take you to lunch at the cafeteria, and then perhaps you'd like to look around a bit."

Chan's eyes sparkled as she led them across the lot and down a street lined with the false fronts of imaginary dwellings. "My oldest girl would exchange the favor of the gods to be on this spot with me," he remarked. "I shall have much to relate when I return to Punchbowl Hill."

They lunched among the film players, grotesque in make-up and odd costumes. "No postman before," said Chan, over his chicken pie, "ever encountered such interesting walk on his holiday. Pardon, please, if I eat with unashamed enjoyment and too much gusto. New experience for me to encounter food I have not perspired over myself in person."

"They're taking a picture on Stage Twelve," the girl explained when lunch was finished. "It's against the rules, but if you're not too boisterous I can get you in for a look."

They passed out of the dazzling sunshine into the dim interior of a great building that looked like a warehouse. Another moment, and they reached the set, built to represent a smart foreign restaurant. Rich hangings were in the background, beautiful carpets on the floor. Along the walls were many tables with pink-shaded lights, and a resplendent head-waiter stood haughtily at the entrance.

The sequence being shot at the moment involved, evidently, the use of many extras, and a huge crowd stood about, waiting patiently. The faces of most of them were vital and alive, unforgettable. Here were people who had known life—and not too much happiness—in many odd corners of the world. Nearly all the men were in uniform—a war picture, no doubt. Bob Eden heard snatches of French, German, Spanish; he saw in the eyes about him a hundred stories more real and tragic than any these people would ever act on the silver screen.

"Leading men and women are standardized, more or less," said Paula Wendell, "but the extras—they're different. If you talked with some of them, you'd be amazed. Brains and refinement—remarkable pasts—and on the bargain counter now at five dollars a day."

A call sounded, and the extras filed on to the set and took their allotted stations at the various tables. Chan watched fascinated; evidently he could stay here forever. But Bob Eden, sadly lacking in that lovely virtue, patience, became restless.

"This is all very well," he said. "But we have work to do. How about Eddie Boston?"

"I have his address for you," the girl replied. "I doubt whether you'll find him in at this hour, but you can try."

An old man appeared in the shadowy space behind the cameras. Eden recognized the veteran player who had been yesterday at Madden's ranch—the actor known as "Pop."

"Hello," cried Paula Wendell. "Maybe Pop can help you." She hailed him. "Know where we can find Eddie Boston?" she inquired.

As Pop joined them, Charlie Chan stepped back into a dark corner.

"Why—how are you, Mr. Eden?" the old man said. "You want to see Eddie Boston, you say?"

"I'd like to—yes."

"That's too bad. You won't find him in Hollywood."

"Why not? Where is he?"

"On his way to San Francisco by this time," Pop answered. "At least, that was where he was going when I saw him late last night."

"San Francisco? What's he going there for?" asked Eden, amazed.

"One grand outbreak, to hear him tell it. You know, it looks to me like Eddie's come into a bit of money."

"He has, has he?" Eden's eyes narrowed.

"I met him on the street last night when we got in from the desert. He'd come by train, and I asked him why. 'Had some rush business to attend to, Pop,' he says. 'I'm off to Frisco in the morning. Things are looking up. Now the picture's finished I aim to take a little jaunt for my health.' Said he hadn't been in Frisco since the 'nineties and was hungry to see it again."

Eden nodded. "Well, thank you very much." With Paula Wendell he moved toward the door, and Chan, his hat low over his eyes, followed.

At the foot of the runway in the bright world outside, Eden paused. "That's that," he said. "One more disappointment. Will we ever get to the end of this? Well, Charlie—Boston's beat it. Our bird has flown."

"Why not?" said Chan. "Madden pays him to go, of course. Did Boston not say he knew all about Delaney?"

"Which must mean he knows Delaney's dead. But how could he? Was he on the desert that Wednesday night? Ye gods!" The boy put his hand to his forehead. "You haven't any smelling salts, have you?" he added to Paula Wendell.

She laughed. "Never use 'em."

They moved out to the street.

"Well, we must push on," said Eden. "The night is dark and we are far from home." He turned to the girl. "When do you go back to Eldorado?"

"This afternoon," she replied. "I'm working on another script—one that calls for a ghost city this time."

"A ghost city?"

"Yes—you know. A deserted mining town. So it's me for the Petticoat Mine again."

"Where's that?"

"Up in the hills about seventeen miles from Eldorado. Petticoat Mine had three thousand citizens ten years ago, but there's not a living soul there to-day. Just ruins, like Pompeii. I'll have to show it to you—it's mighty interesting."

"That's a promise," Eden returned. "We'll see you back on your dear old desert."

"Warmest thanks for permitting close inspection of picture factory," Chan remarked. "Always a glowing item on the scroll of memory."

"It was fun for me," answered the girl. "Sorry you must go."

On the trolley bound for Los Angeles, Eden turned to the Chinese. "Don't you ever get discouraged, Charlie?" he inquired.

"Not while work remains to do," the detective replied. "This Miss Fitzgerald. Songbird, perhaps, but she will not have flown."

"You'd better talk with her—" Eden began.

But Chan shook his head.

"No, I will not accompany on that errand. Easy to see my presence brings embarrassed pause. I am hard to explain, like black eye."

"Well, I shouldn't have called you that," smiled the boy.

"Go alone to see this woman. Inquire all she knows about the dead man, Delaney."

Eden sighed. "I'll do my best. But my once proud faith in myself is ebbing fast."

At the stage door of the deserted theater Eden slipped a dollar into the hand of the doorman, and was permitted to step inside and examine the call-board. As he expected, the local addresses of the troupe were posted up, and he located Miss Fitzgerald at the Wynnwood Hotel.

"You have aspect of experienced person," ventured Chan.

Eden laughed. "Oh, I've known a few chorus-girls in my time. Regular man of the world, I am."

Chan took up his post on a bench in Pershing Square, while the boy went on alone to the Wynnwood Hotel. He sent up his name, and after a long wait in the cheap lobby, the actress joined him. She was at least thirty, probably more, but her eyes were young and sparkling. At sight of Bob Eden she adopted a rather coquettish manner.

"You Mr. Eden?" she said. "I'm glad to see you, though why I see you's a mystery to me."

"Well, just so long as it's a pleasant mystery——" Eden smiled.

"I'll say it is—so far. You in the profession?"

"Not precisely. First of all, I want to say that I heard you sing over the radio the other night, and I was enchanted. You've a wonderful voice."

She beamed. "Say, I like to hear you talk like that. But I had a cold—I've had one ever since I struck this town. You ought to hear me when I'm going good."

"You were going good enough for me. With a voice like yours, you ought to be in grand opera."

"I know—that's what all my friends say. And it ain't that I haven't had the chance. But I love the theater. Been on the stage since I was a teeny-weeny girl."

"Only yesterday, that must have been."

"Say, boy—you're good," she told him. "You don't happen to be scouting for the Metropolitan, do you?"

"No—I wish I were." Eden paused. "Miss Fitz-gerald, I'm an old pal of a friend of yours."

"Which friend? I've got so many."

"I'll bet you have. I'm speaking of Jerry Delaney. You know Jerry?"

"Do I? I've known him for years." She frowned suddenly. "Have you any news of Jerry?"

"No, I haven't," Eden answered. "That's why I've come to you. I'm terribly anxious to locate him, and I thought maybe you could help."

She was suddenly cautious. "Old pal of his, you say?"

"Sure. Used to work with him at Jack McGuire's place on Forty-fourth Street."

"Did you really?" The caution vanished. "Well, you know just as much about Jerry's whereabouts as I do. Two weeks ago he wrote me from Chicago—I got it in Seattle. He was kind of mysterious. Said he hoped to see me out this way before long."

"He didn't tell you about the deal he had on?"

"What deal?"

"Well, if you don't know—Jerry was about to pick up a nice little bit of change."

"Is that so? I'm glad to hear it. Things ain't been any too jake with Jerry since those old days at Mc-Guire's."

"That's true enough, I guess. By the way, did Jerry ever talk to you about the men he met at McGuire's? The swells. You know, we used to get some pretty big trade there."

"No, he never talked about it much. Why?"

"I was wondering whether he ever mentioned to you the name of P. J. Madden."

She turned upon the boy a baby stare, wide-eyed and innocent. "Who's P. J. Madden?" she inquired.

"Why, he's one of the biggest financiers in the country. If you ever read the papers—"

"But I don't. My work takes so much time. You've no idea the long hours I put in—"

"I can imagine it. But look here—the question is, where's Jerry now? I may say I'm worried about him."

"Worried? Why?"

"Oh—there's risk in Jerry's business, you know."

"I don't know anything of the sort. Why should there be?"

"We won't go into that. The fact remains that Jerry Delaney arrived at Barstow a week ago last Wednesday morning, and shortly afterward he disappeared off the face of the earth."

A startled look came into the woman's eyes. "You don't think he's had an—an accident?"

"I'm very much afraid he has. You know the sort Jerry was. Reckless—"

The woman was silent for a moment. "I know," she nodded. "Such a temper. These red-headed Irishmen—"

"Precisely," said Eden, a little too soon.

The green eyes of Miss Norma Fitzgerald narrowed. "Knew Jerry at McGuire's, you say."

"Of course."

She stood up. "And since when has he had red hair?" Her friendly manner was gone. "I was thinking only last night—I saw a cop at the corner of Sixth and Hill— such a handsome boy. You certainly got fine-looking fellows on your force out here."

"What are you talking about?" demanded Eden.

"Go peddle your papers," advised Miss Fitzgerald. "If Jerry Delaney's in trouble, I don't hold with it, but I'm not tipping anything off. A friend's a friend."

"You've got me all wrong," protested Eden.

"Oh, no, I haven't. I've got you all right—and you can find Jerry without any help from me. As a matter of fact, I haven't any idea where he is, and that's the truth. Now run along."

Eden stood up. "Anyhow, I did enjoy your singing," he smiled.

"Yeah. Such nice cops—and so gallant. Well, listen in any time—the radio's open to all."

Bob Eden went glumly back to Pershing Square. He dropped down on the bench beside Chan.

"Luck was poor," remarked the detective. "I see it in your face."

"You don't know the half of it," returned the boy. He related what had happened. "I certainly made a bloomer of it," he finished. "She called me a cop, but she flattered me. The kindergarten class of rookies would disown me."

"Stop the worry," advised Chan. "Woman a little too smart, that is all."

"That's enough," Eden answered. "After this, you officiate. As a detective, I'm a great little jeweler."

They dined at a hotel, and took the five-thirty train to Barstow. As they sped on through the gathering dusk, Bob Eden looked at his companion.

"Well, it's over, Charlie," he said. "The day from which we hoped for so much. And what have we gained? Nothing. Am I right?"

"Pretty close to right," admitted Chan.

"I tell you, Charlie, we can't go on. Our position is hopeless. We'll have to go to the sheriff—"

"With what? Pardon that I interrupt. But realize, please, that all our evidence is hazy, like flowers seen in a pool. Madden is big man, his word law to many." The train paused at a station. "We go to sheriff with queer talk—a dead parrot, tale of a desert rat, half-blind and maybe crazy, suit-case in attic filled with old clothes. Can we prove famous man guilty of murder on such foolish grounds? Where is body? Few policemen alive who would not laugh at us—"

Chan broke off suddenly, and Eden followed his gaze. In the aisle of the car stood Captain Bliss of the Homicide Squad, staring at them.

Eden's heart sank. The captain's little eyes slowly took in every detail of Chan's attire, then were turned for a moment on the boy. Without a sign, he turned about and went down the aisle and into the car behind.

"Good night!" said Eden.

Chan shrugged. "Fret no longer," he remarked. "We need not go to sheriff—sheriff will come to us. Our time is brief at Madden's ranch. Poor old Ah Kim may yet be arrested for the murder of Louie Wong."

CHAPTER XIX

THE VOICE ON THE AIR

THEY arrived at Barstow at half past ten, and Bob Eden announced his intention of stopping for the night at the station hotel. After a brief talk with the man at the ticket-window, Chan rejoined him.

"I take room that neighbors the one occupied by you," he said. "Next train for Eldorado leaves at five o'clock in morning. I am on her when she goes. Much better you await subsequent train at eleven-ten. Not so good if we return to ranch like Siamese twins. Soon enough that blundering Bliss will reveal our connection."

"Suit yourself, Charlie," returned Eden. "If you've got the strength of character to get up and take a five o'clock train, you'll have my best wishes. And those wishes, I may add, will be extended in my sleep."

Chan got his suit-case from the parcel-room and they went up-stairs. But Eden did not at once prepare for bed. Instead he sat down, his head in his hands, and tried to think.

The door between the two rooms opened suddenly, and Chan stood on the threshold. He held in his hand a luminous string of pearls.

"Just to reassure," he smiled. "The Phillimore fortune is still safe."

He laid the pearls on the table, under a brilliant light. Bob Eden reached over, and thoughtfully ran them through his fingers.

"Lovely, aren't they?" he said. "Look here, Charlie— you and I must have a frank talk." Chan nodded. "Tell me, and tell me the truth—have you got the faintest glimmering as to what's doing out at Madden's ranch?"

"One recent day," said Chan, "I thought—"

"Yes?"

"But I was wrong."

"Precisely. I know it's a tough thing for a detective to admit, but you're absolutely stumped, aren't you?"

"You have stumped feeling yourself, maybe—"

"All right—I'll answer the question for you. You are. You're up against it, and we can't go on. To-morrow afternoon I come back to the ranch. I'm supposed to have seen Draycott—more lies, more deception. I'm sick of it, and besides, something tells me it won't work any longer. No, Charlie—we're at the zero hour. We've got to give up the pearls."

Chan's face saddened. "Please do not say so," he pleaded. "At any moment—"

"I know—you want more time. Your professional pride is touched. I can understand, and I'm sorry."

"Just a few hours," suggested Chan.

Eden looked for a long moment at the kindly face of the Chinese. He shook his head. "It's not only me—it's Bliss. Bliss will come thumping in presently. We're at the end of our rope. I'll make one last concession—I'll give you until eight o'clock to-morrow night. That's provided Bliss doesn't show up in the interval. Do you agree?"

"I must," said Chan.

"Very good. You'll have all day to-morrow. When I come back, I won't bother with that bunk about Draycott. I'll simply say: 'Mr. Madden, the pearls will be here at eight o'clock.' At that hour, if nothing has happened, we'll hand them over and go. On our way home we'll put our story before the sheriff, and if he laughs at us, we've at least done our duty." Eden sighed with relief. He stood up. "Thank heaven, that's settled."

Gloomily Chan picked up the pearls. "Not happy position for me," he said, "that I must come to this mainland and be sunk in bafflement." His face brightened. "But another day. Much may happen."

Eden patted his broad back. "Lord knows I wish you luck," he said. "Good night."

When Eden awakened to consciousness the following morning, the sun was gleaming on the tracks outside his window. He took the train for Eldorado and dropped in at Holley's office.

"Hello," said the editor. "Back at last, eh? Your little pal is keener on the job than you are. He went through here early this morning."

"Oh, Chan's ambitious," Eden replied. "You saw him, did you?"

"Yes." Holley nodded toward a suit-case in the corner. "He left his regular clothes with me. Expects to put 'em on in a day or two, I gather."

"Probably going to wear them to jail," replied Eden glumly. "I suppose he told you about Bliss."

"He did. And I'm afraid it means trouble."

"I'm sure it does. As you probably know, we dug up very little down the valley."

Holley nodded. "Yes—and what you did dig up was mostly in support of my blackmail theory. Something has happened here, too, that goes to confirm my suspicions."

"What's that?"

"Madden's New York office has arranged to send him another fifty thousand, through the bank here. I was just talking to the president. He doesn't think he can produce all that in cash before to-morrow, and Madden has agreed to wait."

Eden considered. "No doubt your theory's the right one. The old boy's being blackmailed. Though Chan has made a rather good suggestion—he thinks Madden may be getting this money together—"

"I know—he told me. But that doesn't explain Shaky Phil and the professor. No, I prefer my version. Though I must admit it's the most appalling puzzle—"

"I'll say it is," Eden replied. "And to my mind we've done all that's humanly possible to solve it. I'm handing over the pearls to-night. I presume Chan told you that?"

Holley nodded. "Yes—you're breaking his heart. But from your view-point, you're absolutely right. There's a limit to everything, and you seem to have reached it. However, I'm praying something happens before to-night."

"So am I," said Eden. "If it doesn't, I don't see how I can bring myself to—but doggone it! There's Madame Jordan. It's nothing to her that Madden's killed a man."

"It's been a difficult position for you, my boy," Holley replied. "You've handled it well. I'll pray my hardest—and I did hear once of a newspaper man whose prayers were answered. But that was years ago."

Eden stood up. "I must get back to the ranch. Seen Paula Wendell to-day?"

"Saw her at breakfast down at the Oasis. She was on the point of starting for the Petticoat Mine." Holley smiled. "But don't worry—I'll take you out to Madden's."

"No, you won't. I'll hire a car—"

"Forget it. Paper's off the press now, and I'm at an even looser end than usual. Come along."

Once more Horace Greeley carried them up the rough road between the hills. As they rattled down to the blazing floor of the desert, the editor yawned.

"I didn't sleep much last night," he explained.

"Thinking about Jerry Delaney?" asked the boy.

Holley shook his head. "No—something has happened—something that concerns me alone. That interview with Madden has inspired my old friend in New York to offer me a job there—a mighty good job. Yesterday afternoon I had a doctor in Eldorado look me over—and he told me I could go."

"That's great!" Eden cried. "I'm mighty happy for your sake."

An odd look had come into Holley's eyes. "Yes," he said, "the prison door swings open, after all these years. I've dreamed of this moment, longed for it—and now—"

"What?"

"The prisoner hesitates. He's frightened at the thought of leaving his nice quiet cell. New York! Not the old New York I knew. Could I tackle it again, and win? I wonder."

"Nonsense," Eden answered. "Of course you could."

A determined look passed over Holley's face. "I'll try it," he said. "I'll go. Why the devil should I throw

my life away out here? Yes—I'll tackle Park Row
again."

He left Eden at the ranch. The boy went at once to
his room, and as soon as he had freshened up a bit,
stepped into the patio. Ah Kim passed.

"Anything new?" whispered Eden.

"Thorn and Gamble away all day in big car," the
Chinese replied. "Nothing more." It was obvious he
was still sunk in bafflement.

In the living-room Eden found the millionaire sitting
aimless and lonely. Madden perked up at the boy's arrival. "Back safe, eh?" he said. "Did you find Draycott?
You can speak out. We're alone here."

Eden dropped into a chair. "It's all set, sir. I'll give
you the Phillimore pearls at eight o'clock to-night."

"Where?"

"Here at the ranch."

Madden frowned. "I'd rather it had been at Eldorado.
You mean Draycott's coming here—"

"No, I don't. I'll have the pearls at eight o'clock, and
I'll give them to you. If you want the transaction kept
private, that can be arranged."

"Good." Madden looked at him. "Maybe you've got
them now?" he suggested.

"No. But I'll have them at eight."

"Well, I'm certainly glad to hear it," Madden replied.
"But I want to tell you right here that if you're stalling
again—"

"What do you mean—stalling?"

"You heard me. Do you think I'm a fool. Ever since
you came you've been stalling about that necklace.
Haven't you?"

Eden hesitated. The moment had come for a bit of frankness, it seemed. "I have," he admitted.

"Why?"

"Because, Mr. Madden, I thought there was something wrong here."

"Why did you think that?"

"Before I tell you—what made you change your mind in the first place? In San Francisco you wanted the necklace delivered in New York. Why did you switch to Southern California?"

"A simple reason," Madden replied. "I thought up there that my daughter was going east with me. Her plans are altered—she's going at once to Pasadena for the balance of the season. And I propose to put the necklace in safety deposit there for her use when she wants it."

"I met your daughter in San Francisco," Eden said. "She's a very charming girl."

Madden looked at him keenly. "You think so, do you?"

"I do. I presume she is still in Denver?"

For a moment Madden was silent, regarding him. "No," he admitted finally, "she is not in Denver now."

"Indeed. If you don't mind telling me—"

"She is in Los Angeles, visiting friends."

At this surprising information, Eden's eyes opened wide.

"How long has she been there?" he inquired.

"Since last Tuesday," Madden answered. "I think it was Tuesday—I got a wire saying she was coming here. I didn't want her here, for certain reasons, so I sent Thorn in to meet her, with instructions to take her back to Barstow and put her on the Los Angeles train."

Eden thought fast. Barstow was about the proper distance away to account for the mileage on the big car. But where was the red clay on station platforms hereabouts?

"You're certain she reached Los Angeles safely?" he asked.

"Of course. I saw her there on Wednesday. Now, I've answered all your questions. It's your turn. Why did you think something was wrong here?"

"What has become of Shaky Phil Maydorf?" countered Eden.

"Who?"

"Shaky Phil—the lad who called himself McCallum, and who won forty-seven dollars from me at poker here the other night?"

"You mean his name was really Maydorf?" inquired Madden with interest.

"I certainly do. I had some experience with Maydorf in San Francisco."

"In what way?"

"He acted as though he was trying to annex the Phillimore pearls."

Madden's face was purple again. "Is that so? Would you mind telling me about it?"

"Not at all," replied Eden. He narrated Maydorf's activities at the pier, but failed to mention the connection with Louie Wong.

"Why didn't you tell me sooner?" demanded Madden.

"Because I thought you knew it. I still think so."

"You're crazy."

"Maybe. We won't go into that. But when I saw Maydorf down here, it was natural to suspect something was wrong. I'm not convinced yet that it isn't. Why not go back to the original plan and deliver the pearls in New York?"

Madden shook his head. "No. I've set out to get them here, and I'll go through with it. Anybody will tell you I'm no quitter."

"Then at least tell me what the trouble is."

"There is no trouble," Madden replied. "At least, none that I can't handle myself. It's my own affair. I've bought the pearls and I want them. I give you my word that you'll be paid, which is all that need concern you."

"Mr. Madden," said the boy, "I'm not blind. You're in a jam of some sort, and I'd like to help you."

Madden turned, and his tired harassed face was ample proof of Eden's statement. "I'll get out of it," he said. "I've got out of worse holes. I thank you for your kind intentions, but don't you worry about me. At eight o'clock then—I'm relying on you. Now if you'll excuse me, I think I'll lie down. I anticipate a rather busy evening."

He went from the room, and Bob Eden stared after him, perplexed and at sea. Had he gone too far with the millionaire—told him too much? And how about this news of Evelyn Madden? Could it be true? Was she really in Los Angeles? It sounded plausible enough, and her father's manner when he spoke of her seemed frankness itself.

Oh, well—the heat on the desert was now a tangible thing, wave on wave of filmy haze. Eden was weary with his many problems. He followed Madden's example, and slept the afternoon away.

When he rose, the sun was sinking and the cool night coming on. He heard Gamble in the bathroom. Gamble—

who was Gamble? Why was he allowed to remain on Madden's ranch?

In the patio, the boy had a few whispered words with Ah Kim, telling him the news about Evelyn Madden.

"Thorn and professor home now," the detective said. "I notice mileage—thirty-nine, as before. And bits of red clay on floor of car."

Eden shook his head. "Time is passing," he remarked.

Chan shrugged. "If I could arrest it, I would do so," he replied.

At the dinner table, Professor Gamble was amiability personified.

"Well, well, Mr. Eden, we're glad to have you back with us. Sorry to have you miss any of this desert air. Your business—if I may presume—your business prospered?"

"Sure did," smiled Eden. "And how does yours go?"

The professor looked at him quickly. "I—er—I am happy to say I have had a most gratifying day. I found the very rat I was looking for."

"Fine for you, but hard on the rat," said Eden, and the dinner proceeded in silence.

When they rose from the table, Madden lighted a cigar and dropped into his favorite chair before the fire. Gamble sat down with a magazine beside a lamp. Eden took out a packet of cigarettes, lighted one, wandered about. Thorn also selected a magazine. The big clock struck the hour of seven, and then an air of almost intolerable quiet settled over the room.

Eden paused at the radio. "Never could see the sense of these things until I came down here," he explained to Madden. "I realize now there are times when even a lecture on the habits of the hookworm may seem enchant‹ing. How about a bedtime story for the kiddies?"

He tuned in. Ah Kim entered and busied himself at the table. The sharp voice of an announcer in Los Angeles filled the room:

"—next number on our program—Miss Norma Fitzgerald, who is appearing in the musical show at the Mason, will sing a couple of selections—"

Madden leaned forward and tapped the ash from his cigar. Thorn and Gamble looked up with languid interest.

"Hello, folks," came the voice of the woman Bob Eden had talked with the day before. "Here I am again. And right at the start I want to thank all you good friends for the loads and loads of letters I've had since I went on the air out here. I found a lovely bunch at the studio to-night. I haven't had time to read them all, but I want to tell Sadie French, if she's listening in, that I was glad to know she's in Santa Monica, and I'll sure call her up. Another letter that brought me happiness was from my old pal, Jerry Delaney—"

Eden's heart stopped beating. Madden leaned forward, Thorn's mouth opened and stayed that way, and the eyes of the professor narrowed. Ah Kim, at the table, worked without a sound.

"I've been a little worried about Jerry," the woman went on, "and it was great to know that he's alive and well. I'm looking forward to seeing him soon. Now I must go on with my program, because I'm due at the theater in half an hour. I hope you good people will all come and see us, for we've certainly got a dandy little show, and—"

"Oh, shut the confounded thing off," said Madden.

"Advertising, nine-tenths of these radio programs. Makes me sick."

Norma Fitzgerald had burst into song, and Bob Eden shut the confounded thing off. A long look passed between him and Ah Kim. A voice had come to the desert, come over the bare brown hills and the dreary miles of sage-brush and sand—a voice that said Jerry Delaney was alive and well. Alive and well—and all their fine theories came crashing down.

The man Madden killed was not Jerry Delaney! Then whose was the voice calling for help that tragic night at the ranch? Who uttered the cry that was heard and echoed by Tony, the Chinese parrot?

CHAPTER XX

A H KIM, carrying a heavy tray of dishes, left the room. Madden leaned back at ease in his chair, his eyes closed, and blew thick rings of smoke toward the ceiling. The professor and Thorn resumed their placid reading, one on each side of the lamp. A touching scene of domestic peace.

But Bob Eden did not share that peace. His heart was beating fast—his mind was dazed. He rose and slipped quietly outdoors. In the cookhouse Ah Kim was at the sink, busily washing dishes. To look at the impassive face of the Chinese no one would have guessed that this was not his regular employment.

"Charlie," said Eden softly.

Chan hastily dried his hands and came to the door. "Humbly begging pardon, do not come in here." He led the way to the shadows beside the barn. "What are trouble now?" he asked gently.

"Trouble!" said Eden. "You heard, didn't you? We've been on the wrong track entirely. Jerry Delaney is alive and well."

"Most interesting, to be sure," admitted Chan.

"Interesting! Say—what are you made of, anyhow?"

280

Chan's calm was a bit disturbing. "Our theory blows up completely, and you—"

"Old habit of theories," said Chan. "Not the first to shatter in my countenance. Pardon me if I fail to experience thrill like you."

"But what shall we do now?"

"What should we do? We hand over pearls. You have made foolish promise, which I heartily rebuked. Nothing to do but carry out."

"And go away without learning what happened here! I don't see how I can—"

"What is to be, will be. The words of the infinitely wise Kong Fu Tse—"

"But listen, Charlie—have you thought of this? Perhaps nothing happened. Maybe we've been on a false trail from the start—"

A little car came tearing down the road, and they heard it stop with a wild shriek of the brakes before the ranch. They hurried round the house. The moon was low and the scene in semi-darkness. A familiar figure alighted and without pausing to open the gate, leaped over it. Eden ran forward.

"Hello, Holley," he said.

Holley turned suddenly.

"Good lord—you scared me. But you're the man I'm looking for." He was panting, obviously excited.

"What's wrong?" Eden asked.

"I don't know. But I'm worried. Paula Wendell—"

Eden's heart sank. "What about Paula Wendell?"

"You haven't heard from her—or seen her?"

"No, of course not."

"Well, she never came back from the Petticoat Mine.

It's only a short run up there, and she left just after breakfast. She should have been back long ago. She promised to have dinner with me, and we were going to see the picture at the theater to-night. It's one she's particularly interested in."

Eden was moving toward the road. "Come along—in heaven's name—hurry—"

Chan stepped forward. Something gleamed in his hand. "My automatic," he explained. "I rescued it from suit-case this morning. Take it with you—"

"I won't need that," said Eden. "Keep it. You may have use for it—"

"I humbly beg of you—"

"Thanks, Charlie. I don't want it. All right, Holley—"

"The pearls," suggested Chan.

"Oh, I'll be back by eight. This is more important—"

As he climbed into the flivver by Holley's side, Eden saw the front door of the ranch house open, and the huge figure of Madden framed in the doorway.

"Hey!" cried the millionaire.

"Hey yourself," muttered Eden. The editor was backing his car, and with amazing speed he swung it round. They were off down the road, the throttle wide open.

"What could have happened?" Eden asked.

"I don't know. It's a dangerous place, that old mine. shafts sunk all over—the mouths of some of them hidden by underbrush. Shafts several hundred feet deep—"

"Faster," pleaded Eden.

"Going the limit now," Holley replied. "Madden seemed interested in your departure, didn't he? I take it you haven't given him the pearls."

"No. Something new broke to-night." Eden told of the voice over the radio. "Ever strike you that we may have been cuckoo from the start? No one even slightly damaged at the ranch, after all?"

"Quite possible," the editor admitted.

"Well, that can wait. It's Paula Wendell now."

Another car was coming toward them with reckless speed. Holley swung out, and the two cars grazed in passing.

"Who was that?" wondered Eden.

"A taxi from the station," Holley returned. "I recognized the driver. There was some one in the back seat."

"I know," said Eden. "Some one headed for Madden's ranch, perhaps."

"Perhaps," agreed Holley. He turned off the main road into the perilous, half-obliterated highway that led to the long-abandoned mine. "Have to go slower, I'm afraid," he said.

"Oh, hit it up," urged Eden. "You can't hurt old Horace Greeley." Holley again threw the throttle wide, and the front wheel on the left coming at that moment in violent contact with a rock, their heads nearly pierced the top of the car.

"It's all wrong, Holley," remarked Eden with feeling.

"What's all wrong?"

"A pretty, charming girl like Paula Wendell running about alone in this desert country. Why in heaven's name doesn't somebody marry her and take her away from it?"

"Not a chance," replied Holley. "She hasn't any use for marriage. 'The last resort of feeble minds' is what she calls it."

"Is that so?"

"Never coop her up in a kitchenette, she told me, after the life of freedom she's enjoyed."

"Then why did she go and get engaged to this guy?"

"What guy?"

"Wilbur—or whatever his name is. The lad who gave her the ring."

Holley laughed—then was silent for a minute. "I don't suppose she'll like it," he said at last, "but I'm going to tell you anyhow. It would be a pity if you didn't find out. That emerald is an old one that belonged to her mother. She's had it put in a more modern setting, and she wears it as a sort of protection."

"Protection?"

"Yes. So every mush-head she meet's won't pester her to marry him."

"Oh," said Eden. A long silence. "Is that the way she characterizes me?" asked the boy finally.

"How?"

"As a mush-head."

"Oh, no. She said you had the same ideas on marriage that she had. Refreshing to meet a sensible man like you, is the way she put it." Another long silence. "What's on your mind?" asked the editor.

"Plenty," said Eden grimly. "I suppose, at my age, it's still possible to make over a wasted life?"

"It ought to be," Holley assured him.

"I've been acting like a fool. Going to give good old dad the surprise of his life when I get home. Take over the business, like he's wanted me to, and work hard. So far, I haven't known what I wanted. Been as weak and vacillating as a—a woman."

"Some simile," replied Holley. "I don't know that I

ever heard a worse one. Show me the woman who doesn't know what she wants—and knowing, fails to go after it."

"Oh, well—you get what I mean. How much farther is it?"

"We're getting there. Five miles more."

"Gad—I hope nothing's happened to her."

They rattled on, closer and closer to the low hills, brick red under the rays of the slowly rising moon. The road entered a narrow cañon, it almost disappeared, but like a homing thing Horace Greeley followed it intuitively.

"Got a flashlight?" Eden inquired.

"Yes. Why?"

"Stop a minute, and let me have it. I've an idea."

He descended with the light, and carefully examined the road ahead. "She's been along here," he announced. "That's the tread of her tires—I'd know it anywhere—I changed one of them for her. She's—she's up there somewhere, too. The car has been this way but once."

He leaped back beside Holley, and the flivver sped on, round hairpin turns, and along the edge of a precipice. Presently it turned a final corner, and before them, nestled in the hills, was the ghost city of Petticoat Mine.

Bob Eden caught his breath. Under the friendly moon lay the remnants of a town, here a chimney and there a wall, street after street of houses crumbled now to dust. Once the mine had boomed and the crowd had come, they had built their homes here where the shafts sank deep, silver had fallen in price and the crowd had gone, leaving Petticoat Mine to the most deadly bombardment of all, the patient silent bombardment of the empty years.

They rode down Main Street, weaving in and out among black gaping holes that might have been made by bursting shells. Between the cracks of the sidewalks, thronged once on a Saturday night, grew patches of pale green basket grass. Of the "business blocks" but two remained, and one of these was listing with the wind.

"Cheery sight," remarked Eden.

"The building that's on the verge of toppling is the old Silver Star Saloon," said Holley. "The other one—it never will topple. They built it of stone—built it to stand—and they needed it, too, I guess. That's the old jail."

"The jail," Eden repeated.

Holley's voice grew cautious. "Is that a light in the Silver Star?"

"Seems to be," Eden answered. "Look here—we're at rather a disadvantage—unarmed, you know. I'll just stow away in the tonneau, and appear when needed. The element of surprise may make up for our lack of a weapon."

"Good idea," agreed Holley, and Eden climbed into the rear of the car and hid himself. They stopped before the Silver Star. A tall man appeared suddenly in the doorway, and walked briskly up to the flivver.

"Well, what do you want?" he asked, and Bob Eden thrilled to hear again the thin high voice of Shaky Phil Maydorf.

"Hello, stranger," said Holley. "This is a surprise. I thought old Petticoat was deserted."

"Company's thinking of opening up the mine soon," returned Maydorf. "I'm here to do a little assaying."

"Find anything?" inquired Holley casually.

"The silver's pretty well worked out. But there's copper in those hills to the left. You're a long way off the main road."

"I know that. I'm looking for a young woman who came up here this morning. Maybe you saw her."

"There hasn't been any one here for a week, except me."

"Really? Well, you may be mistaken. If you don't mind, I'll have a look round—"

"And if I do mind?" snarled Shaky Phil.

"Why should you—"

"I do. I'm alone here and I'm not taking any chances. You swing that car of yours around—"

"Now, wait a minute," said Holley. "Put away that gun. I come as a friend—"

"Yeah. Well, as a friend, you turn and beat it. Understand." He was close to the car. "I tell you there's nobody here—"

He stopped as a figure rose suddenly from the tonneau and fell upon him. The gun exploded, but harmlessly into the road, for Bob Eden was bearing down upon it, hard.

For a brief moment, there on that deserted street before the Silver Star, the two struggled desperately. Shaky Phil was no longer young, but he offered a spirited resistance. However, it was not prolonged, and by the time Holley had alighted, Bob Eden was on top and held Maydorf's weapon in his hand.

"Get up," the boy directed. "And lead the way. Give me your keys. There's a brand-new lock on that jail door, and we have a yearning to see what's inside." Shaky Phil rose to his feet and looked helplessly about. "Hurry!" cried Eden. "I've been longing to meet you again, and I don't feel any too gentle. There's that forty-seven dollars—to say nothing of all the trouble you put me to the night the *President Pierce* docked in San Francisco."

"There's nothing in the jail," said Maydorf. "I haven't got the key—"

"Go through him, Holley," suggested the boy.

A quick search produced a bunch of keys, and Eden, taking them, handed Holley the gun. "I give old Shaky Phil into your keeping. If he tries to run, shoot him down like a rabbit."

He took the flashlight from the car and, going over, unlocked the outer door of the jail. Stepping inside, he found himself in what had once been a sort of office. The moonlight pouring in from the street fell upon a dusty desk and chair, an old safe, and a shelf with a few tattered books. On the desk lay a newspaper. He flashed his light on the date—only a week old.

At the rear were two heavy doors, both with new locks. Searching among his keys, he unlocked the one at the left. In a small, cell-like room with high barred windows his flashlight revealed the tall figure of a girl. With no great surprise he recognized Evelyn Madden. She came toward him swiftly. "Bob Eden!" she cried, and then, her old haughtiness gone, she burst into tears.

"There—there," said Eden. "You're all right now." Another girl appeared suddenly in the doorway—Paula Wendell, bright and smiling.

"Hello," she remarked calmly. "I rather thought you'd come along."

"Thanks for the ad," replied Eden. "Say, you might get hurt running about like this. What happened, anyhow?"

"Nothing much. I came up to look round and he"—she nodded to Shaky Phil in the moonlit street—"told me I couldn't. I argued it with him, and ended up in here.

He said I'd have to stay overnight. He was polite, but firm."

"Lucky for him he was polite," remarked Eden grimly. He took the arm of Evelyn Madden. "Come along," he said gently. "I guess we're through here—"

He stopped. Some one was hammering on the inside of the second door. Amazed, the boy looked toward Paula Wendell.

She nodded. "Unlock it," she told him.

He unfastened the door and swinging it open, peered inside. In the semi-darkness he saw the dim figure of a man.

Eden gasped, and fell back against the desk for support.

"Ghost city!" he cried. "Well, that's what it is, all right."

CHAPTER XXI

END OF THE POSTMAN'S JOURNEY

IF BOB EDEN had known the identity of the passenger in the taxi that he and Holley passed on their way to the mine, it is possible that, despite his concern for Paula Wendell, he would have turned back to Madden's ranch. But he drove on unknowing; nor did the passenger, though he stared with interest at the passing flivver, recognize Eden. The car from the Eldorado station went on its appointed way, and finally drew up before the ranch house.

The driver alighted and was fumbling with the gate, when his fare leaped to the ground.

"Never mind that," he said. "I'll leave you here. How much do I owe you?" He was a plump little man, about thirty-five years old, attired in the height of fashion and with a pompous manner. The driver named a sum and, paying him off, the passenger entered the yard. Walking importantly up to the front door of the house, he knocked loudly.

Madden, talking with Thorn and Gamble by the fire, looked up in annoyance. "Now who the devil—" he began. Thorn went over and opened the door. The plump little man at once pushed his way inside.

"I'm looking for Mr. P. J. Madden," he announced.

The millionaire rose. "All right—I'm Madden. What do you want?"

The stranger shook hands. "Glad to meet you, Mr. Madden. My name is Victor Jordan, and I'm one of the owners of those pearls you bought in San Francisco."

A delighted smile spread over Madden's face. "Oh— I'm glad to see you," he said. "Mr. Eden told me you were coming—"

"How could he?" demanded Victor. "He didn't know it himself."

"Well, he didn't mention you. But he informed me the pearls would be here at eight o'clock—"

Victor stared. "Be here at eight o'clock?" he repeated. "Say, just what has Bob Eden been up to down here, anyhow? The pearls left San Francisco a week ago, when Eden did."

"What!" Purple again in Madden's face. "He had them all the time! Why, the young scoundrel! I'll break him in two for this. I'll wring his neck—" He stopped. "But he's gone. I just saw him driving away."

"Really?" returned Victor. "Well, that may not be so serious as it looks. When I say the pearls left San Francisco with Eden, I don't mean he was carrying them. Charlie had them."

"Charlie who?"

"Why, Charlie Chan, of the Honolulu Police. The man who brought them from Hawaii."

Madden was thoughtful. "Chan—a Chinaman?"

"Of course. He's here, too, isn't he? I understood he was."

A wicked light came into Madden's eyes. "Yes, he's here. You think he still has the pearls?"

"I'm sure he has. In a money-belt about his waist,
Get him here and I'll order him to hand them over at
once."

"Fine—fine!" chuckled Madden. "If you'll step into
this room for a moment, Mr. Jordan, I'll call you presently."

"Yes, sir—of course," agreed Victor, who was always
polite to the rich. Madden led him by the inside passage
to his bedroom. When the millionaire returned, his spirits
were high.

"Bit of luck, this is," he remarked. "And to think
that blooming cook—" He went to the door leading on
to the patio, and called loudly, "Ah Kim!"

The Chinese shuffled in. He looked at Madden
blankly. "Wha's matta, boss?" he inquired.

"I want to have a little talk with you." Madden's
manner was genial, even kindly. "Where did you work
before you came here?"

"Get 'um woik all place, boss. Maybe lay sticks on
gloun' foah lailload—"

"What town—what town did you work in last?"

"No got 'um town, boss. Jus' outdoahs no place, laying sticks—"

"You mean you were laying ties for the railroad on
the desert?"

"Yes, boss. You light now."

Madden leaned back, and put his thumbs in the arm-
holes of his vest. "Ah Kim—you're a damned liar," he
said.

"Wha's matta, boss?"

"I'll show you what's the matter. I don't know what
your game here has been, but it's all over now." Madden

rose and stepped to the door. "Come in, sir," he called, and Victor Jordan strode into the room. Chan's eyes narrowed.

"Charlie, what is all this nonsense?" demanded Victor. "What are you doing in that melodramatic outfit?"

Chan did not answer. Madden laughed. "All over, as I told you, Charlie—if that's your name. This is Mr. Jordan, one of the owners of those pearls you're carrying in your money-belt."

Chan shrugged. "Mr. Jordan juggles truth," he replied, dropping his dialect with a sigh of relief. "He has no claim on pearls. They are property of his mother, to whom I give promise I would guard them with life."

"See here, Charlie," cried Victor angrily, "don't tell me I lie. I'm sick and tired of this delay down here, and I've come with my mother's authority to put an end to it. If you don't believe me, read that."

He handed over a brief note in Madame Jordan's old-fashioned script. Chan read it. "One only answer," he remarked. "I must release the pearls." He glanced toward the clock, ticking busily by the patio window. "Though I am much preferring to wait Mr. Eden's come back—"

"Never mind Eden," said Victor. "Produce that necklace."

Chan bowed and turning, fumbled for a moment at his waist. The Phillimore necklace was in his hand.

Madden took it eagerly. "At last," he said.

Gamble was staring over his shoulder. "Beautiful," murmured the professor.

"One minute," said Chan. "A receipt, if you will be so kind."

Madden nodded, and sat at his desk. "I got one ready this afternoon. Just have to sign it." He laid the pearls on the blotter, and took a typewritten sheet from the top drawer. Slowly he wrote his name. "Mr. Jordan," he was saying, "I'm deeply grateful to you for coming down here and ending this. Now that it's settled, I'm leaving at once—" He offered the receipt to Chan.

A strange look had come into the usually impassive eyes of Charlie Chan. He reached out toward the sheet of paper offered him, then with the speed of a tiger, he snatched for the pearls. Madden snatched, too, but he was a little late. The necklace disappeared into Chan's voluminous sleeve.

"What's this?" bellowed Madden, on his feet. "Why, you crazy—"

"Hush," said Chan. "I will retain the pearls."

"You will, will you?" Madden whipped out a pistol. "We'll see about that—"

There was a loud report, and a flash of fire—but it did not come from Madden's gun. It came from the silken sleeve of Charlie Chan. Madden's weapon clattered to the floor, and there was blood on his hand.

"Do not stoop!" warned Chan, and his voice was suddenly high and shrill. "Postman has been on such long walk, but now at last he has reached journey's end. Do not stoop, or I put bullet in somewhat valuable head!"

"Charlie—are you mad?" cried Victor.

"Not very," smiled Chan. "Kindly favor me by backing away, Mr. Madden." He picked up the pistol from the floor—Bill Hart's present, it seemed to be. "Very nice gun, I use it now." Swinging Madden round, he searched him, then placed a chair in the center of the

room. "Be seated here, if you will so far condescend—"
he said.

"The hell I will," cried Madden.

"Recline!" said Chan.

The great Madden looked at him a second, then
dropped sullenly down upon the chair. "Mr. Gamble,"
called Chan. He ran over the slim person of the professor. "You have left pretty little weapon in room.
That is good. This will be your chair. And not to forget
Mr. Thorn, also unarmed. Comfortable chair for you,
too." He backed away, facing them. "Victor, I make
humble suggestion that you add yourself to group. You
are plenty foolish boy, always. I remember—in Honolulu—" His tone hardened. "Sit quickly, or I puncture
you and lift big load from mother's mind!"

He drew up a chair between them and the exhibition
of guns on the wall. "I also will venture to recline," he
announced. He glanced at the clock. "Our wait may be
a long one. Mr. Thorn, another suggestion occurs. Take
handkerchief and bind up wounded hand of chief."

Thorn produced a handkerchief and Madden held out
his hand. "What the devil are we waiting for?" snarled
the millionaire.

"We await come back of Mr. Bob Eden," replied
Chan. "I am having much to impart when he arrives."

Thorn completed his act of mercy, and slunk back to
his chair. The tall clock by the patio windows ticked on.
With the patience characteristic of his race Chan sat,
staring at his odd assortment of captives. Fifteen minutes passed, a half-hour, the minute hand began its slow
advance toward the hour of nine.

Victor Jordan shifted uneasily in his chair. Such disrespect to a man worth millions! "You're clear out of your mind, Charlie," he protested.

"Maybe," admitted Chan. "We wait and see."

Presently a car rattled into the yard. Chan nodded. "Long wait nearly over," he announced. "Now Mr. Eden comes."

His expression altered as a knock sounded on the door. It was pushed open and a man strode bruskly in. A stocky, red-faced, determined man—Captain Bliss of the Homicide Squad. After him came another, a lean wiry individual in a two-quart hat. They stood amazed at the scene before them.

Madden leaped to his feet. "Captain Bliss. By gad, I'm delighted to see you. You're just in time."

"What's all this?" inquired the lean man.

"Mr. Madden," said Bliss, "I've brought along Harley Cox, Sheriff of the County. I guess you need us here."

"We sure do," replied Madden. "This Chinaman has gone crazy. Take that gun away from him and put him under arrest."

The sheriff stepped up to Charlie Chan. "Give me the firearms, John," he ordered. "You know what that means—a Chinaman with a gun in California. Deportation. Good lord—he's got two of them."

"Sheriff," said Charlie with dignity. "Permit me the honor that I introduce myself. I am Detective-Sergeant Chan, of the Honolulu Police."

The sheriff laughed. "You don't say. Well, I'm the Queen of Sheba. Are you going to give me that other gun, or do you want a charge of resisting an officer?"

"I do not resist," said Chan. He gave up his own weapon. "I only call to your attention I am fellow policeman, and I yearn to save you from an error you will have bitter cause to regret."

"I'll take the chance. Now, what's going on here?" The sheriff turned to Madden. "We came about that Louie Wong killing. Bliss saw this Chinaman on a train last night with the fellow named Eden, all dolled up in regular clothes and as chummy as a brother."

"You're on the right trail now, Sheriff," Madden assured him. "There's no doubt he killed Louie. And just at present he has somewhere about him a string of pearls belonging to me. Please take them away from him."

"Sure, Mr. Madden," replied the sheriff. He advanced to make a search, but Chan forestalled him. He handed him the necklace.

"I give it to your keeping," he said. "You are officer of law and responsible. Attend your step."

Cox regarded the pearls. "Some string, ain't it? Kinda pretty, Mr. Madden. You say it belongs to you?"

"It certainly does—"

"Sheriff," pleaded Charlie, with a glance at the clock, "if I may make humble suggestion, go slow. You will kick yourself angrily over vast expanse of desert should you make blunder now."

"But if Mr. Madden says these pearls are his—"

"They are," said Madden. "I bought them from a jeweler named Eden in San Francisco ten days ago. They belonged to the mother of Mr. Jordan here."

"That's quite correct," admitted Victor.

"It's enough for me," remarked the sheriff.

"I tell you I am of the Honolulu Police—" protested Chan.

"Maybe so, but do you think I'd take your word

against that of a man like P. J. Madden? Mr. Madden, here are your pearls—"

"One moment," cried Chan. "This Madden says he is the same who bought the necklace at San Francisco jeweler's. Ask him, please, location of jeweler's store."

"On Post Street," said Madden.

"What part Post Street? Famous building across way. What building?"

"Officer," objected Madden, "must I submit to this from a Chinese cook? I refuse to answer. The pearls are mine—"

Victor Jordan's eyes were open wide. "Hold on," he said. "Let me in this. Mr. Madden, my mother told me of the time when you first saw her. You were employed then—where—in what position?"

Madden's face purpled. "That's my affair."

The sheriff removed his ample hat and scratched his head. "Well, maybe I better keep this trinket for a minute," he reflected. "Look here, John—or—er—Sergeant Chan, if that's your name—what the devil are you driving at, anyhow?"

He turned suddenly at a cry from Madden. The man had edged his way to the array of guns on the wall, and stood there now, with one of them in his bandaged hand.

"Come on," he cried, "I've had enough of this. Up with your hands—Sheriff, that means you! Gamble—get that necklace! Thorn—get the bag in my room!"

With a magnificent disregard for his own safety, Chan leaped upon him and seized the arm holding the pistol. He gave it a sharp twist, and the weapon fell to the floor.

"Only thing I am ever able to learn from Japanese," he said. "Captain Bliss, prove yourself real policeman by putting handcuffs on Thorn and the professor. If the sheriff will so kindly return my personal automatic, which I employ as detective in Hawaii, I will be responsible for this Madden here."

"Sure, I'll return it," said Cox. "And I want to congratulate you. I don't know as I ever saw a finer exhibition of courage—"

Chan grinned. "Pardon me if I make slight correction. One recent morning at dawn I have busy time removing all cartridges from this splendid collection of old-time pistols on the wall. Long dusty job, but I am glad I did it." He turned suddenly to the big man beside him. "Put up the hands, Delaney," he cried.

"Delaney?" repeated the sheriff.

"Undubitably," replied Chan. "You have questioned value of my speech against word of P. J. Madden. Happy to say that situation does not arise. This is not P. J. Madden. His name is Jerry Delaney."

Bob Eden had entered quietly from the patio. "Good work, Charlie," he said. "You've got it now. But how in Sam Hill did you know?"

"Not long ago," answered Chan, "I shoot gun from his grasp. Observe the bandage on his hand, and note it is the left. Once in this room I told you Delaney was left-handed."

Through the open door behind Eden came a huge, powerful, but weary-looking man. One of his arms was in a sling, and his face was pale beneath a ten days' growth of beard. But there was about him an air of authority and poise; he loomed like a tower of granite, though the gray suit was sadly rumpled now. He stared grimly at Delaney.

"Well, Jerry," he said, "you're pretty good. But they always told me you were—the men who ran across you at Jack McGuire's. Yes—very good, indeed. Standing in my house, wearing my clothes, you look more like me than I do myself."

CHAPTER XXII

THE ROAD TO ELDORADO

THE man at the door came farther into the room and looked inquiringly about him. His eyes fell on Thorn.

"Hello, Martin," he said. "I warned you it wouldn't work. Which of you gentlemen is the sheriff?"

Cox came forward. "Right here, sir. I suppose you're P. J. Madden?"

Madden nodded. "I suppose so. I've always thought I was. We telephoned the constable from a ranch down the road, and he told us you were here. So we've brought along another little item to add to your collection." He indicated the patio door, through which Holley came at that moment leading Shaky Phil by the arm. Maydorf's hands were tied behind him. Paula Wendell and Evelyn Madden also entered.

"You'd better handcuff this newcomer to Delaney, Sheriff," suggested Madden. "And then I'll run over a little list of charges against the crowd that I think will hold them for a while."

"Sure, Mr. Madden," agreed the sheriff. As he stepped forward, Chan halted him.

"Just one minute. You have string of pearls—"

"Oh, yes—that's right," replied the sheriff. He held

301

out the Phillimore necklace. Chan took it and placed it in the hand of P. J. Madden.

"Fully aware you wanted it in New York," he remarked, "but you will perform vast kindness to accept it here. I have carried it to outside limit of present endurance. Receipt at your convenience, thank you."

Madden smiled. "All right, I'll take it." He put the necklace in his pocket. "You're Mr. Chan, I imagine. Mr. Eden was telling me about you on the way down from the mine. I'm mighty glad you've been here."

"Happy to serve," bowed Chan.

The sheriff turned. "There you are, sir. The charge, I guess, is attempted theft—"

"And a lot of other things," Madden added, "including assault with intent to kill." He indicated his limp arm. "I'll run over my story as quickly as I can—but I'll do it sitting down." He went to his desk. "I'm a little weak—I've been having a rough time of it. You know in a general way what has happened, but you don't know the background, the history, of this affair. I'll have to go back—back to a gambling house on Forty-fourth Street, New York. Are you familiar with New York gamblers and their ways, Sheriff?"

"Been to New York just once," said the sheriff. "Didn't like it."

"No, I don't imagine you would," replied Madden. He looked about. "Where are my cigars? Ah—here. Thanks, Delaney—you left me a couple, didn't you? Well, Sheriff, in order that you may understand what's been going on here, I must tell you about a favorite stunt of shady gamblers and confidence men in New York—a stunt that was flourishing there twelve or fifteen years ago. It was a well-known fact at the time that in the richly furnished houses where they lay in wait for trusting out-of-town suckers, certain members of the ring were assigned to impersonate widely-known millionaires, such as Frank Gould, Cornelius Vanderbilt, Mr. Astor—myself. The greatest care was exercised—photographs of these men were studied; wherever possible they themselves were closely observed in every feature of height, build, carriage, dress. The way they brushed their hair, the kind of glasses they wore, their peculiar mannerisms—no detail was too insignificant to escape attention. The intended dupe must be utterly taken in, so he might feel that he was among the best people, and that the game was honest."

Madden paused a moment. "Of course, some of these impersonations were rather flimsy, but it was my bad luck that Mr. Delaney here, who had been an actor, was more or less of an artist. Starting with a rather superficial resemblance to me, he built up an impersonation that got better and better as time went on. I began to hear rumors that I was seen nightly at the gambling house of one Jack McGuire, in Forty-fourth Street. I sent my secretary, Martin Thorn, to investigate. He reported that Delaney was making a good job of it—not, of course, so good that he could deceive any one really close to me, but good enough to fool people who knew me only from photographs. I put my lawyer on the matter, and he came back and said that Delaney had agreed to desist, on threat of arrest.

"And I imagine he did drop it—in the gambling houses. What happened afterward I can only conjecture, but I guess I can hit it pretty close. These two

Maydorf boys, Shaky Phil and"—he nodded at Gamble—"his brother who is known to the police as the professor, were the brains of the particular gang at McGuire's. They must long ago have conceived the plan of having Delaney impersonate me some where, some time. They could do nothing without the aid of my secretary, Thorn, but they evidently found him willing. Finally they hit on the desert as the proper locale for the enterprise. It was an excellent selection. I come here rarely; meet few people when I do come. Once they could get me here alone, without my family, it was a simple matter. All they had to do was put me out of the way, and then P. J. Madden appears with his secretary, who is better known locally than he is—no one is going to dream of questioning his identity, particularly as he looks just like his pictures."

Madden puffed thoughtfully on his cigar. "I've been expecting some such move for years. I feared no man in the world—except Delaney. The possibilities of the harm he might do me were enormous. Once I saw him in a restaurant, studying me. Well—they had a long wait, but their kind is patient. Two weeks ago I came here with Thorn, and the minute I got here I sensed there was something in the air. A week ago last Wednesday night I was sitting here writing a letter to my daughter Evelyn—it's probably still between the leaves of this blotter where I put it when I heard Thorn cry out sharply from his bedroom. 'Come quick, Chief,' he called. He was typing letters for me, and I couldn't imagine what had happened. I rose and went to his room—and there he was, with an old gun of mine—a gun Bill Hart had given me—in his fist. 'Put up your hands,' he said. Some one entered from the patio. It was Delaney.

" 'Now, don't get excited, Chief,' said Thorn, and I saw the little rat was in on the game. 'We're going to take you for a ride to a place where you can have a nice little rest. I'll go and pack a few things for you. Here, Jerry—you watch him.' And he handed Delaney the gun.

"There we stood, Delaney and I, and I saw that Jerry was nervous—the game was a little rich for his blood. Thorn was busy in my room. I began to call for help at the top of my voice—why? Who would come? I didn't know, but a friend might hear—Louie might have got home—some one might be passing in the road. Delaney told me to shut up. His hand trembled like a leaf. In the patio outside I heard an answering voice—but it was only Tony, the parrot. I knew well enough what was afoot, and I decided to take a chance. I started for Delaney; he fired and missed. He fired again, and I felt a sort of sting in my shoulder, and fell.

"I must have been unconscious for a second, but when I came to, Thorn was in the room, and I heard Delaney say he'd killed me. In a minute, of course, they discovered I was alive, and my good friend Jerry was all for finishing the job. But Thorn wouldn't let him—he insisted on going through with the original plan. He saved my life—I'll have to admit it—the contemptible little traitor. Cowardice, I imagine, but he saved me. Well, they put me in a car, and drove me up to the jail at Petticoat Mine. In the morning they left—all except the professor, who had joined our happy party. He stayed behind, dressed my wound, fed me after a fashion. On Sunday afternoon he went away and came back late at night with Shaky Phil. Monday morning the professor left, and Shaky Phil was my jailer after that. Not so kind as his brother.

"What was going on at the ranch, you gentlemen know better than I do. On Tuesday my daughter wired that she was coming, and of course the game was up if she reached here. So Thorn met her in Eldorado, told her I was injured and up at the mine, and took her there. Naturally, she trusted him. Since then she has been there with me, and we'd be there now if Mr. Eden and Mr. Holley had not come up to-night, searching for this other young woman who had, unfortunately for her, stumbled on the affair earlier in the day."

Madden rose. "That's my story, Sheriff. Do you wonder that I want to see this gang behind the bars? I'll sleep better then."

"Well, I reckon it's easy arranged," returned the sheriff. "I'll take 'em along and we can fix the warrants later. Guess I'll see 'em safe in the jail at the county-seat—Eldorado can't offer 'em all the comforts of a first-class cell."

"One thing," said Madden. "Thorn, I heard you say the other night to Delaney, 'You were always afraid of him—that time in New York—' What did that mean? You tried this thing before?"

Thorn looked up with stricken face, which had been hidden in his hands. "Chief, I'm sorry about this. I'll talk. We had it all set to pull it once at the office in New York, when you were away on a hunting trip. But if you were afraid of Delaney, he was a lot more afraid of you. He got cold feet—backed out at the last minute—"

"And why wouldn't I back out?" snarled Delaney. "I couldn't trust any of you. A bunch of yellow dogs—"

"Is that so?" cried Shaky Phil. "Are you talking about me?"

"Sure I'm talking about you. I suppose you didn't try to cop the pearls in Frisco when we sent you up there to draw Louie Wong away? Oh, I know all about that—"

"Why wouldn't I try to cop them?" demanded Shaky Phil. "You been trying to cop them, haven't you? When you thought Draycott was bringing them, what did you try to pull? Oh, brother Henry's been on to you—"

"I sure have," put in the professor. "Trying to sneak off and meet Draycott alone. If you thought I wasn't wise, you must be a fool. But of course that's what you are—a poor fool that writes letters to actresses—"

"Shut up!" bellowed Delaney. "Who had a better right to those pearls? What could you have done if it hadn't been for me? A lot of help you were—mooning round with your tall talk. And you"—he turned back to Shaky Phil—"you pulled some brilliant stuff. Putting a knife in Louie Wong right on the door-step—"

"Who put a knife in Louie Wong?" cried Shaky Phil.

"You did," shouted Thorn. "I was with you and I saw you. I'll swear to that—"

"An accessory, eh?" grinned the sheriff. "By gad, just let this gang loose at one another, and they'll hang themselves."

"Boys, boys," said the professor gently. "Cut it out. We'll never get anywhere that way. Sheriff, we are ready—"

"One moment," said Charlie Chan. He disappeared briefly, and returned with a small black bag, which he set before Madden. "I have pleasure calling your attention to this," he announced. "You will find inside vast crowds of currency. Money from sale of bonds, money sent from New York office. Pretty much intact—but not quite. I ask Delaney."

"It's all there," Delaney growled.

Chan shook his head. "I grieve to differ even with rascal like you are. But there was Eddie Boston—"

"Yes," replied Delaney. "It's true—I gave Boston five thousand dollars. He recognized me the other day in the yard. Go after him and get it back—the dirty crook!"

The sheriff laughed. "Speaking of crooks," he said, "that sounds to me like your cue, boys. We'd better be getting along, Bliss. We can swear in a deputy or two in Eldorado. Mr. Madden, I'll see you to-morrow."

Bob Eden went up to Delaney. "Well, Jerry," he smiled, "I'm afraid this is good-by. You've been my host down here, and my mother told me I must always say I've had a very nice time—"

"Oh, go to the devil," said Delaney.

The sheriff and Bliss herded their captives out into the desert night, and Eden went over to Paula Wendell.

"Exit the Delaney quartet," he remarked. "I guess my stalling days at the ranch are ended. I'm taking the ten-thirty train to Barstow, and—"

"Better call up for a taxi," she suggested.

"Not while you and the roadster are on the job. If you'll wait while I pack—I want a word with you anyhow. About Wilbur."

"One happy thought runs through my mind," Will Holley was saying. "I'm the author of a famous interview with you, Mr. Madden. One you never gave."

"Really?" replied Madden. "Well, don't worry. I'll stand behind you."

"Thanks," answered the editor. "I wonder why they gave out that story," he mused.

"Simple to guess," said Chan. "They are wiring New York office money be sent, please. How better to establish fact Madden is at desert ranch than to blaze same forth in newspapers. Printed word has ring of convincing truth."

"I imagine you're right," nodded Holley. "By the way, Charlie, we thought we'd have a big surprise for you when we got back from the mine. But you beat us to it, after all."

"By a hair's width," replied Chan. "Now that I have leisure I bow my head and do considerable blushing. Must admit I was plenty slow to grasp apparent fact. Only to-night light shone. To please this Victor, I hand over pearls. Madden is signing receipt—he writes slow and painful. Suddenly I think—he does all things slow and painful with that right hand. Why? I recall Delaney's vest, built for left-handed man. Inwardly, out of sight, I gasp. To make a test, I snatch at pearls. Madden, to call him that, snatches, too. But guard is down—he snatches with left hand. He rips out pistol—left hand again. The fact is proved. I know."

"Well, that was quick thinking," Holley said.

Chan sadly shook his head. "Why not? Poor old brain must have been plenty rested. Not at work for many days. When I arrange these dishonest ones in chairs to wait for you, I have much time for bitter self-incriminations. Why have I experienced this stupid sinking spell? All time it was clear as desert morning. A man writes important letter, hides in blotter, goes away. Returning, he never touches same. Why? He did not return.

Other easy clues—Madden, calling him so again, receives Doctor Whitcomb in dusk of patio. Why? She has seen him before. He talks with caretaker in Pasadena— when? Six o'clock, when dark has fallen. Also he fears to alight from car. Oh, as I sit here I give myself many resounding mental kicks. Why have I been so thick? I blame this climate of South California. Plenty quick I hurry back to Honolulu, where I belong."

"You're too hard on yourself," said P. J. Madden. "If it hadn't been for you, Mr. Eden tells me, the necklace would have been delivered long ago, and this crowd off to the Orient or somewhere else far away. I owe you a lot, and if mere thanks—"

"Stop thanking me," urged Chan. "Thank Tony. If Tony didn't speak that opening night, where would necklace be now? Poor Tony, buried at this moment in rear of barn." He turned to Victor Jordan, who had been lurking modestly in the background. "Victor, before returning north, it is fitting that you place wreath of blossoms on grave of Tony, the Chinese parrot. Tony died, but he lived to splendid purpose. Before he passed, he saved the Phillimore pearls."

Victor nodded. "Anything you say, Charlie. I'll leave a standing order with my florist. I wonder if some one will give me a lift back to town?"

"I'll take you," Holley said. "I want to get this thing on the wire. Charlie—shall I see you again—"

"Leaving on next train," replied Chan. "I am calling at your office to collect more fitting clothes. Do not wait, however. Miss Wendell has kindly offered use of her car."

"I'm waiting for Paula, too," Eden said. "I'll see
you at the station." Holley and Victor said their good-
bys to Madden and his daughter, and departed. Bob
Eden consulted his watch. "Well, the old home week
crowd is thinning out. Just one thing more, Charlie.
When Mr. Madden here came in to-night, you weren't
a bit surprised. Yet, recognizing Delaney, your first
thought must have been that Madden had been killed."

Chan laughed noiselessly. "I observe you have ignor-
ance concerning detective customs. Surprised detective
might as well put on iron collar and leap from dock. He
is finished. Mr. Madden's appearance staggering blow
for me, but I am not letting rival policemen know it,
thank you. It is apparent we keep Miss Wendell waiting. I have some property in cookhouse—just one moment."

"The cookhouse," cried P. J. Madden. "By the lord
Harry, I'm hungry. I haven't had anything but canned
food for days."

An apprehensive look flitted over Chan's face. "Such
a pity," he said. "Present cook on ranch has resumed
former profession. Miss Wendell, I am with you in five
seconds." He went hastily out.

Evelyn Madden put her arm about her father. "Cheer
up, dad," she advised. "I'll drive you in town and we'll
stop at the hotel to-night. You must have a doctor look
at your shoulder at once." She turned to Bob Eden. "Of
course, there's a restaurant in Eldorado?"

"Of course," smiled Eden. "It's called the Oasis, but
it isn't. However, I can heartily recommend the steaks."

P. J. Madden was on his feet, himself again. "All
right, Evelyn. Call up the hotel and reserve a suite—five

rooms—no, make it a floor. Tell the proprietor I want supper served in my sitting-room—two porterhouse steaks, and everything else they've got. Tell him to have the best doctor in town there when I arrive. Help me find the telegraph blanks. Put in five long distance calls—no, that had better wait until we reach the hotel. Find out if there's anybody in Eldorado who can take dictation. Call up the leading real-estate man and put this place on the market. I never want to see it again. And oh, yes—don't let that Chinese detective get away without seeing me. I'm not through with him. Make a note to call a secretarial bureau in Los Angeles at eight in the morning—"

Bob Eden hurried to his room, and packed his suit-case. When he returned, Chan was standing in Madden's presence, holding crisp bank-notes in his hand.

"Mr. Madden has given receipt for necklace," said the Chinese. "He has also enforced on me this vast sum of money, which I am somewhat loathsome to accept."

"Nonsense," Eden replied. "You take it, Charlie. You've earned it."

"Just what I told him," Madden declared.

Chan put the bank-notes carefully away. "Free to re-mark the sum represents two and one half years' salary in Honolulu. This mainland climate not so bad, after all."

"Good-by, Mr. Eden," Madden said. "I've thanked Mr. Chan—but what shall I say to you? You've been through a lot down here—"

"Been through some of the happiest moments of my life," Eden replied.

Madden shook his head. "Well, I don't understand that—"

"I think I do," said his daughter. "Good luck, Bob, and thank you a thousand times."

The desert wind was cool and bracing as they went out to the little roadster, waiting patiently in the yard. Paula Wendell climbed in behind the wheel. "Get in, Mr. Chan," she invited. Chan took his place beside her. Bob Eden tossed his suit-case into the luggage compartment at the back, and returned to the car door.

"Squeeze in there, Charlie," he said. "Don't make a fool of the advertisements. This is a three-seater car."

Charlie squeezed. "Moment of gentle embarrassment for me," he remarked. "The vast extensiveness of my area becomes painfully apparent."

They were out on the road. The Joshua trees waved them a weird farewell in the white moonlight.

"Charlie," said Eden, "I suppose you don't dream why you are in this party?"

"Miss Wendell very kind," remarked Chan.

"Kind—and cautious," laughed Eden. "You're here as a Wilbur—a sort of buffer between this young woman and the dread institution of marriage. She doesn't believe in marriage, Charlie. Now where do you suppose she picked up that foolish notion?"

"Plenty foolish," agreed Chan. "She should be argued at."

"She will be argued at. She brought you along because she knows I'm mad about her. She's seen it in my great trusting eyes. She knows that since I've met her, that precious freedom of mine seems a rather stale joke. She realizes that I'll never give up—that I intend to take her away from the desert—but she thought I wouldn't mention it if you were along."

"I begin to feel like skeleton at feast," remarked Chan.

"Cheer up—you certainly don't feel like that to me," Eden assured him. "Yes, she thought I'd fail to speak of the matter—but we'll fool her. I'll speak of it anyhow. Charlie, I love this girl."

"Natural you do," agreed Chan.

"I intend to marry her."

"Imminently fitting purpose," assented Chan. "But she has said no word."

Paula Wendell laughed. "Marriage," she said. "The last resort of feeble minds. I'm having a great time, thanks. I love my freedom. I mean to hang on to it."

"Sorry to hear that," said Chan. "Permit me if I speak a few words in favor of married state. I am one who knows. Where is the better place than a new home? Truly an earthly paradise where cares vanish, where the heavenly melody of wife's voice vibrates everything in a strange symphony."

"Sounds pretty good to me," remarked Eden.

"The ramble hand in hand with wife on evening streets, the stroll by moonly seaside. I recollect the happy spring of my own marriage with unlimited yearning."

"How does it sound to you, Paula?" Eden persisted.

"And this young man," continued Chan. "I am unable to grasp why you resist. To me he is plenty fine fellow. I have for him a great likeness." Paula Wendell said nothing. "A very great likeness," added Chan.

"Well," admitted the girl, "if it comes to that, I have a little likeness for him myself."

Chan dug his elbow deep into Eden's side. They climbed between the dark hills and the lights of Eldorado shone before them. As they drove up to the hotel, Holley and Victor Jordan greeted them.

"Here you are," said the editor. "Your bag is in the office, Charlie. The door's unlocked."

"Many thanks," returned Chan, and fled.

Holley looked up at the white stars. "Sorry you're going, Eden," he said. "It'll be a bit lonesome down here without you."

"But you'll be in New York," suggested Eden.

Holley shook his head and smiled. "Oh, no, I won't. I sent a telegram this evening. A few years ago, perhaps—but not now. I can't go now. Somehow, this desert country—well, it's got me, I guess. I'll have to take my New York in pictures from this on."

Far off across the dreary waste of sand the whistle of the Barstow train broke the desert silence. Charlie came around the corner; the coat and vest of Sergeant Chan had replaced the Canton crêpe blouse of Ah Kim.

"Hoarse voice of railroad proclaims end of our adventure," he remarked. He took Paula Wendell's hand. "Accept last wish from somewhat weary postman. May this be for you beginning of life's greatest adventure. And happiest."

They crossed the empty street. "Good-by," Eden said, as he and the girl paused in the shadow of the station. Something in the warm clasp of her slender strong fingers told him all he wanted to know, and his heart beat faster. He drew her close.

"I'm coming back soon," he promised. He transferred the emerald ring to her right hand. "Just by way of a reminder," he added. "When I return I'll bring a substitute—the glittering pick of the finest stock on the coast. Our stock."

"Our stock?"

"Yes." The branch-line train had clattered in, and Chan was calling to him from the car steps. "You don't know it yet, but for you the dream of every woman's life has come true. You're going to marry a man who owns a jewelry store."

THE END

Printed in the United States
43640LVS00005B/207